UNDEAD ON ARRIVAL

JUSTIN ROBINSON

CAPTAIN
SUPERMARKET
PRESS

Captain Supermarket Press
info@captainsupermarket.com

Third Printing, 2017, Captain Supermarket Press
ISBN 978-0-9892781-5-7
eISBN 978-0-9892781-6-4

Second Printing, 2014, Books of the Dead
First Printing, 2012, Solstice Publishing

Cover design by Kate Sullivan – www.fatgreenchicken.com
Book layout and composition by Lauri Veverka
Map design by Alan Caum
Typefaces: DIN, Adobe Garamond Pro

www.captainsupermarket.com

For Lauri.

My heart will always be yours, but if I turn,
you'll have to take the brain too.

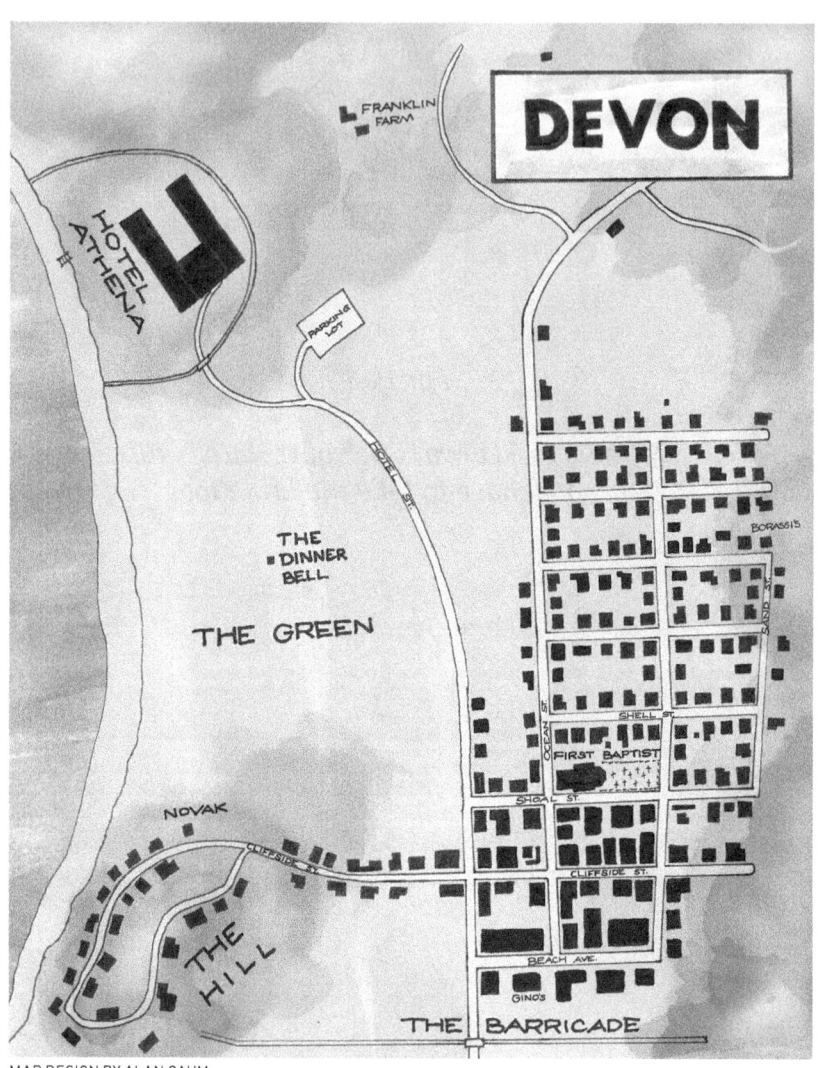

MAP DESIGN BY ALAN CAUM

I'll fix your feet 'til you can't walk
I'll lock your jaw 'til you can't talk
I'll close your eyes so you can't see
This very air, come and go with me

– O Death, Traditional

MOST PEOPLE THOUGHT THAT A shot to the brain was enough to take out a geek. But then again, most people were dead.

It was only half the story. People liked simplicity. The economy was the fault of one guy, the President, or a bunch of easily ID'd outsiders. The problem with reality is that it's always more complex than that. In this case, the complexity had gotten the vast majority of the human race killed.

Glen Novak had it broken down, itemized, and cross-referenced. He drew some amusement from a dark place when a simple headshot was tried. He liked to say, "If I had a nickel for every time some hotshot plugged a geek through the forehead and nearly shit himself when the bastard kept coming, I'd have a giant useless sack of nickels." Stew explained it to him one time, probably from when Judy Bloch had explained it to Stew. Novak didn't remember the whole shebang, just that whatever animated them was deep, the Medusa something. It was a little tube at the bottom that some people called the reptile brain. Stew broke it down: "Geeks don't think, so they don't need the top and they don't remember, so they don't need the back. But they do bite."

The science—what little was actually known—didn't really enter Novak's mind very often. He concentrated on the realities. How to kill.

He had a simple speech depending on what someone had scavenged:

Gun, spear, anything that punctures: aim for the nose or mouth or the top of the head.

Hammer, baseball bat, anything that crushes: aim for the face and peel it.

Machete, sword, anything that slices: cut the top of the head off.

Pick, axe, anything that's a lever with a spike: top of the head, base of the neck.

The real joke was that while killing a geek was a matter of precision, they could kill a man with the slightest nibble.

Of course, there were tons of ways to stop a geek from coming. Just because it was technically possible to drop one in a single swing didn't mean that was the best plan. Headshots were hard, especially when that head wanted to bite. Add to that how scarce ammo had become and bullets were somewhere around Plan E or F. Sometimes, just putting the thing down was enough. Dismemberment could work, as could breaking a leg. Knock the thing over. Lock it someplace. Drop it in a pit. Novak and his guys had come across many geeks that had been hobbled but no one had thought to finish off. The geek would be dragging itself on one arm or slithering like one of those human torsos he'd once seen in a sideshow when he was very little. When he found geeks like that, he destroyed them. It might have seemed pointless, or to the stupid and naïve, it might have seemed cruel. But there was a fact about geeks that everyone should know: geeks attract geeks.

No one knew how or why. Geeks were attracted to sounds, but they didn't make a noise themselves, other than the maddening scrabbling against anything between them and prey. They didn't seem to follow one another by sight. All that anyone knew was that once you saw one geek, chances were that there were one or two more in the area. If that geek saw you, then there were a hundred more zeroing in like sharks.

The geeks were slow, never moving quicker than a stagger. But it was not their speed that made them dangerous. It was their number. Slowly they would surround their prey until it had nowhere to back up. Then, surrounded and hopeless, the prey was killed.

The war that started five years before was over. The human race had lost. But to Novak's mind, that didn't mean opening a vein. Didn't mean feeding the swarm. Didn't mean joining up. It meant destroying them where he found them. He knew he wasn't taking a damn thing back, but it was something to do. Kept him sane and breathing.

He thought of what he did in those terms: destroying the geek. He thought of them, whatever their gender had been in life, as *it*. They weren't human any more. People were killed. Animals were destroyed.

After all, one bite and you were one of them. Not immediately. The infection, the curse, whatever it was, it took around a day and a night to finish the job. It raced through the blood, maybe, shut the body down and turned it into something else. Something mindless and hungry. Sometimes, Novak wondered if the person that the geek had been was still in there. He wondered if that person had become a passenger in their body, slowly losing sanity as they ripped and killed the living.

He thought of all of this in the moment he died.

When the thing tore his finger off at the root, as his hand spouted the blood that seemed to turn black before his eyes. He had one day and one night at the most. One day and one night to find who killed him. One day and one night to put everything in order.

He had so much to do before he ate that final bullet.

- 2 -

ON THE DAY THAT GLEN Novak died, he shuddered awake
with a snore sliced off at the base. He'd been dreaming. Another
nightmare. He never slept peacefully any more, not since the day the
world ended. He'd been past the Barricade, lost in the automotive
labyrinth that used to be the 101 Freeway. Something was all around,
but just out of sight.

The room still smelled like sex. Windows didn't get opened any
more, not even on the good side of the Barricade. It was dark, the
queen-sized bed rumpled. Inez Calomiris was on her side, back
to him. She had a nice back. Skin brown, and because she was
a Calomiris, spine barely showing. Long black hair splayed over
what used to be white sheets.

She was getting bolder. When the thing between them had
started a little over three years ago, she would have to sneak out of
the Athena. They would meet at an abandoned house on the north
side of the Hill. They would furtively fuck and leave separately,
eyes never meeting in the light. For the past year, once a week
she brazenly came to his door and stayed the night. Occasionally,
Novak would even meet her at the Athena, but they had the good
taste not to use the honeymoon suite, opting instead for an empty
fifth floor room in the east wing.

Inez Calomiris was a pretty woman for her time and place.
She was still young, but, like everyone, the apocalypse had aged
her. Lines had deepened to faults on her face, skin had tightened,

fat had hardened to sinew. She was cleaner than most. She traded with all of Devon's scavs for soaps, lotions and perfumes, and she could afford to be extravagant; she had access to the Athena's storerooms. If Walter Calomiris, her husband, noticed, he had yet to stop her. She took sun showers on the east wing's roof every day. She never built up what Novak thought of as the end-of-the-world stink. She was small, her considerable strengths hidden. Deceptive was a word Novak associated with her, in every sense of it.

The drapes were heavy and black, but sun peeked around them. Novak shook her gently. "Time to get up."

She mumbled, turned, blinking those pretty almond brown eyes. "What time is it?"

Novak thought of that as an old question. Time was relative in distance to sunrise and sunset. Seven A.M. had no meaning on its own, only on its proximity to greater or lesser danger. He said: "Just after sunrise."

She sat up. Her breasts were nearly starved away. Maybe if she traded for more food and less soap. She gave Novak a sleepy smile. An invitation: "I'm not awake yet."

"Your husband is probably wondering where you are."

She coughed. It was probably supposed to be a chuckle, turned to dust in her throat. "He doesn't even know I'm gone."

"He knows. He's not that dumb."

She shrugged. "Probably. But if you're going to be like him, I'll just go home then."

She dressed quickly and didn't bother to kiss him when she left, and he didn't bother to give a shit.

He geared up next, pulling the battered footlocker from under the bed. His hunting gear was inside, waiting. When he was dressed and outfitted, he went over everything a second time. Make sure every item is checked off twice or he'd reach for something that wasn't there. That meant he'd be reaching for death.

On his waist: a gun belt taken off a cop and then modified by Jim Sorensen, the leatherworker that lived two houses down the Hill on Pine Ave. On the right hip, a .45 automatic pistol with a single extra clip: fourteen rounds in total. On the left hip, a heavy hatchet and a one-handed sledgehammer, which he used paired. In his backpack: waterproof matches, a roll of duct tape, a compass, a map of California, two empty sacks, and a first aid kit. He wore: Steel-toed work boots, blue jeans, a cup, a t-shirt, hockey shins and shoulder pads, baseball forearm guards, and a heavy leather jacket.

Novak was a short badger of a man. Five and a half feet on a good day, but nearly as broad, and with a powerful wrestler's build. He shaved his head every morning, but that was vanity: he'd lost everything up top. He had clear blue eyes that might have been attractive on a handsome man. On Novak, they just looked cold. He moved like a battering ram; people knew to get the hell out of the way.

Novak's house cut into the east side of the Hill, near the balding limestone peak. Whoever had built it originally had leveled out some of the ground, putting up a cinderblock wall to keep the Hill from falling into the backyard. When Novak moved in, he'd dug a commode in the southeast corner and put up some tarps to cut the wind. Tangerine trees grew in the northeast corner, corn, beans and squash in the central yard. The cannabis plants were all in the front.

He picked a few tangerines and ate them with one of the circular loaves of bread that he traded for weekly from Janelle Ford. She'd trade nearly anything for a jar of Smucker's grape jelly. Maybe that was how Robellada scored her in the first place.

Novak left the house. Night blue fought with the barely risen sun, while slate clouds were beginning to roll in from the ocean. The town of Devon stretched out in front, his home for the last four years. Back in the world, Devon had been a tourist destination, tucked in a dell along the central California coast. After the end, it had become a fortress.

The Hotel Athena was the major artificial landmark. In the old world, it had been a place that made up for chintzy rooms with an amazing view of the ancient Pacific and proximity to wineries and Hearst Castle. It perched on a cliff at the north-westernmost point that could still be called Devon. To the west, a cliff fell to a rocky beach that was all moonstones and tide pools. To the north, a series of cliffs, like shelves, descended back into meandering coastline. To the south, rolling green meadows led to the Hill. To the southeast, the slope turned gentle, leading into Town. The Athena was the beating heart of Devon. It served as capital and keep, in the old sense of the word, as well as a symbol for the inhabitants. The geeks had gotten everything else, but the Athena still belonged to the living.

The Athena was the property of Walter Calomiris and had been since before the end. He took people in, mostly those who couldn't make it elsewhere in Devon. Nothing he did was for free. After the end of the world, that was how things were done. Calomiris charged a high price for safety, but if you paid, you paid. There were other choices: make your own way or starve. Calomiris had the largest gang, but they hadn't added any new blood for at least a year. They were growing stagnant in their castle.

Hotel Street ran southeast past Town, and out to join the main road, which in turn led to the 101 Freeway. Go east along the other streets, Beach, Cliffside or Shoal, and this would be Devon proper. The southern part consisted of restaurants, shops and a gas station: a convenient place to squeeze the first of the tourist dollars. After the end, these had become homes for people or rats. Moving north along the large hill that bordered the east side, like the fold of a colossal rug, there were houses, an elementary school and finally some small farms.

First Baptist was the center of Town, symbolically and nearly geographically. This was the home of Reverend Isador Rippey. If Calomiris was Devon's mayor, Rippey would be the man next in line, one dirty trick away. He lived in the shadow of the Athena. Not for long. His gang was growing all the time, and they would want to expand. If they came at the Hill, Novak was ready to kill every last one of the fuckers, but until they did, Rippey's people weren't his problem.

Take Cliffside to the west, across Hotel Street, then past Dr. Judy Bloch's low one-story office, past the Dinner Bell rising out of the green fields, and find the Hill bursting from the ground. Dotted with pines, the details were hidden until one got close. The Hill was entirely residential, one-stories and cabins, often for seasonal residents. Now it belonged to Glen Novak.

Two hundred years ago, he might have been referred to as a chief. In two hundred years, assuming there were any humans left, that term might be used again. Novak led the Hill's one gang of scavs. The well was in his front yard, between the cannabis plants and the lumpy road. Anyone who wanted water, who wanted a share of the salvage, who wanted protection, paid something to him. He didn't think of it as tribute, even if that was what it was. He did what Calomiris and Rippey did, albeit on a smaller scale. He justified his behavior by creating rules to preserve some sense of himself as, if not a good person, then not a bad one.

Novak had to gather the small group he thought of as his guys. To the rest of Devon, this was Novak's gang. Feared for their ability to tip the balance of power whichever way suited Glen Novak and the Hill, as if there was a difference.

He grabbed his crotch-rocket and wheeled it out onto Cliffside Avenue.

"Mr. Novak?" It was Jim Sorensen, a big redheaded guy with a full beard. Sorensen had a small herd of goats and grew tomatoes to supplement the leather he occasionally worked, either from scavenged pieces Novak provided or from the herd of cows on the Town green, that meadow between the Athena and the Hill. Sorensen carried a bucket in one hand, and something wrapped in cloth, probably goat cheese. Meant he wanted his daily water.

Novak waved him toward the well. Sorensen nodded a "thank you" as Novak rolled his bike down the street. Sorensen would leave the cheese inside.

Christopher Stewart—Stew—was only two houses away toward Town. Stew was already leaving his low green house as Novak arrived. Outside, Stew kissed the man that he called his husband. There hadn't been a ceremony. Not that legality was a concern after the end. Legal was whatever you could get away with. One of the town fathers could get away with more than the scavs, who could get away with more than the farmers, all the way down to one of prostitutes on the Athena's second floor.

Stew found John on one of their runs, hiding in the back of a barred convenience store, living off candy. Stew took him home and two weeks later, he was calling John "husband." Novak felt strange using that term, but Stew had earned the respect it took to make Novak say it.

In the old world, they had hated each other. Novak still thought of Stew as a fag, but the word had softened. Before, it had been an epithet that Susan had scolded him over. Now it was thought affectionately, just another of Stew's quirks. Like the way he had Robellada, Jim Sorensen, Michelle Harmon, and Tigran Gamburyan over every Friday night for Dungeons and Dragons. Or the way he insisted on cleaning his glasses while making a point.

In the old days, Stew and Novak had lived next door, locked with one another over the wars that used to divide neighbors. When the dead rose, whose sweetgum tree dumped two bags of leaves on whose lawn every week suddenly no longer seemed to matter. Over five years, hate had turned to trust, trust to friendship, and Stew had become Novak's right hand.

Physically, they were opposites as well: Stew was tall, lean, and black. He kept his hair short and face clean-shaven. His glasses were immortal by Novak's estimation, and should have been broken a thousand times over, but somehow had stayed intact. Stew fought with a machete and a police riot shield and packed a .45 on his belt.

Stew's house looked like he was trying to forget the world ended. He grew flowers, useless flowers, with the actual functional plants in the back. There was even a gnome on the doorstep, smiling and laughing. Novak hated that fucking gnome, from when they found it in front of that house in Santa Barbara, to when it laughed at him from the bungee web in the sidecar of Stew's bike, to this moment.

Stew whispered something in his husband's ear and nodded to Novak as he wheeled the bike out from the garage. "Morning, Glen," he said.

"Stew." Novak nodded to the husband, who scampered inside with something like terror on his face. No matter how many times the gang left the Barricade, there was the same reaction from some types.

"Hope it waits until we get back." Stew was looking up at the clouds.

"With a little luck, maybe."

Dave Pulaski was next, down a steep side road. He had the house directly below Novak's. If someone knew that one of his guys was a fag, they'd guess it was Pulaski. The makeup would call it, mostly because they didn't have Stew to explain that most transvestites were straight men. Pulaski did his eyes up like a woman and most days he wore lip gloss and liner. That was only visible if he moved the scarf he usually wore wrapped over the lower half of his face. Novak never asked why Pulaski wore the makeup. He didn't really care. It only mattered that Pulaski was a born killer. Some men, like Stew, had to be taught to fight geeks. Not Pulaski. He took to it naturally and liked nothing more than the sound of a blade biting through vertebrae. Pulaski didn't wear armor, just some tight-fitting coveralls with the tails of his scarf tucked down the front. He kept his blond hair short.

The thing of it was, the guy fought with samurai swords. No shit. He had two, a long and a short one that Novak didn't know the proper names for. Pulaski liked the long one best. The handles were covered in graying athletic tape, the blades still mirror sharp. Alone among the scavs, Pulaski didn't bother with a gun. No surprise. Ask him and he'd happily tell anyone that guns were no fun.

He and Stew found Pulaski before they left L.A. They were holed up in an abandoned office building and started to notice that the local geeks were on some kind of exodus. Packs of them wandered west every day right around the same time. Stew laughed, explaining that he never knew geeks were migratory. After the third day, curiosity decided to strangle the cat. They followed the exodus. Then, the tinny sounds of a ghetto blaster.

"Thriller."

Closer, they found the maniac—Pulaski—surrounded.

Pulaski should have been killed, but he was carving geeks up like he was Yo-Jimbo. Piles of body parts littered the place, some of which were actually rotting. It turned out Pulaski had been going to that corner for a full week, blasting "Thriller" until he was good and surrounded. Then he commenced the slaughter.

He thought it was fun.

Stew and Pulaski didn't get along. There were times Novak thought it would turn ugly if he weren't around. There were other times when they seemed more like bickering brothers.

Pulaski came out of his house with those swords over his shoulder, stifling a yawn through that red scarf. His eyelids were green and gold. Go Packers.

They picked up Ricky Robellada next. He was still living alone, but everyone knew he was seeing Janelle Ford, who lived with her brother Jacen in Town. Everyone assumed she'd move in with Robellada before long. Reverend Rippey might even perform that ceremony when it happened.

Robellada was a weird situation. Most people were in one of two categories: those known before, who were all dead, and those met after. Sometimes they crossed over, like with Stew, but in that case, they had survived the whole thing side-by-side. Robellada was one of Novak's students before the end. He still used "Mr. Novak," not out of the new deference others offered him, but because old habits died hard. Stew found him in a barn, hiding out from a small swarm that was wandering around the remnants of Harmony. Robellada joined up after that.

Robellada was a good kid, but was the worst of them in a fight. That wasn't saying much. All of them were terrors, and Robellada was hell with his fire axe. He spoke with a slight sob in his voice and didn't like to meet eyes. He looked to the others for his cues, reckless when Pulaski was closest, cautious when Stew was. He never questioned Novak, who once joked that Robellada acted like Novak could still give him detention.

Robellada wanted to set up a real government. He wanted the return of voting, of taxes, of jury duty, of police. He didn't realize that they were in the Dark Ages again. Novak didn't tease him about his little Constitution. Everyone needed something to do when the nights stretched out and the geeks clawed at the mind.

Robellada still looked like a kid, though he had the same markers as the rest of them: scars on face and hands, although none were teeth-marks, a body turned stringy, skin darker and tougher. He still couldn't grow a real beard, though.

"Morning, son," Novak said.

"Morning, Mr. Novak." Robellada had his eyes down, watching the muddy track in front of him.

Tom Martinez was the last one. He joined up when Stew, Pulaski, and Novak made it to Devon. Martinez was already there, on the outskirts of Rippey's gang. Novak and company took the Hill and Martinez asked for a space. In the beginning, Martinez knew the lay of the land better than any of them, both literally and figuratively. He was good glue for the group: not as strange as Pulaski, not as starry-eyed as Robellada, not as practical as Stew. Martinez was a nice guy, the kind of guy that, in Novak's opinion, you could hang out with and it was almost like being alone.

He was as short as Novak, but a lot thinner. Still, he was strong. They'd all seen him break more than one skull with one of his baseball bats. He carried them in a sack over his shoulder, and when one snapped in half on a geek's head, he'd just pull out another one. He seemed to have an endless supply.

Martinez had a wife, a little homely blonde Novak generally ignored. She was in the doorway when Martinez left the house. She didn't wave.

Martinez said: "Hey, guys." Then he dropped in next to Novak as they walked down the road into Town. A stand of trees to the right blocked the view of the Barricade. Stew was in the lead, next to Robellada. Pulaski lagged behind.

Martinez spoke under his breath: "I have to talk to you about something." There was a shimmer in his voice, like it was a running current.

"Yeah?"

"Look, I just want you to know, some shit is coming."

"You saw something over the Barricade last night? A swarm?"

"Not like that. Look, there are some changes on the horizon."

"Rippey making his move? What've you heard?"

"Just keep your head down for the next couple days."

Novak shrugged. Sounded like some bullshit. He expected this kind of talk from Robellada, what with the Constitution he had written on that ratty legal pad. Robellada had Ideas. Didn't know that they were five years past needing those. Martinez knew it. Made him easy to put up with. If Rippey was angling to take out Calomiris, Novak just had to wait it out. Maybe snap up some of the people that survived.

They made it to the intersection of Cliffside and Hotel. Even at this point, arguably the most important intersection in Devon, the street was still only two-laned, and bordered by gravelly rain gutters. Ahead, Cliffside went into Town, but they turned right, toward the Barricade. On the green, the Athena's herds grazed placidly.

The Barricade had been in its early stages when Novak, Stew, and Pulaski arrived. They'd helped lengthen it, until it reached its present dimensions: a football field and a half, ending just where the Hill got steep, and a good fifteen feet high all the way across. Novak was proud of the Barricade. He and his men had gathered up cars from the 101, drove them back to Devon, drained the gas tanks and tipped them on their sides. From there, Roy Czuchra, the mechanic, had welded the cars together. Novak helped lay the brick for the blockhouse that now stood at the gateway.

Since Novak's arrival, there'd been twelve good-sized swarms, and the Barricade had held for ten of them. When the swarm broke through, the defenders fell back into the Athena where they slaughtered the geeks and pushed back out. Stew liked to draw the comparison of old castle warfare, the wall and the keep. There were times when Stew still annoyed Novak.

Rippey's men manned the gate as they always did. In principle, the gate belonged to all three town fathers. In practice, Rippey decided who went in and out. Forcing Calomiris's men to ask permission reduced Calomiris every time it happened. That might have been what kept him in the Athena, a prisoner in the town he built.

It was the Rosenberg brothers on duty, Jacob, the elder on the inner wall of the Barricade, looking out into the world, with Micah operating the gate. They were tough men, broad-backed, with short wiry hair and patchy beards.

"Five to go out!" Novak shouted.

Jacob scanned the road and the woods beyond. He turned back and nodded. Micah leaned into the wheel inside the blockhouse and the gate let out a hollow creak as it opened.

Novak and his men mounted their bikes and gunned the engines. When the world ended, they thought gas would never run out. After all, a trip to a parking lot that used to be any major freeway could net as much gas as someone was willing to siphon. Unfortunately, within two years, gas decayed into useless sludge. Something about the preservatives. Fortunately, Roy Czuchra, the mechanic, had converted some vehicles to run on propane, which lasted forever. Problem was, Czuchra was killed two years before. People in town knew enough to maintain their bikes, but once it broke, that would be it. Another sign on the slow descent into barbarism.

Other men could modify vehicles in similar ways. The occasional gangs of nomads, with their bikes, RVs, and the like had one of these guys, each one more valuable than a ton of salvage. They tended to get around on back roads, where the cars weren't as thick. They usually had a small swarm of geeks following them, like a wake. Novak's bikes would pull a few geeks, but not enough to matter, especially if they were dealt with quickly.

Today, they raced inland. The close settlements, the little towns, the wineries, the B&Bs, were mostly picked over. They never approached what they called the necropolises. That was a good way to die. The little towns that dotted the California coast, the individual farmhouses, the gas stations, some of those were still untouched. At that point, a few of Devon's people, mostly the scavs and the fathers, had built up stores of food. For them, hunger was a choice. Novak had a pantry stacked floor-to-ceiling with canned goods.

They were headed to what amounted to a rest stop along the 46, a road that joined the 1 and 101 like an H drawn by someone with cerebral palsy. It was a gas station, a convenience store and the house where the owner had lived. They caught a glimpse of it on a previous run, tucked behind an overturned big rig—maybe an improvised barrier, maybe a terrified jackknife.

As the belly of the rig came into view, they turned off their engines and coasted to the crunchy side of the road.

Prey animals pause, cock their heads, and wait. Novak and his men did that. There was nothing. Geeks were usually heard before they were seen, especially through wild areas that had a chance to fill in. They crashed through planted areas and chewed up dead leaves with their feet. Indoors, they ran into walls, pawed at doors, and knocked things off walls and shelves. Novak thought of it as being hunted by drunks with concussions.

He reached to his belt and hooked his fingers around the heads of the hatchet and hammer. A practiced flick and pull, and they were in either hand, ready for action. Stew wrung the handle of his machete as he slipped his riot shield into place. Martinez rested a baseball bat across his shoulder. Only Pulaski didn't draw, but kept a hand on the hilt.

The group approached the rig with caution, looking for geeks that had gone dormant.

Ahead, the white gravel of the rain gutters expanded into the parking lot of the gas station. The pumps were dark, but probably still had a good amount of gas in them. The mini-mart was at the edge of the greenery, and beyond that, down a short path, they could see a nice white two-story farmhouse barely peeking in. Novak listened to the forest noises: the birds, the insects. As long as those kept up, they were safe. Animals couldn't turn into geeks, but they counted as food. That was why the dog was extinct.

Pulaski scaled the rig like a monkey and scrambled to the cab. He glanced through the driver's window, then looked back and shook his head before jumping back down.

The mini-mart was a little better. Some *Chocodiles* still in the wrapper, some soda still in the can, some gorp miraculously ignored. A few cartons of smokes, as good as money after the end. Then, the treasure: eight cans of mixed nuts, unopened and probably covered in fat salt grains the size of a baby's fist. Those went in the sacks.

The rest of the place was quiet. That meant it was time for the house.

Houses were bad: lots of last stands happened inside houses. Geeks got locked in, trapped, sometimes even lost. Turn a corner, get a face full of snapping teeth. Still, this wasn't Novak's first dance.

He motioned, to his men, sending Martinez and Pulaski around the back. Novak took Stew and Robellada up the front way. One of the first things anyone learned, and what every parent taught the few children being born, was never to go anywhere alone unless there was no other option. Within the Barricade, everyone spent a good deal of time making that rule breakable.

The house had a nice wide porch. Good place to sit, if it looked out on something other than a gas station and a tipped-over big rig. The door looked relatively intact. That worried Novak. He tried the knob. Unlocked.

He eyed Stew, who had his war face on. He flicked his eyes; this said enough. They knew every look and gesture of the other.

Novak turned the handle gingerly, then slid the door open. He had the hatchet raised high, ready to open the skull of any trapped geek that heard dinner coming in through the front. Nothing. He slid inside, followed first by Robellada, trailed by Stew.

To the right, there was a dining room. He was relieved that there was nothing on the table. More than once, he had come across a last meal, and that, more than anything else, took him back. After the end of the world, going back was never a good thing.

A loose swinging door led deeper into the house, probably a kitchen. To the left, there was an empty living room.

In terms of scavenging, the most important thing was food, but books weren't far behind. It didn't matter to Novak, but he knew he could trade books to Judy Bloch or Walter Calomiris. Calomiris had a good library in rooms 101 and 102 that was open to anyone who signed the ledger.

Ahead, stairs went up and a hallway led to the back of the house. Just beneath the stairs, he saw an alcove. Didn't like that. He nodded to it and hugged the wall, while Stew made sure nothing lunged out of one of the doorways. The alcove was empty.

Out back: a crash.

A shout.

Martinez cursing. A dry sound.

Martinez begging. A wet sound.

Silence.

Novak accelerated through the back. Not a run, but a jog. A balls-out run had the potential to blind him to the threats all around. No matter how bad it was there, it could always get worse. He wouldn't let his guard down until he was back at home in his chair, sipping at his evening's Jack.

Pulaski was standing in the backyard, watching the treeline. His posture was relaxed, his eyes scanning through the undergrowth. He held his bloody sword out in front of him. At his feet: the corpse of a female in a ragged sundress. Her skin was fishbelly white. She was missing the top half of her head, and was only just starting to leak that jellylike geek blood.

Next to the dead geek: Martinez's body. The top half of his head sat next to him, meat-down, almost like he'd been buried up to his nose. Novak scanned the corpse of his friend: there was a bite wound on Martinez's left hand, between the middle and ring knuckles.

Pulaski smoothly turned. There was no expression in his eyes. Martinez had been bitten. Get bitten, turn into a geek. No cure, no hope. Pulaski had done the right thing. Novak had done it many times. More than he liked to think about. Still, there was no one as eager as Pulaski when it came time to put a potential geek down.

Robellada's voice, quavering: "Oh. Oh, God. Mr. Novak, Tom."

Stew's voice, steady, thick: "It's okay. Keep your eyes open. Where there's one, there's more."

Novak took the stairs. Pulaski took a graceful step back, almost like he thought Novak was going to take a swing. Novak said: "Stew, take Robellada inside. Bring a sheet for Martinez." Novak pronounced the *L*s in the kid's name, even though no one else did.

"Mr. Novak!"

Novak ran back up the stairs. They didn't have time. There would be more geeks, and they'd be coming. He didn't need Robellada crumbling. Novak got in the kid's face. "Martinez is fucking dead, got it? You whining isn't going to bring him back, but if Pulaski hadn't chopped his head off, that might have. Understand?"

Tears welled up at the corners of Robellada's eyes. "Yeah. He's fucking dead." He nodded repeatedly. "No whining."

Novak wanted to slap him. Instead, he just grabbed Robellada's collar and leaned in, washing him with sour breath. "Yeah. That's it."

"Glen. Glen, I got this." It was Stew, taking Novak's hands off the kid.

Pulaski said: "Let him keep blubbering. Might bring the geeks out."

Stew fixed Pulaski's eyes: "Shut your mouth. He doesn't need this."

Novak grunted. "Neither do I. Take Robellada inside. Clear the house."

Stew was gentle. He talked to Robellada quietly and led him back inside. And Stew managed to do this without dropping his guard. He was ready for any geek that was lying in wait inside. Robellada was nearly helpless. A hidden geek would mean the end of him, just like it had with Martinez.

This thought pushed Novak's attention down to Martinez's body, cooling in the sun. He made a decision: they'd bury Martinez back in Devon. He'd earned that.

There was a crash inside. Novak resisted the urge to run up— Stew was cautious, if it got bad, he'd sing out. Instead, Novak put his back to the stairs and got ready for the inevitable. He heard thrashing up ahead, in the bushes. What had been a backyard was overgrown, disappearing into a solid green wall.

A grin grew across Pulaski's face. "Sounds like someone's hungry."

Novak didn't bother to answer. Pulaski didn't need encouragement.

One geek shambled through the green. The crashing farther off in the darkness said at least two more were following. Hopefully, that was the end of it. The geek held its arms out, opened its mouth, picked up its stagger as it got visual contact.

Pulaski said: "Your show, boss."

Novak let the geek get some steps away from the green before he closed the distance. He ducked low and swept the geek's legs out from under it and planted the hatchet in the base of its head. No blood. Geeks didn't circulate. It collected in the feet and legs to putrefy, only leaking out when someone dropped one and gravity did its work.

Two more geeks crossed the line, one male and one female; though they had gender, they were *its*. They were something less than animals, as male and female, rather than man, woman or, worst of all, child.

Pulaski made an arc in the grass with his sword: his line in the sand.

Novak planted a foot on the geek's shoulder and yanked the hatchet free.

Pulaski advanced and beheaded the male, cut into the female's outstretched arms before chopping her head in two. The male's head bounced away into the trees where it would snap at anything that got too close. Both wounds were bloodless. Both bodies were still.

The door opened. Novak turned, half-expecting another geek. It was Stew, dragging another dead geek, minus a head. Robellada appeared a moment later, pulling another geek, this one with a caved-in face. Stew said: "The house is clear."

Novak said: "Good. Stack the geeks here. Pulaski and I are on geek detail. You two, ransack the house."

Robellada pulled a wadded up sheet from his backpack. "I brought a sheet for Tom." He handed it over rather than tossing it.

Novak knelt by Martinez's body, retrieved the top of his head and placed it on his chest, then wrapped him in the sheet. It was a shitty job, but he tried to do it with a little respect. At the very least, Martinez would never become one of *them*.

Novak hefted the first geek. Pulaski watched Novak's back as he hauled the dead weight to the bikes, one by one, tying a corpse to the back of each one. Finally, he put Martinez respectfully in Stew's sidecar, the only bike they had with one.

Stew and Robellada emerged after Novak had packed the last geek. Their bags were partway full, and Stew had what looked like a box gently packed with a shredded pillow. Stew approached Novak and held out the box. "Found these for you."

Novak pulled some of the synthetic stuffing aside and found long-stemmed wine glasses. They were dusty, but they looked new. "Thanks."

It was a decent run, but not one that was worth Tom Martinez.

As they revved the engines, a geek rounded the corner of the house. Female. Might even have been pretty in her old life. She, and Novak didn't catch himself mentally. He thought of her as she before he could issue the mental correction to it, to make her an object that could be broken apart. She had long hair, now hanging in greasy vines. Her mouth was wide, but some of that was shredded meat: something had worked over the left side of her face badly. Her left eye was a black void, the right a milky cataract. An earwig crawled over the teeth marks in her breast. She wore what used to be a white terrycloth bathrobe, but as she walked, it flapped open. She was wearing nothing else. The sight of the dark triangle under her soft belly turned Novak's stomach. He didn't want to get off the bike now and kill her. He thought about shooting her, but he only had fourteen rounds.

Let her wander. He gunned the engine and followed his men back along the 46 to Devon. When they arrived several hours before sundown, the clouds were coming in good now, blocking a large section of the sky. Rippey's men—now it was Gray Hervey and Louis Chu—opened the gate without a word. This was custom: give trouble on the way out, but never coming back.

As they drove up Hotel Street, Novak glanced to the meadows to his left. In the middle of them, the ramshackle tower of the Dinner Bell was the single beige accent in the green. A tiny shape sat in the lengthening shadows: Barrett Cheeseman, the bellringer, watching the Athena's herds returning home. Novak didn't have to get closer to know that Cheeseman was sipping from a warm can of Coke. The ground surrounding the Dinner Bell was crackling with discarded cans.

Novak and his men turned right on Shoal, and left before they hit First Baptist. They were headed for Paul Borassi's place. Before the end, Borassi had worked at some kind of Renaissance Faire. Novak was unclear on the details, but Borassi had a skill that had all but died out even before the apocalypse. He knew how to make candles.

His shop was in Town, flush against the eastern hill and on a dead end street called Sand. Most days, the stench blew over a single farm and out through a small gap at the top of the hill. Some days, the stench settled in to throttle Devon.

Borassi's place was a restaurant that had been converted from a craftsman mansion. The wide porch now held headless human bodies hanging upside from meat hooks, like chickens in the window of a Chinese market. Rising from the lawn, Borassi had constructed elaborate sculptures of tanned human leather and bone. It was a compulsion, but it was a compulsion that many shared. Not in the specifics, but in the broader sense. To stay sane, they all had to go a little crazy.

Borassi was out front, strapping longbones to longbones in something that looked like the playground equipment in Hell. He was a big man, broad across the shoulders, with gray hair and a beard. He wore a leather apron over his clothes and rubber gloves. Half-Santa and half-serial killer.

He gave them a headcount before addressing Novak. "They got Tom?"

Novak nodded, while his men started pulling geeks from the bikes and dumping them in front of Borassi. They made grotesque smacking sounds as they fell. "Five geeks for you."

"Say ten per?"

"Say twenty."

Borassi hesitated, as if he thought about haggling. Maybe he realized that Novak losing Martinez meant winning wasn't possible that time. Maybe he saw the cold look in Novak's eyes. "Twenty it is."

Twenty candles per geek body. He'd take the fat off these geeks, render it, make more candles. Bring him raw material, let him turn it into something he could trade in town. Novak did the math in his head: *That'd be four, no, five candles per for each of us.*

Borassi handed over a thick bundle. Novak stuck them in his pack, to be distributed later. They left Borassi without another word, retracing steps back to First Baptist. The somber white building dominated its corner. There was no fence: a sign of Rippey's arrogance. Novak's destination was around the back, the cemetery. The church was closed and locked, gold light falling from the windows and pooling on the verge.

Novak hoped that they would be ignored. He wasn't sure if he could take Rippey today. Novak picked up the shovel from where it leaned against the toolshed and started digging. The others found picks and shovels, some leaning against cracked wooden markers, others by the church, and helped. Most of the markers were wood, and looked like the Boot Hills of the westerns he used to adore.

The graveyard was bigger than it had been. Before Devon was a fortress, the cemetery was a garden. It had since spread to eat the old backyard of the church, into the alley beyond, and then to the yards of the houses on Shell Street. There would be a time when the whole town would just be the graveyard.

"Someone should get his wife," Stew said. He was looking at the dead roots sticking from the side of the trench.

Novak knew he was the one who should have to do it. He was in charge. He knew the woman—whose name he couldn't remember—would blame him, the same way Stew's husband or

Janelle Ford or whatever skinny piece of Athena trash Pulaski was banging would, if circumstances were different. He could count on tears, maybe fists to the chest, name-calling, shouting. She would want him to ask forgiveness just so she could refuse to grant it. She'd want Novak to comfort her even though she was inconsolable.

Novak knew that when it was his time, they wouldn't have to tell anyone.

He hated the words even as he said them. "You do it." He sent Stew because Robellada might cry and Pulaski was as sensitive as a brick.

They waited in silence while Stew trudged back to his bike. Then, the sound that Novak dreaded: footsteps coming up the back hall. The church's door opened and Gloria Wu poked her chubby face out. There were different standards for thin and fat after the end of the world. Gloria was the kind of woman who would always have a little extra meat on her face, even if the rest of her melted away to nothing. She still dressed like she thought it was the old world, but the gray suit, complete with a skirt, was worn through in a few places, with a couple stains that would never come out.

She fixed her eyes on Novak, then the trench, then back to him. "Mr. Novak, I'm so sorry." The tone was too sincere to be sincere.

"Yeah, thanks."

"Tom Martinez and Chris Stewart?"

"No. No, Stew's getting Martinez's wife."

"Thank the good Lord for small favors."

"That only one of my guys is dead?"

"In His divine mercy."

Novak considered telling her exactly where she could shove that mercy. Instead, he looked down at the shadow of his shovel.

Gloria said: "You probably want someone to deliver last rites."

"That's okay. We're fine."

"I'll get Reverend Rippey."

"Martinez was Catholic." Novak wasn't sure if this was true, but it seemed right.

"No Catholic priests in Devon. Maybe no Catholic priests in the world." She sounded smug. Before Novak could tell her not to bother herself, she disappeared back inside.

"Come on," he said, "let's lower him in."

He hopped into the grave and guided the body in with help from Pulaski at the head and Robellada at the feet. He took the dead weight and set Martinez in the damp earth as gently as possible. Down in the grave, it was unlikely that the others could hear him, but Novak didn't whisper to his friend. There were several things he thought of to say, but nothing seemed quite right. He reached up. Pulaski took him by the forearm and pulled him back to the land of the mostly living.

The back door opened again. Reverend Isador Rippey stepped into the bleeding sunlight. He was in his early fifties, but that was mostly seen in the creeping around his eyes and the gray at his temples. His thin mustache was still totally black, and his hairline was mostly intact. His skin was on the lighter side of brown, his eyes deep and dark. He probably used to be strong, but he had gone to seed. Rippey always dressed in stark black and white, and was likely the cleanest man in Devon. He clutched a worn Bible in one hand, and might have been the only person in Town unarmed.

Gloria Wu, Micah Rosenberg, and one of the Reverend's wives followed. Novak couldn't tell them apart: they were all thin and blonde, except for the newest one. Since she was only ten, she tended to stand out. As a group, they were known on the Hill as the Rippettes. Novak never bothered to learn their names.

Micah Rosenberg looked like he was trying to hide a smile. Novak thought about making Martinez's grave a party.

Rippey didn't smile, but he stuck his hand out. It was smooth, the handshake firm and sympathetic. "I am deeply saddened by your loss. Gloria informed me we are waiting on the widow?"

"Did Gloria also tell you that we're good?"

Rippey didn't acknowledge that. "I recall performing that ceremony. One of the Lord's greatest mysteries is separating husband and wife."

"Not much of a fuckin' mystery, Rev."

Pulaski chuckled.

"What is common is not necessarily manifest. And please, leave the language on the Hill."

Novak considered adding Rippey's request to the Lord's mercy, but the buzz of Stew's returning bike silenced that.

Stew brought the red-faced blonde whose name Novak still couldn't remember up to the lip of Martinez's grave.

Reverend Rippey nodded to her, but he seemed to ignore Stew.

"Mrs. Martinez, let me be the first to console you on this darkest day. There is a callow tendency to place blame at the feet of the Almighty, but look instead within. Our God is glorious. He is Holy, Holy, Holy. He saved me and He keeps me all by His infinite grace. Bless the Lord, oh my soul."

He seemed to remember that they were there to honor a dead man, and finally turned his attention to the pit. "Though Tomas Martinez was not among the saved, we have high hopes for the soul of his widow. In the Lord's wisdom, He has denied a soul that will never be His, to save one that He still can. His is the power, the wisdom and the glory forever and ever. Amen."

Of Novak's people, only Robellada said, "Amen."

Novak said: "Anyone want to say anything?" When Rippey opened his mouth, Novak held up a hand and fixed Rippey with the steely blue eyes. "Anyone who actually knew him."

Novak's eyes moved from Rippey to sweep past his guys and the gently crying blonde in Stew's arms. Robellada looked like he wanted to speak up. He shuffled his feet and wrung his hands, but he couldn't summon the courage. Not with Mr. Novak and the right Reverend seething. The kid was sensitive. Death still touched him. Novak had no idea how Robellada made it out of L.A. with that softness intact. He almost told Robellada to speak his mind when the widow let out something between a snort and a sob, a uniquely female sound that disgusted Novak, although he could not say why.

Finally, Stew spoke up. "Tom was a good man. He was good to have at your back, good to have at your side. He always brought more to the table than he took off it. We'll miss him."

Rippey shook the widow's limp hand.

Novak and Pulaski filled the hole.

The clouds filled in the sky.

They separated from there. Stew took the widow back home to the Hill. Robellada went home, probably meeting Janelle. Pulaski gunned his bike for the Athena. Novak headed back up Cliffside, past Hotel, toward Dr. Bloch's office. As he passed the intersection, he saw the tiny shape of Barrett Cheeseman. The little man threw his soda aside and started across the heath toward Novak.

As Novak pulled the bike over, that's when he heard the shouting.

"You faggot! Saw one of your men bit the fucking dust!"

Cheeseman was a dwarf. He was perfectly proportioned, he just looked like a child with a bizarrely wrinkled face and a helium voice. He seemed to fetishize soda, and always had a can whenever he wanted it. There were rumors that he had a cache hidden somewhere in Devon, and those rumors prompted the few children to hold scavenger hunts in the summer when the memory of cola was strongest.

He also hated Novak.

"Fuck off, freak."

"No, fuck you, Glennie! You think you can duck me, you pussyfag? You fucking crowbait shitbag motherfucker? Eat a geek's rancid cock!"

"Get back in your fucking tower before I put you there."

Novak ignored the rest of the abuse and went to the door of Bloch's office. He knocked.

After a minute, Dr. Bloch opened the door. She was maybe an inch taller than Novak, dark hair, dark eyes, and looked tired. She had brown freckles across the bridge of her nose. She was beginning to show, too. No one sober would ever call her beautiful, but she did more than turn Novak's head. Something about her modest beauty. The arch of her brow as it flowed into the freckles of her nose seemed at once exotic and familiar.

"Mr. Novak," she said. "Come on in." He kept things on a formal level: Mister and Doctor. Kept him safe.

Her office was her house. There was a waiting room that she'd turned into a living room, although the differences were minor, amounting to nothing more than a full ashtray and some glasses she'd forgotten to take back to the kitchen. Novak guessed her bedroom was one of the offices, but he never saw it.

"What do you have for me?" She took one of the seats and put a hand on her belly.

Novak fished into his bag. Antibiotics. He tossed them her way. She didn't make the catch, and so had to lean over to retrieve them. She held them up to examine, shaking each one like a rattle, as if to verify the contents.

She said: "Fuckin' ay. Half a bottle. Not bad. Thanks."

"It could be better."

"Every little bit counts."

"Right."

She was silent. Novak was almost ready to get up. Then: "I need a sample."

"Sample of what?"

"I need a living one."

"A living what?"

"A geek. One of them."

"They're not alive."

"You know what I mean."

Novak said: "Yeah, I guess I do. Begs the question."

"What for?"

"No. Are you fucking crazy?"

She took it in stride. "Maybe."

"One bite. One little nip, you're dead. And not good dead. Slow burn for a day, then you're a monster. You're the doctor here. You go, and we're all one more step beyond fucked."

"Don't you want to know why?"

"Not really."

"I thought you were a teacher."

"I was a gym coach."

She saw that he'd closed the avenue off, but she decided to open it up as best she could: "Look, we need to know what the infection actually is. Viral, bacterial, maybe fungal. Once we do, maybe we can cure it. Maybe we can immunize."

He shrugged. "And? Then what? In case you hadn't noticed, we're down to a couple hundred people here. Not exactly enough to rebuild. In a couple generations, we'll all have one eye and flippers."

"There are the nomads. And there have to be other settlements like this one."

"Okay, so that goes up to maybe a couple thousand. Twenty, tops."

She took a breath. "Have you ever heard of the Toba Event?"

He gave her a look: of course he hadn't heard of the fucking Toba Event.

She started up: "About 75,000 years ago, a volcano erupted. Not a normal volcano, either. We're talking an eruption that measured in the thousands of megatons. The ash thrown into the atmosphere plunged the earth into a sort of mini-Ice Age. Humanity nearly went extinct. All the other species of hominid died out. Every single one. Scientists think we were down to maybe ten thousand individuals. *Homo sapiens* was right at the brink. And we recovered."

"Yeah, without ever discovering a cure for volcanoes."

"This is our Toba. It's not the end until the last one of us is dead."

"Give it another couple years."

"You're a ball of sunshine," she said.

Novak rolled it around in his mouth then said, "Martinez died today."

That got her. "I'm sorry."

"It happens."

"You need to talk about it?"

"Just wanted to drop those off. When your crop comes in, take my share to my place. That is, if you can still get around."

She rubbed her belly. "I'll be fine."

"So you're the one." Novak left then, time to head for home.

The sun was down by the time he leaned his bike under the small awning on the north side of the house. It was a good house. Not his. When Novak had found it, it had been abandoned, probably since the end. Maybe the owners decided to run to one of the military evacuations that turned into geek smorgasbords. They had left one of the few places that could be called safe with a straight face. Novak wondered if he'd ever run into the owners someday, paler and hungrier than the pictures he consigned to the attic. Every sign of the owners had been purged, and the interior of the house looked strangely bare, even after four years of inhabitation. Novak didn't add to it. He only took away.

He stepped into darkness but found the candles on his end table by memory, the book of matches below them. The light of two candles was more than enough. Their subtle stench invaded the room. There was a part of him that wished he hadn't gotten used to that dead smell, like distant roadkill.

He took off the armor, dropping the stuff on the couch next to the box of stemware Stew had given him. He went outside to the front and drew up a bucket of water from the well. He sipped, barely noticing the plasticky taste.

Dinner was some corn, beans, and squash: Dr. Bloch once told him that added up to a perfect protein diet. He didn't know what the hell that meant, but he was never hungry afterwards, so that's what he grew out back. He made some extra and portioned it out into three Tupperware containers. He looked them over and added a couple tangerines and a can of peaches.

He grabbed a bottle of Jack from the cupboard and two tumblers. Those were set on the table next to his chair. He took the box of stemware under one arm and went outside. A cruel wind flipped in off the Pacific. He moved through the swaying pines toward the crest of the Hill. The peak abruptly dropped away to a cliff, the angry ocean roiling a couple hundred feet below. He opened up the box and took out the first glass.

Probably had never been used. Perfect form, maybe even hand-blown. Delicate, beautiful, subtle.

He kissed it once and threw it over the cliff.

He couldn't hear the shatter, but he pretended he could, washing through the wind like spice.

He threw each glass over one by one. When he was finished, he kicked the cardboard box after them and walked home.

He settled into his chair and poured two fingers of Jack into each tumbler. He drank one. He refilled it and thought about the broken glass at the mouth of the Pacific.

His doorbell rang.

He knew who it was. He swallowed his second and poured a third. "Come in."

It was Karen Harmon, a canvas bag under one arm. She didn't look tired, but she didn't meet his eyes either.

He unzipped, let her take him out and into her mouth. She worked quickly and he shut his eyes and tried to think of nothing at all. When she was finished, she swallowed, picked up the other tumbler of Jack and threw it back.

He said: "It's in the kitchen."

She went in there and put what she found on the counter in her canvas bag. "See you next week," she said.

He nodded.

She shut the door. She'd take the food to her husband and daughter. It was a good arrangement. She got food and water and paid what she could. Novak justified it: *If I was a real bastard, I would have demanded more than a blowjob. If I was a real bastard, I'd want her daughter, who just turned sixteen and looked like Karen would have without the crow's feet and emerging dewlap. If I was a real bastard, I would just take both of them and leave the husband to rot.*

He watched the far wall and drank more Jack. Past midnight, when the rain just started to tap on his roof, he decided to go to bed. Despite the liquor, he was barely wobbly. He picked up his gear and the candles and went into the blacked out bedroom. He pulled the footlocker from under his bed, opened it up and reached in without bothering to look.

The pain was nearly blinding. He felt the crunch, the give of the first knuckle of his left pinkie, the pop of the tendon and the rip of the skin.

Then the pain washed away: shock.

He pulled his hand back, felt the skin tear loose.

He looked.

In the footlocker, placed just so: a geek head.

Mouth open: his finger sticking out like a cigarette.

He looked at his hand: blood flowing down, across, black gold in the candlelight.

He was bitten.

He was a dead man.

- 3 -

FOR A SECOND, NOVAK HAD the urge to chop his hand off, burn the stump, hope for the best. Try to beat the infection to the source. That was the natural reaction. He'd seen it tried. It never worked. There's no beating the infection.

In the old days, they said twenty-four hours at the outside from the moment of the bite to death. First, the fever burns, cooking the brain, making it see things that weren't there. Blood would turn thick, tacky. Skin would go fishbelly-white. Cataracts would bloom on the eyes. Organs shut down, one at a time.

Then death.

Then reanimation.

Novak hadn't gotten a death sentence; he'd gotten something worse.

He looked at his hand. The pinkie was bitten off at the first knuckle, just popped off. Blood spurted from the wound and slashed down his hand. He wrapped it into a burning fist and rushed into the kitchen. He was going to have to stop the bleeding.

When he unclenched the fist, the spurting had already stopped. That was the infection. Already taking a ride through his body.

The blood burbled up like a swamp. Soon it would turn into a poison scab. He wrapped the wound tightly in gauze, wincing as it burned. On the bandage: an eclipse, haloed in red. Anyone who got a good look at it would know immediately. He was a carrier. He was the enemy.

Once bitten, anyone in town would kill him. Some might enjoy it more than others. He had flashes of Pulaski beheading Martinez, of Rippey's smile when they killed Rodney Gautreaux. Novak saw himself killing those who had been bitten. He'd lost count of how many died that way. See the wound, and anyone who liked could try to take him out. Better to kill him when he was weak from the transformation than when he was freshly risen and endlessly hungry.

He went back into the other room.

The geek head saw him, snapping its jaws. He ended it with his hammer.

He felt a bubble rising in his chest. He forced it down. Blinked his eyes. Kept things clear.

He picked up his gloves: fingerless, black leather. He pulled the right one on. Then the left. It burned. He pulled harder. It snapped into place, the bandaged nub barely poking free. He bit his lip to keep from making a sound. His left hand was heavy, wet.

Then, the tapping of the rain grew louder. No, not the rain. The door.

For a single mad moment, he saw Pulaski on the other side, ready to kill him. No, Pulaski wouldn't know.

Novak ripped open the door, hoping the dim light would hide his terror.

Robellada stood outside in the light rain. "Mr. Novak?"

He could hardly focus on the kid. The infection was burning through his body. It had already killed him. He was just too dumb to know it. "What do you want, kid?"

"What do I want? Mr. Novak, I wanted to talk..."

Novak tried to force the normality into his voice. "Robellada. Not now. It's late."

Robellada looked up, like he hadn't realized. "It's late. Yeah.

I'm sorry, Mr. Novak."

He shut the door, leaned against it. He was going to die. He had no way to head that off. He shut his eyes.

In the silent room, he listened to the gentle tapping of the rain. The geek's head was smashed inward, like a pumpkin after Halloween. It had been beheaded, and not cleanly. A couple hacks had taken it off its shoulders. He couldn't tell gender and couldn't remember what it looked like before he'd hammered it to pieces.

He realized something: it hadn't crawled there with its lips.

Someone put that goddamn thing in my locker. Someone too pussy to settle his differences with me like a man. Someone who would turn me into one of those things. Someone who I was going to find. Someone who was going to spend as much time as I could manage in excruciating fucking pain.

It all fit. It wasn't going to be a great question. He knew instantly who had murdered him. Jackson Harmon, whose wife had been servicing Novak a couple hours before.

He didn't bother with his gear. Wouldn't need it. If Harmon was a real man, he wouldn't have had to turn his wife into a whore to feed his family.

He was through his door and into the lightly falling rain.

The Harmon house was close, downhill and up a short, winding driveway.

The house was like its inhabitants. Cheerful from far away, but look closer, see that the hummingbird feeder was empty, except for a red crust. See the cobwebs just outside of hand traffic. See the dirt collecting at the corners of the dark windows, the dead flies on the sill. See the rotted plants and rocky soil.

Novak kicked the front door in.

A scream tore into him. A silhouette hugged a wall ahead. Small, thin.

Novak said to it: "Who the fuck is that?"

No response. It melted into shadow.

Another shape, skinny and tall, suddenly detached from the shadows. It was holding something. Maybe a baseball bat. It spoke: "What the hell...?" A man's voice.

Novak said: "You."

Harmon didn't have a chance to swing. Novak hit him low, shoulder in Harmon's guts, and lifted him off his feet. Harmon slammed into the ground, Novak on top between his knees, like Novak was fucking him. He dropped three hammer-fists on Harmon. He gurgled. Novak had perfect control over the other man; he could move him into any position he liked, batter him to unconsciousness and death if he wanted. Harmon had no leverage, no power, no hope.

Just like Novak.

Then, a scream from above.

Light.

Flickering, golden light.

Jackson Harmon was holding his hands up, not even trying to fend off Novak, just trying not to get hit. He had a cut under his left eye, blood coming from his nose and mouth. His brown eyes were wide, uncomprehending. His baseball bat rolled not far away.

"Get the hell off my husband!" Karen's voice.

Novak looked up.

Karen held a candle in one hand, her daughter Michelle with the other arm. Both were terrified.

Novak said to Harmon: "Go on, you pussy, tell them. Tell them what you did."

"I don't know..."

Novak hit him again. Twice.

Karen screamed. Michelle ripped free and grabbed the bat. She was shorter than Karen, growth stunted from the five years of apocalypse living. She was prettier than her mom, with sharper features that made her look more like an ideal than a girl. Novak's eyes crawled up her skinny arms, arms that were skinny because she ate only what Novak gave her.

"Go on, kid."

He fixed her with his bloodshot eyes.

Her brown eyes looked gold in the candlelight.

He whispered again: "Take your swing."

Her lips trembled. Her eyes watered. She dropped the bat.

He wished he was silent, but he couldn't help himself. He looked down at Harmon. "That's why you live under me. Now tell them what you did before I drag you out of the Barricade and feed you to the geeks."

"Please, you can't!"

"Tell them!"

"I don't know what you're talking about!"

Novak wanted to hit Harmon again. He was bleeding freely now. Harmon's life was Novak's. Not like before, when it was in some metaphorical sense. This was the power of the barbarian, his for the taking. This was a case of being able to kill a man with bare hands and get away with it. Harmon was helpless. Weak. *Goddamn it.*

Novak stood up, turned to Karen and the kid. Both were crying, but trying not to; Michelle harder than her mother. She had just been broken for the first time, and it would never hurt this bad again. Novak looked down at his victim. He was a skinny man, short beard. Dressed for bed: wifebeater and boxer shorts. Blood spotted along the yellowed undershirt. Panicked, Novak looked at his hand. The bandage had held.

Karen said: "Worried you hurt yourself on my husband's face?"

He tried to think of something to shoot back at her. He thought Harmon had killed him.

Novak saw it in Harmon's eyes. He really had no idea what was happening. The attack was out of the clear blue sky. Maybe he thought Novak was just exercising his rights. Novak fed them. Novak used his wife. Novak could do what he liked.

Goddamn it.

Novak wanted to hit him for that.

Michelle was biting back her tears, but they still rolled down her cheeks like tree sap. He reckoned that she hated herself for crying. She hated herself for letting Novak see that. Novak wanted to comfort her. He wanted to beg her forgiveness for what he'd done then and forever. He opened his mouth, but the words stuck in the back of his throat.

Instead, he said: "You had your chance. Should have taken it."

She shut her eyes, freed up more tears to form slick rivers on her cheeks.

Novak stalked out.

He looked out over the Hill. A few lights still twinkled in windows, giving off that deadstink. There was another option: downhill, curtains like shrouds. Martinez's widow. She could have been that mad, and she would have had the time. But could she have a geek's head in her place? The thought of going in there made him want to throw up. If she was innocent, he didn't think he could handle that. Not after what he'd done to Jackson Harmon.

He went home.

It wasn't Harmon, but he wasn't the only one with reason to want Novak dead. He paced the house, putting the list together in his mind.

Name one: Walter Calomiris. Motive: jealousy. Every time Novak fucked Inez, he was hammering another nail into his coffin. Calomiris found out, maybe someone on the Hill did for extra food, maybe from one of his own men. He sent one of his men to plant the head; Calomiris wouldn't do that on his own. Inez said he didn't care. She said he never touched her. That could have been a lie to ease a conscience that wasn't bothering Novak.

Name two: the right Reverend Isador Rippey. Motive: power. Novak was a Calomiris ally in that Novak supported the status quo. The Hill was the Hill and Calomiris liked it that way, while Rippey would rather see it made part of Town. Less of a motive, but Rippey's people had been getting antsy. A thought flickered through his mind: *Could be that's what Martinez was trying to warn me about.*

Maybe there were other names. Smaller people on the food chain, thought they were doing right by the boss. Take out Novak the one way they knew they could do it. The one way they wouldn't have to face him. All of Devon remembered what he'd done to Gautreaux's group.

Novak strapped the gear back on. The pads were heavy until they slipped into the grooves they'd worn. If he was going to die, he was going to die armed and armored. He shut the twice-dead head in the otherwise empty footlocker. Let that be his suicide note.

The wound throbbed. Any movement, any finger twitch, sent a sharp stab up through the arm. He tried to ignore it. He couldn't.

He walked out into the rain. It wasn't heavy enough to soak through his clothes. The trees caught most of it, only to drop in fat blobs when the sea exhaled inland. He took the Hill in long strides.

The sounds of the ocean were far below. The moon was nearly full. The Hill dropped away at the edge of his feet.

Five years after the world ended. That was a good run. Five years longer than he probably had a right to. Five years ago, that terrible Thursday when what they thought was rioting broke out. Five years ago, looking into the eyes of his kids, telling them he had to get home, telling them they should do the same.

He remembered Ricky Robellada in that moment. The kid's eyes were huge. Novak could tell the kid wanted to say something, but he couldn't make himself. Novak left the kids in the gym that day and ran to his car. Even with all of that, he had been too late.

His gun was loaded. Seven shots in the clip, seven more in the spare. Thirteen more than he needed.

He could eat that bullet under the full moon and pretend that the rain somehow washed away what he did. If he did it right, he wouldn't come back.

Somehow, the gun ended up in his right hand. The perfect right hand. He flexed the left, winced as it bit back. The palm felt sticky inside the leather.

One bullet. Let the body *(not the body, me)* fall into the Pacific. They would never know. The Harmons would say that he'd gone crazy. Jackson Harmon could show them what Novak had done to a man that never did anything to deserve it. No one would piece it together.

No one except the piece of shit who planted the head.

The pistol was heavy.

He could lift it easily.

It would taste like rare steak but only for an instant.

He shoved the pistol back into the holster.

Whoever had done it was in Devon somewhere. Probably one of two men, one of the most powerful men in town.

He would show them real power. The power that comes with ultimate freedom.

He turned his back on the ocean. Ahead and below, blinking through the trees, scattered lights in Town. To the left, the Athena, a few windows like the golden eyes of lions. A small flame burned on the roof of the south wing.

Good idea.

If he had to burn Devon down, he would find his murderer.

There were only so many holes in which to hide.

For a moment, he saw Michelle's face, tear-streaked. It changed to another face briefly. He shut his eyes to banish the ghosts.

He banished them with images of Devon in flames.

He knew just where to start.

- 4 -

BEFORE THE WORLD ENDED, GLEN Novak had been a wrestling coach. He taught P.E. But that wasn't a passion, getting the overweight kids to climb the rope or learn the basics of basketball. His passion was coaching the wrestling team. He'd been a wrestler himself, but he had failed.

Not failed exactly, but he didn't succeed. For collegiate wrestlers, the only place to go was the Olympics, and Novak hadn't been good enough. It hurt for a while. Teaching burned some of that away, but the sting of failure never left entirely.

Failing was about a loss of control, and wrestling was all about control. Controlling the opponent, controlling oneself. Wrestling was, in essence, about who controlled whom. Who used the pillars of strength and leverage to break down the opponent. Novak understood control very well.

And he had lost all of it.

The Hotel Athena looked out over Devon. In the light of the full moon it seemed to brood, with its eyes flickering balefully as he approached. Maybe before the end, it had once been welcoming. It was intended as a home away from home, but it had become a fortress. Before he had arrived, the transformation had already been completed. They had installed the sliding metal gate over the front doors and the bars on the ground floor windows. The smaller barricades around the south and east sides had fallen, but geography limited the avenues of attack. There was a long wooden staircase that led to the beach below; but the beach had been artificial and the currents washed it away until all that remained were jagged rocks. Geeks did wander out of the surf every now and again, but they were always spotted on the long walk up.

Novak walked to the Athena. The rain still fell, just heavy enough to let him know he was awake, light enough to make him think he was dreaming. His left hand throbbed with his heartbeat.

The Athena was almost L-shaped. The bulk of it consisted of the long six-story wings that faced south and east. The lobby, facing southeast, was only one story, and connected both. In the crotch of the L that faced the ocean, that was where the hotel pool had been, along with a low stage for local bands. It had become a garden, complete with pens for a small herd of goats, cows and some chickens. In the daytime, the herds grazed on the meadows between the Athena and the Hill. The Athena's well was large, and sunk right next to the hotel, across the way from the outdoor meth lab.

The front doors were open. In its time, the hotel had been something. It was a place for people who wanted easy access to the central coast. Short drive to Hearst Castle, short drive to half a dozen wineries, short drive to pretty much anywhere worth going on vacation. Not that any of it was worth going to any more. Right after the infection, a group of people barricaded themselves up in Hearst Castle. Novak went there a year before to salvage and what he found was death. Walter Calomiris had owned the Athena before the apocalypse, and he owned it still, mostly because no one took it from him.

The floor used to be white, some kind of fake marble. Over the last five years, the constant tread of dirty feet created a shit-smear of dirt that led almost to reception. That's where Calomiris posted the first of his guards. They were big bullyboys who might have stopped Novak if he'd been someone else.

He stalked past them. First, he planned to check what used to be the hotel bar. Turn left into the south wing, first door on the right. It would have looked out on the bikinis at the pool, but both were dried up.

The bar was still a bar. It sold liquor from the still out by the east wall, but prices were pure barter with cigarettes being the preferred currency. Sometimes it sold the real booze that scavs like Novak found.

A stage had been set up against the back wall, covering the tinted windows in cheap black curtains. There was a spot, though who dragged that fucker back was a mystery. If they spent their time looting things like that, they were either living the good life on the sixth floor, or they were shambling around in the woods waiting for Novak to plant a hatchet in their head.

It wasn't full, but it wasn't empty either. It was the middle of the night. Could have been a weeknight, but it wasn't like anyone kept track of those nowadays. More than half the people in here didn't have far to stagger home, either.

All eyes were on the stage. It took him a minute, but Novak was pretty sure he'd seen her around the Athena before. She was a blonde, and skinny, even for the current time. She was mostly bones with a little skin stretched over, and what she was doing wasn't really dancing, but she was doing it naked. He'd seen worse.

He turned away, not out of disgust, but because the little dancer didn't matter. Inez wasn't in the bar, but at a table in the corner, the next best thing. Her cousin, Rudolfo Marcos, wasn't just her cousin; he was also her bodyguard. He was maybe half a head taller than Novak, but quite a bit slimmer. Marcos was drinking out of an old water bottle, but Novak could smell the coffin oil from where he was standing. He sat down next to Marcos, both of them facing the stage.

Marcos gave him a sidelong look. "Hey, Novak."

"Marcos. Where's your cousin?"

"I got a lot of cousins."

"Then where's the one that's still alive?"

His head snapped around. He watched the tendons in Marcos's arm draw tight. He refused to look directly at Marcos: *Let him swing if he has the balls for it.*

Turned out he didn't. "She's in her suite. Sleeping."

"Alone?"

He took a long drink. "Well, you're down here."

Of course he knew. He was the woman's bodyguard. Someone had to alibi her, and Marcos made good sense. He said: "I need to talk to her."

Marcos shook his head. "She's sleeping. It's the middle of the fucking night."

"Yeah, I know. I saw the moon."

The music stopped to dusty applause. The girl stopped dancing, just held her ribs like she was cold and kept looking at nothing. Jones the emcee, in his suit that might have once been white, stepped into the spot and didn't even squint. "A big hand for Stacy, everybody!" A little more applause.

Stacy picked up a coat, wrapped her bones in it and scurried backstage.

Jones went on: "We have something special for everybody. Fresh from the Bakersfield necropolis, Mr. Tanner and his exotic Pink Snapper!"

More applause, some of it even sounded genuine. Tanner lived on the third floor of the Athena. He was a scav, and a good one, too. His gang of three ranged farther inland than Novak's, but the guy didn't have a good eye for what was needed and what wasn't. When he came back, there was even odds he'd be hauling a load of porno mags as he would be bringing canned goods.

Tanner was dressed in a leather harness and not much else, his skin crinkling like a cooked pig. He dragged a geek on an animal control leash, female, probably would have been gorgeous back when it was breathing. It wore some filthy lingerie, hiding absolutely nothing. The bite marks were still livid on her inner thighs. Her nipples had been bitten clean off. Tanner's erection was bad enough, but the look on his face was worse. Novak felt like putting his hatchet in both of them. It'd be a favor for all concerned.

"What the fuck is that?"

"I think she was a stripper or something."

"It'll bring others."

Marcos shrugged. "One geek ain't so bad. Besides, where is it gonna bring 'em? Up the stairs? No problem. The Barricade? Fine by me."

"This is fucked."

Marcos said: "Have to do something for entertainment."

"That thing gets off its leash..."

"There's a roomful of motherfuckers who will put her down."

"Drunks who probably wish they could remember the time they were only seeing double."

"We ain't had an outbreak for... shit, going on three years now. Not since Rodney Gautreaux's kid got bit."

Everyone knew the story. Gautreaux was a scav, used to be the other number one guy in Town, back when there was a question over whose neighborhood it would be. Gautreaux believed that practice was essential to survival, so he used to catch live geeks—as live as geeks got—and bring them back. He was anal about security, but that didn't matter. He didn't remove the bite, so they were just as dangerous as they always were. The true danger of geeks, that like attracted like, was only half-known then, the kind of thing that some people believed implicitly while others dismissed as an urban legend.

Gautreaux strung them up for target practice. He tied them down for close in practice. One of the fuckers got free. No one ever figured out how, just that its tether was frayed through. Maybe the geek figured it out, maybe some animal chewed it up, maybe the tether rubbed up against a rock too many times. Didn't matter. Gautreaux found his kid with a fresh wound, and after putting the geek down, hid the little boy away. Everyone who survived the first year of hell said they would kill anyone with the bite. It's one thing to say, and another thing to face your own flesh and blood, crying and begging.

Two days later, Gautreaux and his whole family were turned. Two days after that, geeks roamed Devon. A swarm massed from inland, broke through the Barricade and joined up. Devon was on its way to becoming a tiny necropolis.

Reverend Rippey assembled a group to go out before it got too bad. Rippey went himself, the last time he would do that, along with some of his guys and a few people from the Athena, including Marcos. Novak took Pulaski and Martinez, leaving Stew in the Athena to look after their people. That group butchered every geek in Devon. They went to the buildings that the geeks had gathered around and found what they knew they would: survivors, some of whom had been bitten, some of whom hadn't.

The bitten were slaughtered.

Rippey forced the bitten survivors to the cliff, a somber look on his face. Novak saw the light in his eyes. He was enjoying it. He put them on their knees. These were people they knew. Dr. Judy Bloch had freed herself from the Athena, and she tried to stop them. She didn't beg; she demanded. She tried to interpose herself. She asked for samples, to study the process of the change. She asked to make sure that everyone was in fact bitten.

Pulaski took the heads off one by one, speared the base of the neck and dumped the bodies in the Pacific.

Bloch got nothing.

Novak said: "Yeah."

Marcos grinned. "Maybe we're about due. If I had to put down money, I'd... you know Booker? Lives on the third floor here, came in about a year back? Yeah, he's my guess for ground zero. Guy like that... strange."

Novak knew who Booker was, a creepy little fucker, with thin lips and a prematurely gray beard, but nothing beyond that. "What do you mean 'strange'?"

"I mean that if we were in the old days, we'd all be doing interviews about how nice and quiet he was."

"I get it."

"Yeah."

Novak stood up. "Nice talk."

"Going home?"

"No, I'm going to talk to your cousin."

"I thought we went through that."

Novak kept walking. "You can try to stop me if you want."

Marcos thought about that. He looked at his table, and what Tanner was doing to Pink Snapper onstage. Maybe that kept him in his seat. Maybe it was the booze. Whichever excuse he wanted was fine by Novak.

Novak found the service stairs next to the bar and took those up. Walter and Inez Calomiris lived in the honeymoon suite on the top floor of the south wing, so it was a hell of a walk. The story of the Calomirises was common knowledge to everyone in Devon. Inez had been a maid in the old days, her cousin Marcos a groundskeeper. When the world ended, Walter's wife had gotten the bite. No one ever admitted to putting her down, but most fingers pointed at Marcos for the job, and he never denied it. Inez moved in with the big man. Novak wasn't sure how official the marriage was, by the old standards of the term, but it was enough that they said they were married and no one could challenge a damn thing Walter did.

Novak's footsteps seemed to aggravate the wound. He tried to ignore it, but every three steps he'd get a sharp pain that crept into the rest of his hand to settle in the center of his palm. He wanted to look at it, but the stairs were dark, with only a single candle burning at each landing. The entire stairwell was thick with the candle smoke.

Something clattered hollowly past Novak. He pulled the hatchet reflexively and looked where it came from rather than where it went—reflexes bred by the end. He saw a shape at the fifth-floor landing, small enough to be a child, but get closer, and it would be no kid. A snap and a hiss from the top confirmed this.

Novak didn't have to look to know the clattering thing was a Coke can.

He rounded the landing, facing the exit to the sixth floor. Sitting on the top step, sucking on an aluminum can with half a six-pack sitting next to him: Barrett Cheeseman, the bellringer.

Cheeseman said: "Thought I smelled shit and lube."

"Keep talking. I might decide it's time to drop you out a fucking window."

"I was going to ask what you were doing up here, but we all know the answer to that. Fuck, I bet old Walt knows the answer to that." In the dim light, Novak saw Cheeseman's wrinkled childface twisting into something that might have been a smile.

"So he knows?"

Cheeseman shrugged. "You gone faggot or something? As big a pussy as you are, I think maybe you could fuck Walt's brains out his ears." He took a pull on his Coke.

"Where do you get those? You never trade with me."

"Up your mother's fuckhole."

Novak passed Cheeseman on the stairs and kicked the half a six-pack down them. As they tumbled, one burst, spraying sticky soda over the wall.

Cheeseman got up to fetch them. "You piece of shit."

"My mother's buried in Glendale Forest Lawn if you want to get some more."

Novak shut the door on Cheeseman and went out into the sixth-floor hall. It was cleaner on the top than the rest of the hotel. Some of that was because barely anyone came up here, just the Calomirises, bodyguards and Novak. Still, the carpets were wearing down in the middle and some smudges on the walls had become permanent.

He turned left. The honeymoon suite was at the end of the hall. So was the sentry. He knew the man, Tigran Gamburyan, a friend of Stew's who came over to the Hill every Friday for D&D. Absurdly, he remembered at that moment that Gamburyan played a half elf, whatever that meant, but occasionally Stew would talk about whatever weird thing Gamburyan had done the way a father talks about a problem child he really loves.

Gamburyan was a pretty rangy guy, and calling him hairy didn't justify it. He was practically a sasquatch. He watched Novak with hard eyes that glittered like onyx. He leaned back in a chair by Inez's door, balancing himself with a baseball bat he used like a cane.

As Novak approached, Gamburyan righted his chair with a thump. A few steps away and he stood up. Novak only looked right at him when Gamburyan finally spoke: "Mr. and Mrs. Calomiris ain't seeing anybody." He had the traces of an accent that Novak identified from teaching in Glendale before the end. Armenian.

"Tell Mrs. Calomiris I'm here to see her."

"Don't understand, bro. They're not seeing anybody. Come back tomorrow and it's cool."

Novak looked up at Gamburyan. He had maybe a head on Novak, but both men knew that probably wasn't enough. Novak saw it in those black eyes: Gamburyan was psyching himself up for a fight that he believed to be inevitable.

He was right.

Novak bulled into Gamburyan's midsection, mashing his stomach between shoulder and wall. The air in his lungs whooshed out of him.

Novak pushed off the wall for separation. Gamburyan wobbled, trying to suck air into crushed lungs. Novak punched him in the jaw with the right hand, then the gut with the left. He instantly regretted that as the fire bloomed up his wrist.

That agony gave Gamburyan the time to recover enough to throw a punch, but it was a looping, lazy thing. Novak stepped inside the taller man's reach and grabbed the side of his head. At that moment, Novak knew he could hurt Gamburyan as much or as little as he liked. A quick heave using his body as a fulcrum and Gamburyan was on the ground, drooling over the rug. Novak picked up the chair and broke it over the other man. He was gentled after that.

Novak tried the door. Locked.

He kicked it in.

Inez was already coming out, wrapped in her robe and brandishing a .38 Special at head level. Novak read the panic on her face: *the geeks made it in somehow.*

"Glen?" she said. Novak winced inwardly. Anywhere Calomiris could hear, either with his ears or those of his men, Glen was Mr. Novak.

"Where's your husband?"

She shrugged. She had told Novak that Calomiris hardly ever slept in the same room as her. Sad, considering they were still sort of newlyweds. At least they'd passed the paper anniversary. They'd be coming up on the... whatever the five year one was. Susan would have known.

She said, quavering, and not putting the gun down yet: "What are you doing here?"

He could take Inez, but not from fifteen feet away and not when a gun was involved. He had no idea how good a shot she was, but this wasn't how he wanted to find out. "Someone tried to kill me."

"Who?"

"Your husband maybe. You gonna put your gun down?"

She didn't. "Are you here to kill him?"

"The thought crossed my mind."

"I heard your man was killed?"

"Tom Martinez."

"The same time? When the person tried to kill you?"

"No. Martinez was bitten. When we were out."

"And you finished him off?"

"That was Pulaski. I didn't show up until Martinez's head was already on the ground."

Her shoulders slumped a little.

He said: "Why the fuck do you care?"

"Worried about you. You think Walter tried to kill you?"

"How much does he know?"

Inez relaxed the gun, walked past Novak and glanced into the hall. "*Madre de dios*. What did you do to him?"

"Convinced him to let me in."

She shut the door on her downed man. The concern was palpable. She turned back to Novak. "Walter doesn't know about us."

"You sure?"

"As sure as I can be. Even if he did, he wouldn't care anyway. Never even tries to touch me any more."

Deadpan: "That's a shame."

"His loss is your gain. Did you come here to beat up my guard or did you have time for something else?" She let the robe fall open, giving him a look at one smooth leg. Inez was one of the rare few that still shaved.

He thought about it. No time. "If it wasn't your husband..."

She shrugged. "Reverend Rippey? It's not a secret that he wants your support."

"Hell of a way to get it."

"It almost got you to take out his rival."

"True."

"Besides, if you were gone, he could get someone else to take the Hill—maybe Gloria Wu or Jack Finger. If he did that, then the power you had would be his. Town and the Hill, that's more than the Athena."

Novak thought about that. True, all of it. If Walter Calomiris didn't care about the affair, he had less than no motive. Novak was basically a supporter in that he didn't work against Calomiris.

Inez watched him. "Are you okay? You look pale."

"I'm fine. Sorry about the door. And what's-his-name."

Inez crossed the distance. She was still holding the gun, even when she pulled him close. "It's okay. You had a scare. You sure you don't want to stay? No. Don't answer. I need to get a new guard. Don't go anywhere."

She opened the door and went out into the hall.

Novak contemplated staying. If he stayed, that might turn into the rest of the night. There were a couple more hours of that, hours he couldn't lose. Inez would be soft and willing, but that didn't get Novak anywhere.

He opened the door.

Gamburyan was stirring.

Novak nudged the beaten man with a steel toe.

Gamburyan looked up.

Novak said: "Tell Mrs. Calomiris that I have some business to... you know."

He couldn't tell if he'd knocked the English out of Gamburyan, but he looked like he didn't understand. *She'd get the message when she realized I wasn't fucking her.*

Novak went out. Cheeseman was no longer in the stairwell, probably scampered back to the Dinner Bell. The rain had petered into a soft drizzle. It covered Novak in a cold sweat.

He hoped it was only the rain.

- 5 -

NOVAK WALKED DOWN THE SOFT slope of Hotel Street. The lights that flickered below were few and far between. Off to his left, Borassi's necrosculptures looked like some kind of giant spider waiting in the dark.

His left hand felt wet. He tried to pretend it was his imagination, maybe the dying rain, maybe his sweat. No, the slushy feeling in his palm was the wound, weeping. Every footstep, every heartbeat, sent the pain shooting up his arm. If he bent it at the elbow, held it steady, just a little ways from his body, the pain dulled to a biting ache. That was the best he could do.

The lights were still on in the right Reverend's church. He wasn't a night owl. He had men awake around the clock, even though there weren't any working clocks in Devon, but he was sure to get his eight hours when it was dark out so he could wake up fresh at dawn. Dawn was still a couple hours off.

The church was one of those pure white Protestant numbers that seemed to sprout by the sides of roads. Classic lines, peaked roofs, and just barely cross-shaped, possibly for God's benefit when looking down. There had been concessions to the end of the world. The big double doors had been reinforced, and Novak knew from Robellada who still attended church, that there was a medieval crossbeam on the inside. The ground floor windows had bars biting into the walls over and under. The attic windows were removable, letting defenders drop things on an attacking swarm.

Nice to see a church getting back to its roots.

From his vantage point on Hotel, Novak could see the shapes of sentries at the church doors. If he wanted to take Rippey out, he knew he would have to get in close, which meant talking his way past the sentries. No way he could take them all, not solo, and not before the alarm went up. He went to the front. That's what respectable visitors did.

As he turned down Shoal, he saw the man leaning against the front door: Jacen Ford, Janelle's big brother. He was twice Novak's size, probably twice Novak's strength. If there was one person in town he wasn't sure he could take one-on-one, it was Jacen Ford, and Novak knew for damn sure he couldn't in anything less than tiptop condition. He was already a couple hours past that.

Ford kept his head shaved, and when Novak got close, he could count the little red razor bumps on Ford's scalp and chin like zits. Made him look like a juicer. His skin was dark, but not African dark. His nose had never been broken, so Novak had that on him. Ford looked like he could move a mountain if he wanted to, and he had Novak fixed with dark eyes as he fiddled with a buck knife.

Novak said: "I need to see Rippey."

"The Reverend is busy, Novak. Come back later."

"Getting a lot of that lately."

"Busy time."

"Look, Ford, I don't want to—"

"Then don't."

Ford hadn't moved, but he had tensed. He would be ready. Novak wondered if Ford actually knew how to fight, or if he let his strength and size talk for him. Didn't really matter, once the knife and the bite were factored in.

Novak locked his eyes on Ford's. "It's the middle of the night."

Ford looked up at the sky. "Well, that explains it."

"What's Rippey doing up in the middle of the night?"

Ford shrugged. "Don't think that matters much. You're out here, he's in there, it's gon' stay that way."

"Right."

"I can tell the Reverend that you stopped by."

"How long's he busy?"

"Till tomorrow. Maybe the next day."

Novak wanted to test Ford right now. It was going to happen sooner or later, and later was no longer an option. It gnawed at the corner of his mind and would until it was settled. Time was running out.

He ground his teeth. No. Ford wouldn't have planted that head. If Ford had a beef, he'd settle it head on, like a man. If one of Rippey's men planted the head freelance, it would've been that toad Finger or that fat bitch Gloria Wu. If Ford wasn't the guilty one, then there was no time for him. No time to fuck Inez, no time to fuck up Ford, no matter how much he wanted to do both.

He finally settled on what to say: "Okay. You tell the Reverend I was here."

Ford nodded. "Maybe you get some sleep, huh? You look like you need it."

"Fuck you."

"Suit yourself."

He stalked away, turning right on Reef, heading toward the Barricade. He wasn't going to stray far. When Rippey poked his head out, Novak planned be there: playing whack-a-mole with a minister and a real sledgehammer. He briefly considered waking his guys up. Stew would tell Novak that going after Rippey was stupid. It was. Robellada wouldn't have the stomach to kill people that weren't geeked. Pulaski, well, Pulaski would probably wonder what the hell took Novak so long.

There were still candles flickering in windows. Janelle Ford was up, as usual, baking bread that Novak would trade for on a normal day. She was in her yard, putting the lumps of maggot-white dough in the large oven, then stoking the coals until they looked like the eyes of wolves. She turned, saw Novak, and waved.

He turned away.

Instead, he found Gino's at the end of Reef, so close to the Barricade that there was only a narrow alley between them. Someone was staggering out, even at that time of night. It almost could have been a geek, but there wasn't enough purpose to it. The people of Devon still called it Gino's because that's what the sign said, even if the real Gino had probably died long before the apocalypse. It used to be an Italian restaurant, but it mostly only served drinks with the occasional substandard burrito.

It was the only place that served drinks in Town, and excepting the small plots in the backs of a couple of the northern farms, the only place that catered to any kind of mind-altering substance. Novak figured that Rippey tolerated the sin because Gino's was the canary in the coalmine. If the geeks made it through, Gino's would be the slaughterhouse and the righteous could fall back to the Athena where the real sin took place.

Novak went through the heavy front door. It swung freely, but on the other side, it had enough bars, locks, and chains to secure it in the event of an attack. The bar was along the south wall, with the main dining room closed off. Roberto Nuñez, the owner, used the rest of the place as his home. People drank the homemade stuff out of old glasses, with mason jars and unadorned bottles lined up behind the bar where the expensive liquor used to be. Geek candles flickered in the corners, giving off just enough light to squint by. Behind the bar, Nuñez kept the bulk of his collection: Donald Duck. Cheap plastic figurines, some cups, one of those old-style tins. Nuñez would and did trade for every piece of junk that had that duck on it. His way of staying sane.

Novak was a little surprised to see Pulaski at the bar, drinking from a chipped tumbler and barely swaying on his stool. Novak slid in next to him. Pulaski's presence seemed like a sign. Maybe something was signing off on his proposed rampage. Maybe that was wishful thinking. Maybe he should have thought it through before sitting next to a killer like Pulaski.

He cursed inwardly. So glad to see one of his guys, he hadn't thought of the obvious. He wanted to turn around. After all, if Pulaski got a glimpse of the bite, that was it. Chop. The end.

But then, Pulaski turned, recognized him and lifted his glass, and cut off escape. "Hey, boss."

He was trapped. He nodded to Pulaski, turned to Nuñez, who was behind the bar trying not to fall asleep, and held up a finger from his good hand. Nuñez poured some yellow stuff out of a mason jar, whatever Pulaski was having. Novak clenched his left hand into a fist and kept it in his shadow.

Novak said: "What are you doing up?"

Pulaski slurped another. "I was thinking that Tommy needed a drink in his honor."

"And here I am."

"Never see you in here. Figured you'd be in dreamland or Inez Calomiris."

Novak glanced around. No one reacted to what Pulaski said, so they missed it or it was old news. Either way: "Keep your fucking tongue off that."

Pulaski shrugged. "Kind of thing would make you king shit around here. Fuck you in the Athena, sure, but we're not in the Athena."

He was probably right. Novak was a dead man before tomorrow. Not like he needed to be popular in the Athena. Just as long as the Barricade held from now till he wore the blood of his killer.

He tossed one back, making sure to use his right hand. The liquor strained against the throbbing in his left hand. A thought popped into his head: *Booze supposedly thins the blood, to the point that alcoholics can't clot like normal people. Once my blood turns to jelly, clotting will be the least of my problems.* He laughed.

Pulaski joined in. He didn't know why, but he didn't care either.

Novak signaled to Nuñez for another.

Nuñez came over, scowling. "That first one was on his tab, but he's out."

Pulaski locked Nuñez's eyes. "How do you figure?"

Nuñez shrank a little, but this was his livelihood. "Two bottles last week, two cans this week? You're done."

"Keep me drinking and I'll get you a delivery tomorrow. Smokes."

Nuñez thought about it, then nodded. "Okay. You been good for it. Two packs?"

Pulaski nodded. Deal made. Nuñez refilled and left them alone.

Novak said: "What have you heard?"

"I guess I saw her leave your place one time—"

"No, you dumb shit. This morning, Martinez said something about how things were going to change."

Pulaski shrugged. "It started raining."

"I don't think he was talking about rain."

Pulaski thought about it. "Then I got nothing."

"The way he said it... I don't know."

Pulaski searched Novak's face.

Whatever drunkenness Novak thought he saw in the green-and-gold-rimmed eyes, Pulaski now looked completely sober. "That geek that got Martinez... what happened?"

Pulaski turned his attention back to the moonshine. "Same thing always happens. Bad luck."

Novak motioned for him to continue.

Pulaski sighed, took another drink, and started up: "We circled the house, like you said. We knew we had probably pulled a couple in with the bikes, so we were on guard. I guess she was in the bushes or something—you know how they do sometimes, when they just stand like statues? She was probably doing that, waiting for whatever geeks wait for. She came out and Tommy brought up his hand, like to fend her off. She got him instead."

Novak reflexively clenched his hand again, wincing at the fresh fire.

Pulaski sloshed the liquor around. "I killed Tommy first."

He never thought Pulaski would be that sentimental. Pulaski was a stone killer when it came to the bitten. It was the one thing he never took a risk on. As soon as he saw the bite, there'd be a flicker of quicksilver metal, and that goddamn samurai sword would finish the person. If Pulaski saw the hand, Novak was a dead man. Pulaski was the only one of Novak's guys that might be able to take him.

Kill him at that moment, and I wouldn't have to worry about him down the line. Novak hated that he thought that, of pulling the hammer and tapping Pulaski on the base of the skull. It would be quick. Pulaski might see a flash of light, and then nothing. No pain, no bite. But he couldn't kill Pulaski. Not yet. He might be needed.

He lifted the drink to his mouth. He heard the door opening and glanced, not expecting to see anything interesting, just another drunk looking for a way to stop the nightmares.

He wasn't expecting to see a gun.

He pushed off the bar with his feet, falling backward off the stool.

Pulaski reacted a split second later, jumping in the other direction, over the bar.

Thunder cracked through the bar. Yellow-white lightning flashed. Mason jars exploded. Wood sprouted smoking burrows.

Novak kicked over a table and dove behind it.

The shots stopped, but the echoes reverberated in his head. Through the blue smoke that stank of the old world, a silhouette ducked aside.

He pulled his gun and tried to find a target. He couldn't.

The thunder cracked and bullets thudded into the table. He took cover and did the math: Pulaski wasn't carrying a gun. If this was going to get finished, Novak would have to do it himself, and he'd have to get closer.

All without eating a bullet.

The rest of the bar had taken cover, hiding in corners, behind tipped over tables. Novak thought for a moment of telling people to calm the fuck down, that this guy was here to kill him. *Fuck that. Last thing I need is them deciding to help.*

The gunfire stopped. Feet on the linoleum floor. Squeaking. Closing.

He scooted around the far side of the table. He wasn't going to get close enough to take the shooter down. The bitten left arm throbbed with every one of the killer's steps.

Probably wouldn't help to tell the fucker I'd be dead in a day anyway.

The shooter sounded like he was about level with the bar. Novak breathed in time with his hammering heart and ran for the door. He hoped he'd have a clear path.

As he cleared the table, he saw the assassin leveling his pistol.

Pulaski vaulted over the bar.

The assassin fired his gun.

Novak dove.

The bullet tore a hole in the air an inch over Novak's back.

Then: a grunt. Something wet.

He turned.

Pulaski had a foot and a half of that samurai sword sticking out of the front of the assassin. The guy looked surprised. It was the first time Novak had gotten a clear look at the gunman. He recognized him. The gray beard over the black hair, the thin lips and the rat teeth. Booker, one of Calomiris's boys. The same guy Marcos mentioned.

Pulaski had a grin on his face. "Hey, can I have my sword back?" He ripped the blade out, readied it, and took Booker's head off.

It tumbled forward, end over end. Novak stopped it with his foot. He picked up Booker's gun: now empty. He patted Booker down and found no more ammo.

He swore at the headless man, then said to Pulaski: "Good hit."

Pulaski wiped his sword blade on the bar towel and grinned.

Nuñez popped up from behind the bar. He opened his mouth, but whatever he planned to say died when he must have realized that Pulaski had just beheaded someone and was in no mood to get yelled at by an unarmed man.

Pulaski said: "What was that about, you think?" The tone was casual, honestly curious.

Novak picked up the head with his left hand. It took some effort. His fingers puffed and locked when they tried to bend. The hand burned all over, except the at the point of the bite. There, it felt numb, like nothing at all.

To answer his man, Novak showed Pulaski the head. He seemed to recognize the face, but there was nothing else, no guilty eyes flickering, no suddenly dry lips. This meant Calomiris. Getting tired of waiting for Novak to keel over. Wanted to make sure the job got done quick.

He was damn close to taking the head back to the Athena when the door burst open behind him. He couldn't even turn before he felt a gun pressed to the back of his neck.

- 6 -

THE VOICE, JUST A LITTLE too far to belong to whoever was holding the gun, said: "Drop the weapon, Mr. Novak. We'll take it from here."

Novak holstered his gun. The barrel came away from his neck.

He turned to find Gloria Wu and two of her men, one right up in his face.

Gloria Wu was either the number two or three in Town, depending on where she stood against Jack Finger, Rippey's other number two or three. She wasn't as creepy as Finger, but she was a hell of a lot more annoying. He'd heard somewhere that back in the world she had been some kind of lawyer. He never got a full story on that, mostly because he never cared to ask, but be figured she was one of the ambulance chasers as opposed to Grisham crusaders. It fit her best.

She had shown up a little before Novak and his gang, and climbed Rippey's organization ruthlessly. She took the evangelical part of her faith more seriously than Novak liked: he caught her on the Hill more than once, talking to his people. Each time he chased her off. She took this as an excuse to lord her power over Novak in Town.

He thought of her as fat, but she wasn't, not in the old sense of the term. She was one of those people who packed on the weight easily, packed it on in her neck, cheeks, waist and hips. But she didn't eat three times a day any more, and she was mostly vegetarian, the same way they all were. Still, by virtue of being the number two or three in Rippey's organization, she had access to sweets when they came in. She never missed a meal she didn't want to miss. And no matter what sanctimonious shit came out of her tiny mouth, she never passed a single meal onto anyone else.

"I said 'drop the weapon.'" Gloria Wu was trying to smirk at Novak, but it looked funny on her.

"Best you're gonna get."

She opened her mouth to threaten him. He tossed her Booker's head. "You're probably going to want this."

She let out a yelp and took a step back, so the thing sort of bounced off her tits and crunched at her feet. It left a nice splotch of blood on her blouse.

Pulaski stepped up next to Novak, grinning ear to ear.

Novak kept his smirk inward.

She composed herself and gestured to one of her boys. He picked the head up gingerly, by the hair. It had mostly bled out by that point. She said: "Ah. Yes. That was what, I, uh... what happened?"

Pulaski said: "He came in shooting. I killed him."

She pointed at the sword. "With that?"

"It was that or my dick, and the katana was already in my hand."

She scowled. Her eyes went to Pulaski's makeup. He didn't seem to notice, or if he did, he couldn't give a fuck.

"Self-defense," Novak said.

"So it seems."

"Ask anyone here." She opened her mouth, but Novak closed it with: "We're not going anywhere."

Novak and Pulaski righted their stools and sat down at the bar. There was a new bullet hole right in front of Novak, and he traced it with his index finger. The splinters in the wood felt like the pins and needles that were going over his other hand. He wanted to run out of here, but there was no point. *Calomiris showed his hand, I could kill him, then eat a bullet. Easy peasy, Japanesy.* He could afford a little time to placate Rippey's hounds.

Gloria Wu went from drunk to drunk and got the same story from all of them. They slurred their way through Booker's move and Pulaski's counter. Novak wondered for a moment what she would have done if they had killed someone in cold blood on Rippey's land. Booker was Calomiris's anyway. Depended on who she wanted to hurt more, he guessed.

Novak glanced at the guards, making one of them put a hand on his holstered pistol. He added the distance and the hand speed the guard just displayed. *Move quick enough, Pulaski and I could take them both.*

He said, in a nice, loud, starting-some-shit kind of way: "Happy? He came in, started shooting and now he's dead."

Gloria Wu wasn't done lording over them quite yet. She knew that the longer she delayed, the more likely she was going to get even more backup sent her way and the more she could lord. It was a hell of a snowball effect. It depended on Novak and Pulaski not losing patience, and the one thing she didn't know was that Novak didn't have much left to lose. She said: "Do you know him?"

"His name's Booker. He lives over at the Athena."

She decided that getting right up in Novak's face was her best play. He wasn't about to argue with anything that put her within hammer's reach. "You knew him, then?"

"Not really. I knew who he was."

"Did you have some kind of quarrel with him?"

"I do now."

She sighed. "Before tonight?"

"No. Like I said, I knew who he was, not why he had a beef."

"Don't fudge around with me, Mr. Novak. This is official."

Novak chuckled. "Believe me, if I was *fucking* with you, you'd know it."

The door opened, letting out some warm air and Novak's chances of taking Gloria's people if it came to it. Two more of Rippey's soldiers, with Jack Finger at the head. Novak was relieved that Ford hadn't come in. That would tip the balance of power irrevocably the wrong way.

Finger was short and lean, and looked like he was made of leather. Novak never knew what Finger did back in the world, but always pictured him selling cars. He had a sleazy smile and always looked scrubbed, his hair perpetually oiled flat and smelling like rotten artichokes. He didn't wear a suit, but he was one of the few people suicidal—or confident—enough to wear a tie; this one was red, like a shout. He had a wet windbreaker over middle-manager office wear.

"Hello, everyone. Gloria, the Reverend wanted me to make sure that everything was okay." Brightness in his voice nearly hid the malice underneath.

The look on her face said she wanted to throw a curse Finger's way, but she was in public. "I'm not finished questioning the witnesses."

Novak snorted. "She's gotten the same story from everyone and still won't get the fuck out."

Finger barely winced at the curse, sidling over to Novak. "And what, pray tell, is the same story?"

Novak repeated the story. He was beginning to think that sudden head trauma was in everyone's immediate future.

Finger turned to Gloria. "Seems pretty cut and dry to me."

She smiled as sweetly as she could. "And what do you think I was going to report?"

Finger nudged Booker's corpse with his foot. "The real question is what does Walter Calomiris know? This man is one of his. He came to Town to kill a respected, if non-native man. If Mr. Booker had been successful, there's a good chance that Mr. Novak's men would have come here to take revenge."

Pulaski said: "Fuck, yeah. I'd have gutted all of you."

Finger flinched, but recovered in time to point to Pulaski as evidence. "See?"

"It's a good thing you were here to tell me everything I already realized," Gloria said.

"You have the... uh... head?" Finger glanced around, finding it in a guard's hand. He went on: "Good. We should take it to Mr. Calomiris. One of his people is dead and he has a right to know."

Novak said: "And you can shake him down for it."

Finger shrugged. "If it happens, it happens."

"You two," Gloria said, "you're coming with us."

Pulaski looked at Novak. He arched one plucked eyebrow, which said *is she kidding here?*

"Please, Gloria! These men aren't ours to order around." Finger turned to Novak. "Mr. Novak, will you and your man consent to accompany us to the Hotel Athena? We would appreciate having the victim of the crime present when we speak to Mr. Calomiris."

Hell, I was going there anyway. "Sure thing, puddin'."

Finger smiled at Gloria. "Honey, Gloria. Not vinegar."

She scowled and snapped her fingers at her men.

Pulaski and Novak followed the six out the door. The rain had let up. The ground squelched underfoot, and the sky was cloudy overhead, but they were no longer walking through the mists. The Athena loomed large ahead, a few windows gold. The roof was dark: the fire up there had gone out.

Novak's hand had stopped throbbing. He flexed it. No pain, except for a dull ache in the wrist. He touched the fingers of his left hand to the right. The left hand felt like someone else's. The hand wasn't his. It belonged to the thing in his footlocker.

I'll have to kill Calomiris soon.

There was still the matter of hiding the bite. Pulaski only needed a hint before he would take Novak's head off. Of the others, only Gloria Wu and Jack Finger weren't hardcases. But everyone still alive had some experience detecting bites, and everyone knew exactly what to do.

They weren't a large group, and it was late enough to be called early, so they weren't met out front. Gloria Wu had her face set in a scowl. Finger looked like he was thinking about something else entirely. Novak turned back to the Athena, now eclipsing the skyline.

They stopped on what used to be the car roundabout. In the old world, a valet would have taken their car to the crumbling lot on Shore, now empty. The dirt was slowly claiming what used to be asphalt, stubborn grass poking through the multiplying cracks. They would scrape it out eventually, when they had turned the world to dirt and the only things left moving were already dead.

Gloria was about to head in, but Finger put an arm up in front of her. She flinched; the worst thing on her mind was him feeling her up. Couldn't really blame her for that one.

She hissed something at him. He spoke back, low and calm. Novak didn't bother with the eavesdropping. Those two could have their little power struggle without him.

Finally, Gloria shoved Finger lightly and shouted up at the Athena: "Walter Calomiris! We have one of your men! Come down!"

Nothing. Gloria rested her voice for a second. Then got back up to the shouting. She called Calomiris out. Practically challenging the man. She had some stones for that. She had four people, and Finger, who would back her up if Calomiris decided to throw down. She was taking the chance that Novak didn't care more than didn't like her, or she thought that he'd back her in that fight in light of the assassin.

She might have been right.

More of the windows lit up with the guttering glow that passed for bright in the new world. Pitted eyes peered down at the small group at the roundabout.

Every breath she spewed up at the walls put another wraith at a window. Finger let her talk, waiting for his precise moment. In the meantime, Novak tried not to think about his hand. Tried not to flex it. Tried not to touch it.

He had no idea how long Gloria Wu shouted. Short times like seconds, minutes, hours; those were things of the past. Old ways of thinking. In the new world, there were days, there were nights. There were seasons. Real time. They sometimes talked about units like hours, fifteen minutes, thirty, but these were abstracts that were agreed upon in a ballpark sense. Fifteen minutes was longer than five, but not necessarily three times longer. Time had become a fluid thing, a perpetual late summer afternoon where these things bled their meaning out.

After she had shouted for God knew how long, and her voice skinned like a knee, that's when Walter Calomiris came down into the lobby. Novak recognized the faces with him: Calomiris's bodyguards. His top guys. Individually, Novak would put any one of his guys—except Robellada—against any one of Calomiris's guys. But they had numbers. Calomiris wasn't looking at Novak.

He was looking right at Gloria Wu.

Calomiris had a body type that was rare. In the old days, Novak would have pegged him for an accountant or something. He was tall, well over six feet, with long limbs that had some muscle on them. The unique part was the gut. It was a hell of a gut, looking like a golf ball stuck in the middle of a drinking straw. Thick hair poked up out of his open collar, and his bare forearms looked like they belonged to a bear. He had dark eyes with deep purple rings around them and wiry black hair like a crown.

Those eyes, looking like they hadn't seen the insides of his eyelids in days, were focused on Gloria Wu. His eyes were nearly black, reflecting a tiny glitter in each one, making them look like negatives. He was unarmed.

But his men weren't. The lead guy was Craig Sakimoto. Novak wasn't sure where they had hooked up, but Sakimoto had been with Calomiris since Novak's arrival. Sakimoto was a little taller than Novak, and sinewy muscle on top of that. He was famous in Devon for his judo; Novak had seen him throw geeks twice his size around with ease. He was the kind of person who liked to put on a good front. Though it was the dead of night, he wore a full suit, all dark colors so the dirt and sweat stains wouldn't show. He kept the hair and mustache cut nice and short. His eyes were on Gloria's boys, knowing, not thinking, that he could take the lot of them.

Each side had good killing tools: heavy blades, bludgeons. If it came to it, the fight would be bloody as hell.

Calomiris said: "What exactly do you want?"

Novak could swear Gloria Wu blanched, and that's all Jack Finger needed. He slithered to the front. "Mr. Calomiris, we're sorry that Miss Wu chose to approach you in that manner..."

"Play those games down there, Jack. What exactly do you want?"

Gloria looked like she was about to step in. Finger had to stammer the first part of his sentence to cut her off. "Th-th-that buh-brings me to the point. One of your people attempted to kill a citizen at Gino's."

Calomiris's eyes went from person to person. When he came to Novak, his eyes narrowed. It seemed like confusion, but there was no way to be sure. He wiped his hands on his pants and turned his attention back to Finger. "I don't see any of my people here."

Gloria Wu said: "Steve, the—"

Finger gestured. Gloria's man who held the head tossed it forward. It landed in the shallow muck at Calomiris's foot. Calomiris never flinched. He looked down at it, snorted a throatful of mucous, swallowed, and looked back at Finger. "Problem solved."

Pulaski leaned over to Novak: "That's what I said."

Novak reflexively balled his left hand.

Finger clasped his hands together. "Not exactly."

Here, Gloria cut in. "One of your people, Mr. Calomiris. Don't you recognize him?"

Calomiris gave the head another look. He squinted, but made no other movements. Finally, he was able to work through the death mask, through the dirt and mud. "Charles Booker. Third floor."

"Charles Booker!" Gloria said, like it proved something.

Finger cut back in. "Charles Booker was part of your, well, security force."

Calomiris said: "And who are you claiming he attacked?"

Gloria pointed at Novak. He wanted to hit her for that. "Glen Novak."

Calomiris looked to Novak. "And you're okay?"

That was a loaded question. "He didn't get me."

Finger said: "Mr. Novak was at Gino's, enjoying himself as is his right, when a member of your security force entered and started shooting."

"I understand the situation. I just don't understand why you're telling me."

Gloria Wu looked completely flummoxed. Finger wasn't much better, but he recovered enough to get something out. "Well, ah, your man, and he was your man, tried to kill someone, in, ah, in Town. That's a crime."

"And you dealt with it."

"Maybe. We dealt with the assassin, not necessarily who sent him."

"You're implying that I sent Charlie Booker to kill Glen?" Another man would have laughed, but Calomiris turned to Novak with a serious look on his face. "What do you think?"

Novak shrugged. "Could be."

"There's... Glen, there's no way I did this and you should know that."

Novak shrugged again.

Calomiris turned to Finger and Gloria. "So you two thought you might as well show up here with this bullshit."

"It's not—"

"Shut up, Jack. Isador wants to call me out but he lacks the guts to come out of his church, so he sends you two. His gofers."

Calomiris started to walk in Novak's direction.

Gloria Wu's men tensed.

Pulaski was loose. That was how he was just before unsheathing three feet of steel and making someone eight inches shorter.

Gloria said: "Stay away from him."

"You tell Isador if he wants to come at me, he should come himself." Quieter, to Novak: "Glen, you can't believe this."

Their eyes met, and Novak thought he saw real confusion in there. Possible, even probable, that Calomiris was a good liar, but Novak didn't see anything that he would have expected. No anger. No hatred. No fear.

Novak said: "Believing it less and less by the moment. Fact remains though, your man did come in and did try to kill me."

"Then look into it. Look, Glen, if that's what it takes, that's what it takes."

Finger sidled up to them. "Mr. Calomiris, you can't expect us to turn over the investigation to the victim. It happened in Town and it's a crime for the Reverend to investigate."

Calomiris's head snapped around, and he loomed over Finger. "The Reverend isn't here. Soon as he finds his backbone, he's welcome to look around."

Finger opened his mouth.

Calomiris kept talking. "In the meantime, get the fuck off my lawn, and if your friend wakes my people up again, I'll have to investigate another murder, and believe me, I won't be looking into it very closely, got it?"

Finger swallowed, recovered, smiled. "Thank you very much for your time, sir. We'll, uh, we'll take the body to the church." He returned to Gloria Wu, and they had a hissing conversation with each other. In a moment, they were heading back into Town, defiantly keeping their backs turned.

Calomiris said: "Glen, I'd like to sort this out. Would you come in for a little while?"

Novak had some time, though not a lot, and if it was Calomiris, this would be the time to bury the hatchet in his head.

- 7 -

THE SKY WAS ALREADY GETTING a little lighter, showing off the clouds that hung low and gray. Walter Calomiris led the way inside.

Pulaski was about to follow them, but Novak turned to him. "Go home. Get some rest."

"No offense, boss, but you're the one that looks tired."

He was probably right, but Novak didn't have time left to waste it on sleep. "Difference is, I have shit to do."

"You sure you want to go in there alone? If he sent that other motherfucker, you should have some backup."

"He's not going to try anything."

Pulaski didn't believe him. They had that in common.

"Boss—"

"Just fucking go, okay?" He said it a little harsher than he meant to and regretted it instantly. But he couldn't apologize, especially not in front of Calomiris's boys.

Pulaski was silent for a second, then nodded. "Sure thing, boss. See you when I see you."

Pulaski walked down the hill. Novak hoped Pulaski understood. If he didn't, he could be mad at Novak in a day or two when they stuck him in the ground. Maybe Pulaski would understand then. Novak flexed his hand again. Pain shot to his elbow.

He turned back to Calomiris, who had stopped, watching Novak, brow furrowed, searching him with those glittering black eyes. Finally, he said: "You didn't have to send your man away."

Yeah, I did. No need to get him killed.

"You wanted to talk," he replied. "You can talk to me."

Calomiris nodded, turned to Sakimoto. "Craig, you're done for the time being."

The two of them had a conversation consisting entirely of eyebrow movements, before Sakimoto took the guards away. It was just Novak and Calomiris. Arm's reach. Novak knew he could have Calomiris on the floor bleeding out from a cracked skull in seconds. No stopping it.

"Walk with me, Glen."

Calomiris was a hard man to read. That he was a deeper thinker than Novak was a given, but there was something more that bothered Novak. Everyone went a little crazy, allowing their quirks room to grow or collecting useless trinkets of a dead world. Novak knew the comforting insanity in himself, in his men, and in most of the people he associated with, but he didn't with Calomiris. The man had to have something, but that something was a mystery.

The other possibility was that he had nothing, and had quietly lost his mind.

Calomiris led Novak away from the front desk, down the hall, past the hotel bar. Novak glanced inside: it was the girl stripping again. He couldn't remember her name, but he could count the shadows under her ribs. There was no one on the Hill that was so skinny. He looked up at Calomiris's thoughtful face and wanted to cave it in just for that.

He went from Novak's face to the girl. "You like Stacy?"

"A little skinny."

"All my men who've used her say she's good."

That might have been it, the use of others as he liked. But

something in Novak said that Calomiris had something else, something far darker waiting to be seen.

"Did you call me in here to talk about the girl?"

"No. No, I didn't."

They kept walking. Novak smelled the tension coming off Calomiris in waves. He was unarmed. Novak wasn't. If Calomiris did send that son of a bitch to Gino's, this was a hell of a risk. Maybe he knew that Novak couldn't get out of the Athena if he attacked. Maybe Calomiris knew that Novak didn't care about that.

Finally, Calomiris said: "You don't believe them, do you?"

"Not sure what to believe."

"You don't trust me."

"Aw, puddin', you hurt?"

Calomiris's head snapped up at that, processed it, and broke into a grin. "Okay, fair enough. But it's not like you and I have been at each other's throats. You've never challenged me for the Athena, and I never bother you on the Hill."

"True." Novak shivered in the sudden chill of the hall.

"Makes no sense for me to. You control the Hill, and you do it well. Hell, there's less violence there than there is here, let alone in Rippey's cesspool." Calomiris wasn't mincing words, but he was right. Town was the most dangerous. It was also the most alive and the only one that was growing, albeit slowly. Calomiris continued: "The Hill isn't one of the active borders, but it is a border."

"Yeah, I know."

"It's not one I want."

"And you don't want to be outnumbered."

"And I don't want to be outnumbered."

"Booker was your man."

"Glen, I swear to God, I didn't send him. There's literally no reason I'd want you out of the way. If I was going to have someone killed, it'd be Isador Rippey."

"Why haven't you?"

"Who says I haven't tried?"

If he thought failing meant he was stone cold or something, he had one on Novak. He didn't want to explain to the man the finer points of strength. After all, Calomiris had been running Devon since the first outbreaks.

"Maybe you should have sent someone who wouldn't fuck it up then."

"Probably. My point is this: I have no reason to come after you and I didn't. I'd be happier if you publicly joined me, but what we have is the next best thing. I'd take that over some kind of power vacuum on the Hill any day."

Novak probed Calomiris's defenses. He couldn't see the lie, but that didn't mean it wasn't there. Could be Inez was right: Calomiris didn't know, or he did and he didn't care. Novak would believe either. The fact remained though, that Booker was his man.

"Prove it to me."

He saw the rage pass over Calomiris's face like a shadow, but he worked to keep that expression blank. "Of course. You want goods? I have some cans I could part with."

He nodded, but didn't break eye contact.

Calomiris went on: "How about a girl? Look, you wait in Room 213 and I'll have it all brought to you."

He thought about it. Not a bad deal, but what the fuck good were cans and pussy when he was a dead man? The pain reached up his elbow with tendrils.

He said: "What I really want is a look inside Booker's room."

Calomiris blanched. "What for?"

"What do you think? If he came for me and you didn't order it, then he came for me just because. Maybe he left behind a reason."

"I don't think he left a typed confession."

"Me neither. Doesn't mean he left nothing."

Calomiris considered it. "Fine."

"What room?"

"310." He rattled it off quick. There were a lot of people in the Athena by the end's reckoning, but Calomiris had that info on the tip of his tongue. He didn't seem to register that he'd made a mistake. Maybe he hadn't. Or maybe he was good at hiding it. It would be a hell of a lot easier just to pound it out of him.

Later.

"Key?"

Calomiris sighed, took out his key-ring and handed it over. "Skeleton key. Opens every room in the place. I'm going to want that back."

Novak didn't answer, instead heading for the stairs. The stairwells were dark. It was late enough that the candles had either gone out or burned to nothing. They would be replaced if Calomiris cared enough.

Booker was on the third floor. That alone meant the man had status. Not a lot, but some. With a few exceptions, it broke down thus: The first floor was uninhabited. Storerooms in the interior, and the outer were boarded up. The mezzanine held the library and supplies for defenders. The second floor was for refugees. Those who didn't show up with much, who were mostly going to make a living trading their bodies in one way or another, they lived in the interior and toward the edges. The outer rooms, especially those over the main doors were specifically for defense. They had stockpiles of rocks, bricks and the like. Some had Molotov cocktails. The third floor was for low-level Calomiris men or rich refugees. If a family showed up with a camper stuffed with goods, they got the third floor. If a tough man was willing to use his baseball bat for Calomiris, he got the third floor too. Calomiris's few scavs like Tanner were on the third too. The fourth floor was for Calomiris men. Novak was fairly certain that his security force had twenty-odd of these hardcase members, and they would be on the fourth floor, along with their families, girlfriends and entertainment. The fifth floor was for top lieutenants. Sakimoto lived on the fifth, as did Inez's cousin Marcos. The sixth floor, that was for Walter and Inez Calomiris in the honeymoon suite. Novak heard about a message up the roof from the early days, when people still expected the government to bail them out, but he'd never been up there himself.

All of the doors were shut on the third floor, most of the occupants were asleep, or trying to after Gloria woke them up. Novak was covered in a thin sweat, which gripped the cold and froze into tiny crystals. The smells in the hall were mostly sweat and breath. Someone had been burning incense to cover it. That hadn't worked.

Room 310 was closed and locked. There was a scuffmark at kick level. Novak touched it with his shoe. Booker probably unlocked, kicked the door open. He had no idea what that told him. He opened the door like Booker did. *a feeling for the guy.* It didn't.

The first thing that hit him was the smell. Unlike most rooms, it didn't smell like a locker room. Most rooms went that way. Cleaning supplies were easy to come by, but scavenging them over, say, food, took a special kind. Trading for them even more. Charles Booker's place smelled like fake pine trees.

He stepped inside. There was five feet of hall, with a doorway on the right that went into the bathroom. Beyond that, the room opened up to the right. He could see the foot of the bed, which was made with military corners. Straight ahead, the hotel curtains over the sliding door that led to a balcony. There was a table and chairs with an ashtray and a neat stack of magazines.

He got closer. Beneath the pine scent was the stale stink of cigarettes. The ashtray had been used, but washed out, so that only little limpets of black ash still caked the bottom. He checked through the magazines, expecting some kind of porn. He hoped not: all of it was *Cat Fancy* and *Boy's Life*. Each one had been thumbed into oblivion; a couple were missing covers, one had lost the staples. Nothing in there against Novak, unless Booker resented that Novak used to be a Boy Scout.

He went to the end table. There was a glass, one of the ones from the hotel, only slightly chipped and cloudy. The Gideon Bible lay next to it. Bookmarked, even. He opened it up. Luke, Chapter 19. He didn't know enough about the whole thing to attach any significance. He put it down.

There was a barrier around the bottom of the bed. It kept guests from losing things back when people had enough things to lose. He went to Booker's dresser. He had some candy and a few useless coins. In the bottom drawer was a wind-up monster that spat out sparks when it walked. Novak turned it over in his right hand. When it encountered resistance, he jumped, looked back at it. The resistance was from the numb fingers of his left hand, unconsciously holding the toy. He threw it across the room. It shattered against the far wall. He flexed his good hand.

No pain.

He looked at the bad one. The glove shone at the last knuckle. He took the glove off, wincing when the pain shot into his elbow. The bandages were thick, black. The wound had been weeping. He wondered how much of that stuff he'd left behind. *Was there a puddle on the bar at Gino's? Had Inez found something on her? Had I even touched her?*

It was dry now: an ugly scab. He thought about taking the bandage off, investigating further. Why bother? It had already killed him.

He put the glove back on, and this time when the agony ripped into his elbow, he let it.

He went to the closet. Booker had a raincoat, and his supply of pine-scented cleaners. A bloody pipe wrench leaned against the wall. Novak smiled a little at that. In the old days, something like that would have said, loud and clear: "I'm a murderer, take me in." These days, all it said was that he'd survived. It was a good weapon. Novak took it. Someone on the Hill could use it.

He turned back to the bed. He started staring, not really knowing why. He remembered a story his dad had told him when he was a kid. A couple was on their honeymoon, and they checked into this motel on the way to the airport. They slept on the bed the first night—Novak's dad had cleaned up the story— but they noticed a horrible smell. The next day they complained. The manager went in to look, lifted up the mattress, and found a decomposing body in the box spring.

What the hell. Based on the smell, maybe he'd find a pine tree that smoked. He lifted up the mattress and pushed it aside. No body in the box spring. But there was something else, something soft and purple.

He got closer. It was one of those bags that used to hold whiskey. He picked it up. Something clicked in there, but there was more, something else, softer. His left hand was still agile, even if he couldn't feel it. It still listened to what he was telling it to do. He wondered when that would change. He wondered if it would just die on the vine. He wondered if it would rebel.

He opened up the bag, tipped it upside down and shook it. The first thing that fell out was a bracelet: plastic beads on an elastic string. In the old days that meant kid, but these days it could mean almost anything. Real jewels weren't prized in the same way. Heirlooms were, but the rest were mostly just shiny rocks. He kept shaking.

Just because plastic beads didn't always mean kid, they sometimes did. Because certain things always said kid. Like the panties he'd just shaken into his good hand. Old ones. Worn. Stained.

He dropped the whole thing back into the bed, wiping his hand on his pants. After a minute, he picked up the bracelet and replaced the mattress. They could tell it had been disturbed, but fuck them, let them find out that their man was a pervert. Let them explain that to Isador Rippey.

He went to the door, turned into the hall and nearly bumped into Craig Sakimoto, Calomiris's top guy, leaning against the wall like he'd been there a while. Novak was close enough to smell his breath: fresh coffee.

Sakimoto said: "Doing some remodeling in there?"

Novak tried to recover. "Calomiris said I could look around. So I was looking."

"Find anything?"

"Nothing that says why he tried to kill me."

"Maybe he's met you." Sakimoto grinned at that.

He wanted to hurt Sakimoto. There was no reason to it, just an animal rage that commanded Novak to put his hands on Sakimoto and tear him apart.

He fought the impulse. "Go fuck yourself."

Sakimoto ignored that. "I need your key."

"Calomiris gave me Room 213."

"It's unlocked. You don't need the skeleton any more. Give it up."

"What do you know about this guy?"

"Who, Charlie Booker? Quiet guy. Kept to himself. He was a good soldier, though."

"Why was he still on three then?"

"Spent too much time in Town. Can't trust a guy like that."

Novak nodded. Town meant Rippey. If Novak was going to find whoever owned those panties before Booker got them, that person would be under Rippey's protection. Protection was a funny fucking word.

He dropped the key on the floor and walked past Sakimoto. "Take it easy."

One floor down, and Room 213 was open, only a crack. Novak shivered in the cold.

He nudged the door. He smelled her first. Not perfume, not soap. Her.

The bite pulsed in his elbow, reaching for his shoulder. He tried to ignore it. Ignore her. He wasn't fooling himself.

He walked in the room, which was laid out in mirror image to Booker's. He didn't glance at the bed to his left, but he saw her out of the corner of his eye. Just a slip of flesh, lounging on the bed, trying to look as sexy as she could. He sat down at the table by the window and looked straight ahead. A bag, the bag of food Calomiris had promised, sat where the TV used to, in the corner. Most of the TV sets had already been dropped on geeks, and those few that hadn't were waiting to be.

"Hi," she said.

"Hi."

"Don't you want to look?"

He didn't. "Aren't you cold? Fucking drafty in here."

"It's warm enough to me."

He shivered, mopped the sweat off his head. Maybe she thought he was shy. That thought nearly made him laugh.

She got up. Her robe was piled in the corner, by the bed. He wondered if she had clothes any more, or if she just went from bed to bed to pay for her next meal.

She was in front of him. She looked like she was entirely made from the webbing between fingers. Her face might have been pretty, but she'd forgotten how to smile.

He met her eyes and she tried for a come hither. It didn't work out.

"Mr. Calomiris said you liked me. He said I was supposed to

do whatever you want."

He sighed and unzipped his pants. She knelt down, took him in her mouth and got to work. He looked through the open door out into the hall. There was a part of him that hoped someone would pass by, see what he was doing. Know what he was.

She hit a good spot. He shut his eyes. His elbow pulsed with red, sending out its tendrils once again. The bite carried the infection. That meant saliva, maybe blood. Maybe semen.

Goddamn it.

He grabbed a handful of her blonde hair. It was thin. Some gave. He yanked her off and tossed her down in front of him. Her eyes were wide, but she recovered, laid back, spread her legs.

"Get up," he told her.

Her face was a void. Not used to being rejected like this. He put his cock away, wishing the goddamn thing didn't look so proud.

She said: "What did I do?"

He ignored the question. "When was the last time you ate?"

"A couple hours ago. After my first show."

"What was it?"

"A couple crackers. Some broth."

"No, when was the last time you ate a meal? A real meal?"

She shrugged. She saw an opportunity and got to her knees, knotted hands going for his pants. "I was trying to have—"

"Shut the fuck up with that. Get your fucking robe, wait for sunrise, and go to the Hill, got it? There's a green house near the top. Guy who lives there is Dave Pulaski. He'll take care of you. Place you, feed you. You'll only have to pay him from now on."

She frowned at him. "You're Glen Novak, right?"

He nodded.

She crawled forward, hands on his thighs. "You run the Hill. You're the boss. I'd rather be with you."

He thought about that. The rage burned from his crotch to his hands. He pushed her away, tried to keep his voice even: "Maybe I don't want a fucked out cunt like you."

He stepped over her, grabbing the paper bag and walked.

He never looked back.

Even when he heard the wispy sobs.

- 8 -

DAWN WAS APPROACHING FAST. THE clouds were breaking up overhead into gray smudges like something badly erased. Novak breathed in the cold and wet air like a sneeze. The pain was moving from the elbow to the shoulder. Other than that, he felt alive, balanced on a razor's edge.

He looked down the sloping hill of Hotel Street where Town nestled in the uneven ground. Ocean Street ran parallel to Main and served as the main drag, with gas stations, restaurants, and gift shops. His gaze swept north, into the residential part of Town, up to the few larger farms that were directly to his left, almost in the Athena's shadow. Candles still burned in the church's windows, guttering in the morning's judgment. *Rippey was doing something. Getting ready for me to die?*

He walked past First Baptist. Rippey still had guards at the doors, but Ford wasn't one of them. They watched Novak as he walked by. They would report it; where Novak went was news. They knew about Gino's. They probably knew how Rippey was planning to frame Calomiris for it.

Gino's was still lit. It would close in the early hours, open up in the late afternoon, as soon as the sun started thinking about bed. Criminals return to the scene of the crime; did victims?

He opened the door. There was only one of the drunks left. At least there was that. Only one man to witness what Novak was already feeling guilty about doing.

Nuñez jumped when Novak shoved through the door. He couldn't be sure if it was the suddenness of the door, or if Nuñez saw what was in Novak's face.

"Glen! You okay?"

"Never been better."

"You look like you have flu or something."

Novak smiled. "Could be. Could be I haven't slept."

He sat in front of his bullet hole, tracing the shredded edges with his finger.

Nuñez's voice betrayed fear. *Good.* "Can I get you something? On the house. Call it the psycho special."

Novak didn't answer. He just put the plastic bracelet on the bar.

Nuñez looked at it like it was poisonous. He said: "So… about that drink?"

Novak nudged the bracelet. "What do you know about Charlie Booker?"

"Nothing much."

"Bullshit, Nuñez. You know everyone in Devon, especially Townies."

"Booker never hung out here."

He heard the lie. He didn't have time for lies. He was a dead man. He popped up from the stool, reached out with his right hand and caught the back of Nuñez's neck with a wet slap. He tried to bring Nuñez closer, but when Novak hauled, the other man felt lighter than he should have. Novak got him half onto the bar before loosening just enough to let Nuñez get his feet on the ground.

"First time, we'll call that an oversight. Second time, a misstep. By the third time, you're lying to me."

No more lies, just fear. "I know Booker. Not well. But I know him."

"That's good. Now what do you know about him?"

"Nothing!"

He slammed the side of Nuñez's face into the bar and pressed down. He would stay there as long as Novak liked. He pulled his sledgehammer and let that hover over Nuñez's nose. "Do we understand each other?"

The floodgates opened. "Booker never had anything to say about you, but he did come here. Three, four times a week. Usually well after dark."

"Who did he talk to? You?"

"No. No! He didn't talk. Just drank!"

Novak used the sledge to nudge the plastic bracelet under Nuñez's nose. "Where would he have gotten this?"

"Once, just once, I was late coming in. I was coming down from the Athena, and I saw him heading over to the Franklin place! That's it!"

The Franklin place was one of the farms at the edge of Town, pressed up against the series of hills to the north.

"Was that so hard?" Novak put the hammer away and let Nuñez go. His eyes darted to the line of Donald Ducks behind the bar. He saw the smudges of dirt, the cracks in the plastic. He flexed his hand and was almost out the door when Nuñez said, "You can't do this. This isn't the Hill. This isn't your place. You can't do this."

"Tell Rippey. Let him try to stop me." Novak turned to go, but stopped. "Threaten me again, Nuñez. See what happens."

He didn't bother turning to face Nuñez. His shallow breathing hissed in the dim silence. Nuñez had a clean shot at Novak's back, but he didn't take it, and Novak was certain he would be thinking about that for the rest of his life.

Novak said: "See you around," and left.

Walking out of Gino's, Novak looked at his mushy footprints in the mud. Somewhere, under those, were Booker's, and under those, Novak's again. And Booker's, and Novak's, all the way down to the bedrock. Novak kicked a lip of mud.

The lightening sky showed him the way to the Franklin farm. The Athena loomed large to his left. Part of him wondered if Inez was watching him from on high.

The Franklin farm was nestled in the crotch of the hills. The first thing Novak saw as he moved past the other farms—the Duman vineyard, the Wong cornfield—were the ten flagpoles and the tattered flags already snapping in the morning breeze. Franklin collected flags, and in fact Novak had once traded a giant Stars and Stripes he'd found at a car dealership for two baskets of squash. The Franklin farm almost looked like the UN, if the flags were faded and rotten, and the USA represented half the banners. Other than the poles, Franklin hung flags from his porch, used them as curtains, and even had a scarecrow that was an effigy of Uncle Sam. It was the single largest farm in Town, which should have given Robert Franklin some power, but it hadn't. Novak had seen him around Devon before, a thin, beaten-down man of which there were entirely too many. Novak wondered if the Franklins had been there before the end. Probably not. Like most everyone else, they fled a necropolis and grabbed what they could. Possession was nine-tenths of the law, after all.

Not that there was law in Devon. But there was order.

The place had a craftsman look to it, with a wooden porch that stretched the whole width of the house. Novak opened the screen and pounded on the door. It was good wood, probably reinforced from the inside with a makeshift barricade. The ground-level windows had bars on them, but the second story windows were clear. He pounded on the door again. That's when he heard stirring. In the old days, visiting in the moments before dawn would have been rude, but after the end, working people woke with the sun.

He pounded on the door again.

Finally, it opened. Franklin was on the threshold, rubbing his eyes on the sleeve of his bathrobe. He had a large nose, a dark beard and a hairline making tracks for the back of his head. Tall and reedy; Novak sized him up immediately and found him lacking. "Yes?"

"Good morning, Franklin."

Franklin nodded and seemed to get a better look at Novak. "Morning, Mr. Novak. If you want to trade, I'd appreciate it if you came back this afternoon."

"You have a daughter? Maybe ten years old?"

Franklin blinked. This wasn't how he thought this would go. "Melissa's eleven. What do you want?"

"Do you know Charlie Booker?"

That woke him up. His voice sharpened to an edge. "What do you want exactly?"

"Here's the thing. I found this," and he held up the plastic bracelet, "in his room. I found something else. Something that might provoke a father. You know, like you."

"What do you—?"

"Her panties."

Franklin blanched.

Novak caught the scent of blood and bulled ahead. "It's pretty clear what Charlie Booker wanted from your kid. The question is, did you let him have it, or did he just take it?"

"Goddamn it, you—" Franklin lunged for Novak, but the farmer was too heavy from sleep.

Novak reached up, grabbed the side of Franklin's head and introduced it to the doorjamb. He collapsed, giving Novak a view into the hall. Mrs. Franklin was coming down the stairs and saw her husband, on the floor, holding his head, blood leaking through his fingers.

Novak had already scared the shit out of a better family. He grabbed Franklin by the collar, let him smell Novak's breath. He had the question on his teeth, ready to tear the confession out of the man.

"Leave him alone, Novak." The voice came from behind. He recognized it immediately. Ford.

He turned. Ford and another man were twenty feet off, holding rifles. Ford's face was calm. The other guy looked about to piss his pants. *I could use that.* Novak let Franklin go and stood up straight.

"This is between me and him, Ford."

"He's one of ours. It's our business."

Novak took a step toward them. Pisspants brought his rifle up quick. Novak stopped. "We were just having a little conversation."

"Looked like a little more than that."

"An important conversation."

"Then it's a conversation you can have with me."

"You want to try to take me, Ford? Go ahead. Give it a shot."

"You don't want this."

"Who says I don't?"

Ford's eyes searched Novak. "You're the one sweating."

Novak touched his forehead and immediately regretted that tacit admittance of weakness. In that moment, he'd lost. Ford knew it, Novak knew it. Franklin and Pisspants probably knew it.

At that moment, the sun poked its brilliant face up over the hills to the east, right in Novak's face, as though God wanted to put a spotlight on his failure. He was momentarily dazzled, and put up a hand to block it. As his eyes readjusted, he saw Pisspants glance back from the direction of the Barricade.

Novak tried to squint, but Ford was still a silhouette. Then Novak heard it: a rumble of engines. A lot of engines. Probably a convoy, coming from the main road. Could be traders, could be refugees, could be an attack. One thing was certain, that level of noise would call to the geeks.

Novak started walking south, away from Franklin and Ford. Pisspants shouted: "Hold it!"

"We're zeroed, kid. You want to shoot me, go ahead, but we need men at the Barricade. Now."

Ford pushed Pisspants's barrel down and whispered something to him. Ford then spoke louder, to Novak: "You're free to go, but the Reverend's going to hear about this."

"Great. Maybe that will get him to climb out of God's ass long enough for a heart to heart."

Novak started running for the Barricade.

Town was alive, houses emptying into the streets. Ford and Pisspants peeled off from Novak at the church to meet up with the men already gathering there. Reverend Rippey stood in the middle of them, looking at nothing and everything. He was already dressed, his black clothes and white collar crisper than the morning. He was unarmed, but had ten men around him not only willing but eager to take a bite for him. Three of the Rippettes, blond hair looking faded, watched him fearfully from the doorway.

Rippey and Novak's eyes met. Novak tried to know what Rippey was thinking, but the old minister's face was a Gordian Knot. Rippey was a planner, a plotter, a thinker. Novak knew himself that he was none of those things and never would be. The Reverend seemed to be sizing Novak up, extrapolating his timeline, but that could have been projection.

Ford got to him and Rippey held up a finger. The men around him fell silent and backed off one step. Ford whispered in Rippey's ear, and the Reverend nodded silently, his eyes never leaving Novak's, his face locked in that same frustrating serenity. Novak had the sudden insane inspiration that Rippey was trying to control him: forge a connection through their eyes and manipulate Novak like a puppet.

That was another thing that he was not and never would be.

He broke the contact and jogged to the road.

Rippey's boys were on the gate, shouting to each other. Novak glanced to the Hill. Shapes were coming down Cliffside, just coming free of the treeline. Even at this distance, he picked out Stew and his husband, Pulaski, and Robellada. People were beginning to come out of the Athena as well, but they were too far to see.

The gate creaked open. The guys on the gate, Micah the younger Rosenberg and Gonzalez, were already waving the people on the other side in. Novak shouted: "Hey! Goddamn it!" It was too late. Through the gate, a Winnebago was already moving forward, inching up Hotel Street. It had been modified: bars across the windshield, ram plate on the bumper, razor wire across the top where two men armed men sat and probably an engine that ran on propane or natural gas. Rumbling next to it: five motorcycles, two cars and a VW bus, all modded to greater or lesser degrees for the hazards of the postmodern world. The people inside were armed and armored.

Why Rosenberg and Gonzalez felt the need to let the motherfuckers in was another story. They should have waited for Calomiris, or failing that, Novak and Rippey. But they hadn't.

"Hey, dumb shits!" Novak was at a near run.

Gonzalez was up on the battlements about ten feet off the ground while Rosenberg cranked the gate open.

The bikes were all in, the Winnebago halfway.

Rosenberg looked at Novak. He was a big guy, skinny through the body but with shoulders like basketballs. His beard had a little red in it, and his eyes looked like he'd been up all night. "Yeah?"

"What the fuck do you think you're doing?"

"Letting these people in."

"Not your call."

"Yeah, I give a fuck what you think."

"What was that?" Novak got a little closer.

"There's nobody on the Hill. You got, what, four guys up there? A couple families? You might want to think about the future a little bit. Join up with us before we just make you."

"That right?" Novak considered it, then hit Micah Rosenberg in the gut. He went down, so Novak stomped his head one time before coming out of the blockhouse. No one had seen the assault.

The convoy was already in. Rippey had arrived along with most of his people, smiling and waving the convoy to the side of the road with the lazy wave of a dictator. The bikes were parked, the Winnebago sliding to the side like a barge. Rippey's men were scattered along the road, all armed, all stern. A show of force. Pisspants was still watching Novak and wiped his hands on his pants.

"What the hell is going on?" Stew. Novak's three men had surrounded him in a loose semicircle. Stew looked worried, Pulaski eager. Robellada glanced between the two, scared.

Pulaski grinned. "We're going to get a swarm. First, new fur, then new kills. I knew it was gonna be a good day."

Robellada almost nodded until Stew shot back: "You idiot. A lot of people are going to get killed."

Pulaski shrugged. "Not me."

Novak stepped in. "Cut that shit out. All I know is that the gate crew just let these people in."

Stew: "Didn't wait for permission?"

Novak shook his head.

Robellada looked at the people getting out of the vehicles. "They look hungry."

Novak said: "The geeks that are following them look hungrier, I guarantee it."

Robellada flinched. "Yeah. Hungrier."

Behind them, more of the Hill was gathering, twenty feet from the four people that were the top of the Hill's food chain.

Novak tried to ignore the Harmons, but Jackson Harmon looked like he'd been hit by a truck. Barrett Cheeseman was halfway across the green, thoughtfully sucking on a can of soda. Dr. Bloch waited in the doorway of her house, hiding her belly behind the doorjamb. Novak paused when he saw her, his eyes tracing the aristocratic arch of her brow. Part of him wanted to go to her and tell her everything, hope she would forgive him and comfort him as he died. Part of him hated that.

The leader stepped out of the Winnebago. He was a huge man, well over six feet, with long black hair and a beard, skin freckled by the sun. He wore biker's leathers and carried across his back what looked like an authentic medieval mace, the flanges caked with old meat. He approached Rippey, hand out, and the two men shook. They had a quick conversation, voices low, bodies relaxed.

Rippey motioned to the man and then to the gathering throng: *take the floor, it's yours.*

Something about it looked wrong.

Calomiris and his group were coming down Hotel Street at a brisk walk. Novak couldn't yet make out faces, but it was an easy bet they were ready for a fight.

More of the nomads spilled out of their vehicles. Novak did a quick head count. Five bikes, all males. From the cars, five more, three males and two females. Two more females and a male had come out of the VW bus. No one else, other than the two men on the roof, were out of the Winnebago. There were more shapes in the Winnebago, faces of women and children that Novak forgot as soon as he saw them. A total of twelve men and four women, from appearances, all of which were ready to fight. It was more than enough to tip the balance of power.

The leader started up. "First off, I want to thank everyone, especially the Reverend here, for the nice welcome! We've been moving through Arizona, Utah, Nevada, and California, and we have a lot of salvaged goods to trade. We're hoping to stay for a few days, and maybe longer depending on how we like it here."

Rippey stepped in for a perfect politician photo op. "We're pleased the Lord has blessed us with your presence. I hope everyone can join me in welcoming Mr. Hendrie and his group, and offering a prayer to the Most Holy for His grace!"

Novak was already walking forward. Stew barely got out a protest.

Hendrie, senses keened by the dead world, watched Novak approach with amused confusion.

Rippey was immediately on guard and said: "Thank you for taking the initiative to welcome our guests, Mr. Novak. Mr. Hendrie, this is Glen Novak, one of our leading citizens—"

Novak turned to Rippey. "Did you order your men to open the gates?"

"Of course. No doubt the undead had caught their scent. It is our duty to offer sanctuary to any who ask."

"Fuck that. The geeks eat them, that's their problem, not ours."

Hendrie put a hand on Novak's chest. "Hey. We have women and children in there."

"So do we. And more than you do."

Rippey said: "Christian charity demanded that we open the gate."

"If you gave two fucks for Christian charity, we wouldn't have people hungry in Town."

"No one goes hungry in Town."

"No one starves to death. There's a difference."

Rippey allowed a thin smile. "I never thought you to be one of the righteous."

"No one is." Novak turned to Hendrie. "And you, lay another hand on me and I open you up like a melon, got me?"

Hendrie grinned. "Big talk from a midget." No matter how big Hendrie was, Novak wasn't going to take that on a good day, let alone his last day on earth.

"What was that?"

Hendrie touched Novak's chest again. Novak grabbed the wrist, gave it a twist that brought Hendrie to his knees and down to size. Then Novak tackled him. Novak's speed surprised Hendrie; he didn't start moving until Novak was sitting on his chest. Hendrie didn't have leverage. He was not a wrestler. He didn't understand control.

Novak did.

He rained fists down on the other man, some connecting flush with Hendrie's cheek, chin, temple, face, nose. He had his hands up, trying to fend off Novak, but it was useless. Hendrie had been hurt too much and too quickly to mount an effective defense. The fight, the man, belonged to Novak utterly.

Every hit from his left hand sent a dull ache through his shoulder, but the hand itself was a cushion that felt nothing at all. He didn't care. He heard nothing but the roar of blood in his ears, saw only the destruction of the man below him. This man he could hurt with impunity. This was not a friend. This was not an ally. This was not a face he had to see day in and day out.

Suddenly, he felt hands under his armpits, hauling him away. He turned to hit the owner of the hands, saw Stew's face, kept the punch in check.

Rippey, far off: "Someone get him off him!"

An unfamiliar voice: "Shoot him! Fucking kill the shrimp!"

Then, Ford: "No! Nobody shoots nobody!"

Stew said: "Glen! Calm down! Glen!"

Novak tried to push the adrenaline out of his system, but it roiled with the poison turning black and thick.

Hendrie tried to get up, blood from his smashed nose pooling in his eye sockets. One of the women, a pretty brunette, was next to him, cradling his head and talking to him.

The other nomads had guns on Novak, guns on Rippey's

soldiers. Rippey's men had guns on the nomads. Pulaski stood in front of Novak, a grin on his face and a challenge in his eyes.

Rippey shouted at Stew: "Control your friend!"

Robellada seemed to obey instinctively, going toward Novak, but backing off as though his old teacher were red hot.

Stew whispered in Novak's ear: "Calm down, man. It's cool. You're cool. You're cool."

Robellada nodded along, though he probably could not hear the exact words.

Calomiris arrived at that moment. "What's going on here?"

Rippey stepped up. Finger was at his left shoulder, grinning like a reptile. Ford was at his right. Rippey said: "Glen Novak just assaulted our guest, without warning or provocation."

"I don't buy that," Calomiris said.

"There are plentiful witnesses."

Calomiris snorted then swallowed the wad of phlegm he jarred loose. He swept the area with those glittering eyes, then turned his attention back to Rippey. "On the subject of our guests, I don't remember asking you to let them in."

"The gate is mine, Walter."

"So you decide who to let in? I don't think so. Glen, did you agree to let them in?"

Novak had calmed down. He shook his head.

Calomiris said: "I didn't think so." He turned back to Rippey. "You endangered all of us when you opened that gate. After all, what if one of them has been bitten?"

The brunette helped Hendrie to his feet. He had recovered enough to glare, the smeared blood making his cheeks blush. His voice had a cracked and nasal quality now. "We're clean."

Calomiris turned his attention on the larger man. "And I have, what, your word on it? No. Before you go any further, you will submit to a medical exam."

Rippey nodded. "I was going to announce that right before Mr. Novak lost his mind. Dr. Bloch can get started right away."

Calomiris said: "I don't think so. You let them in without a consensus. You forfeit your rights to any new settlers. Besides, we should show our guests the right kind of hospitality. What, you're going to put them in the field behind the gas station?" Calomiris turned to Hendrie. "Take your people up to the Hotel Athena, and I'll see to it that you have nice soft beds in the east wing."

Hendrie wiped the blood from his nose, looked from Calomiris to Rippey to Novak. Finally, he said: "Show me the way."

Calomiris smiled. "Right up this road here. When you're squared away, my people can have a look at you. Welcome to Devon."

Something was wrong, a crack in what had happened, growing deeper into a fault. Novak could not name it, instead letting it nag at his burning mind.

- 9 -

THURSDAY WAS IN SOME WAYS arbitrary. The rioting had been going on for a couple weeks before that, and the exact flashpoint date, that elusive patient zero, was never known. It had become irrelevant. They were far closer to the last human than the first geek.

But Thursday was the day of the fall, when the swarms hit the big cities. At that point, they had an idea that it might be more than rioting. The fishbelly faces, the milky eyes, those grainy images on the news hinted at something worse.

Novak woke up that day as Mr. Novak, gym teacher and wrestling coach at Glendale High. He worried about the troubles that had just reached Santa Clarita, and he hoped they wouldn't come to his doorstep. He hoped he wouldn't come down with Susan's flu because of the big meet the following Friday. He wanted to get home, watch *Cosby* and *Night Court* with Susan and drift off in a comfortable and dreamless sleep.

That didn't happen. Not when the sirens and smoke started around 10 a.m. He looked over his third period class of 10th graders, including Ricky Robellada, five years younger and a hundred years greener. Novak looked at them and told them he was leaving.

He left them, one and all.

He left them for Susan.

And he was too late.

First kill, and like a light, humanity gone.

Novak pushed the memory of Susan away. If there was an afterlife, maybe he would meet her again. Probably not, no matter how that theological debate got handled. Best not to think about her. Easier said than done.

He sat down heavily by the side of the road, back to the caravan rolling past, feet in the drainage ditch that ran alongside. He stared at the Dinner Bell, where Barrett Cheeseman stood outside, drinking his soda and watching the caravan. Cheeseman looked down, saw Novak, and shot him the finger, then went back to watching the vehicles.

Rippey's men grumbled to each other, but they didn't try to stop anything that transpired. Calomiris, smiling in his triumph, led the way up Hotel Street to the top of the hill where the Athena waited for her new guests.

Novak enjoyed the sun on his shoulders, but the clouds were already spreading like spilled ink.

Stew settled next to him. "Are you okay, Glen?"

Thirty feet off, Dr. Bloch watched Novak, face unreadable. He looked at the gold freckles across her nose, the ones that made her look young, no matter the root system by her eyes. He might have told her, in that moment, had she asked.

"Been better."

Pulaski stood on the road, Robellada in the drainage ditch in front of Stew and Novak. Stew looked to Novak's cheeks and forehead. "You look feverish."

Novak shrugged. "Possible. Haven't slept."

"Then maybe you should get some sleep."

Pulaski: "Talk to us, boss."

Novak was very aware of Pulaski so close. The signs had to be getting more apparent. They had all seen every stage of the bite at that point. Sure, the early stages could be confused with any number of things, especially a bad flu, but one glance at the wound, one count of Novak's fingers, and they would know. The leather glove groaned as Novak balled his left hand into a fist. He anticipated pain, but there was no feeling, not in the hand, arm or shoulder. Three sets of eyes bored into him. He knew he had to give them something. "Someone tried to have me killed last night."

Robellada: "Someone tried to kill you? Who?" Eyes big. Poor kid was probably scared that he was next. He immediately glanced at Stew and Pulaski, as though hoping they would approve of the question as worthy.

"I don't know. That's why I said 'someone.'"

Pulaski scanned the departing factions. Janelle Ford had joined her brother, walking back to the church. She was looking in Robellada's direction, but Ford's attention was on Novak. Pulaski said: "A couple hours ago at Gino's, some guy tried to gun the boss down."

Stew was quiet, searching Novak's face.

Novak said: "Charles Booker, Athena resident. A low-ranking scav. Turns out he's been after the Franklin girl."

Robellada said: "After?"

"Like you're after Janelle Ford."

"Oh! Oh." Robellada's face crumbled, then set.

"I was talking to Robert Franklin about it when Ford showed up to ask me to stop roughing up one of Rippey's people."

Robellada, eager: "You think Robert had something to do with it?"

"He's got a connection to the assassin. More than I can think of with anyone else. Maybe Rippey worked through him? I don't know."

"Maybe we should go ask him." Robellada had a fire in his eyes Novak hadn't seen before. Usually, this would have been Pulaski, spoiling for a fight and ready to cause some shit. It was nice seeing the kid get a killer instinct. Robellada didn't even look for approval, even though he was channeling Pulaski.

Novak stood up. That was a little harder than it should have been. "Good idea, kid."

He expected Stew to drop some counsel. Tell Novak to slow down. Tell him to get some sleep. Tell him to look somewhere other than a guy whose daughter had been raped by some freak gunman. But Stew was completely quiet, falling in right next to Novak. Robellada forged on ahead. Pulaski was behind them, whistling something Novak was pretty sure Michael Jackson had written.

After Calomiris publicly beat Rippey like that, Novak half expected to see Town gearing for war. They would gather on the front yard of the church, all fifteen of his hardcore soldiers, the inner circle and maybe a couple of pissed off civilians. Rippey could probably draw a mob of twenty-five or thirty if things were that bad. The church was full, but no more full than it was every day around sunrise.

Rippey had been beaten twice in the last couple hours and he was taking it lying down. Maybe Robellada had somehow gotten Rippey's balls without Novak's knowing it.

The sun was up over the eastern hills and already disappearing into the low clouds. Franklin's porch was in shadow. There was furtive movement on it, then the door slammed. Robellada and Stew pulled their pistols. Pulaski was right behind Novak. A glance from him, a momentary drop in Novak's guard, and the secret would be out. He probably wouldn't get a word out before that sword did its slick work.

"Stew, take Pulaski around the back. Kid, you're with me."

Within thirty feet of the house, Stew and Pulaski peeled off. Stew was low, but Pulaski looked like he was wandering into a garden party.

Novak was first to the porch, Robellada next.

He put one foot on the first stair. It creaked. Nothing. He made it up and across the porch. Wasn't going to stand in front of the door. Robellada got on the other side. Novak did a little mental calculation and hoped he was right: Stew and Pulaski should be on the other side of the house. He stretched a hand out and knocked.

"Mr. Franklin, it's Novak. We haven't finished our conversation."

No sound. He nodded to Robellada and twisted the doorknob, still out of the line of fire.

A shotgun blast went through the open doorway.

Novak heard what sounded like the scrape of a chair, followed by a shout. He went through the door first, gun leveled, knowing Robellada would be right behind him.

They found Franklin, back to them, a small wooden chair tipped over beside him. He was holding a sawed-off shotgun, pointing back down his hall, toward the kitchen. Beyond that, Stew and Pulaski were nearly invisible behind cover.

Novak said: "Nice shot."

Franklin whirled. Novak brought the gun up. Robellada came through the door, pistol trained on Franklin's head. Stew and Pulaski stepped out of cover, Stew pointing his pistol, Pulaski looking mildly amused, his sword still slung on his back.

Novak said: "Try it."

Pulaski flopped down on the couch and put his feet up.

Franklin glanced around, realizing how outnumbered he was. He dropped the gun.

He was dressed—blue jeans and flannel—like any good farmer. The cut on his head had stopped bleeding and didn't look as bad as Novak initially thought. He would have a nasty bruise, though. It was then Novak noticed that Franklin's eyes were nearly all white. He looked like a trapped animal.

He sort of was.

"Where'd you hide your family?"

"They're not here."

Novak opened his mouth to threaten the guy, but Robellada pistol-whipped him before Novak got a word out. Franklin fell to the floor, clutching his nose.

Novak picked up the shotgun and tossed it to Stew, who barely caught it. "Mr. Novak asked you a question, *maricon*."

"Upstairs. I told them to wait for me!"

Novak nodded to Pulaski. "We don't want them going to Rippey before we're done here."

Pulaski sighed but went up the stairs. Stew closed to Novak and spoke low: "You're not threatening this guy's family." It was a demand, and one Novak had already conceded to in his own mind.

"No. They're off limits." Novak raised his voice. "I think your daughter's been fucked with enough already, don't you?"

He kicked Franklin in the short ribs, who then curled up like a pill bug. He hauled Franklin up and tossed him on the couch. At that moment, Pulaski came downstairs with Mrs. Franklin and little Melissa. Both of them had the same curly blonde hair, pretty and not painfully skinny. The mother saw her husband, shrieked his first name and Pulaski had to hold her back. The little girl looked at the room almost like she expected it. She didn't feel one way or the other. It was just something that was happening, and there wasn't a thing she could do about it. It was a horrible resignation in her eyes.

Novak said to Pulaski: "Keep them company in the kitchen. They don't need to see this."

The wife said: "Please! Don't hurt him!"

"Everything we do is up to him."

Pulaski dragged her from the room. The little girl followed, turning her head away.

Franklin, his nose bleeding a sluggish trickle, said: "What do you want?"

"Talk to you. We established earlier that a man tried to kill me.

A man you know. Practically an in-law."

"You son of—"

Robellada punched Franklin in the face before he got the rest out. Novak had never seen the kid like this. Pissed as hell. Nice to know someone cared. "You sent the fucking guy, now tell us why."

Franklin's eyes were wide on Robellada, more scared of the kid than he was of Novak. "Sent the guy?"

"Charlie Booker. You sent him to kill me. Why?"

"I didn't—"

Robellada punched Franklin in the belly this time. "We know what you did. Admit it!" If the kid kept it up, Novak was going to adopt him.

Stew said: "If you're going to ask the man questions, let him answer them."

"Not if he lies," Robellada said.

Stew said to Franklin: "Did you send Charles Booker to kill Novak?"

"No. No! I knew Booker, but we weren't friends! I tried to kill him the other night!"

Robellada hit Franklin with a right cross. Stew grabbed the kid and pushed him away. "That's enough, goddamn it! Jesus, I didn't think I'd have to say this to you, but hit him one more time and you're waiting outside."

Robellada glared at Stew, but Stew stared him down. That was the Robellada Novak knew.

Novak said: "You tried to kill him. Why?"

"You know." Franklin couldn't look at Novak, and chose to watch the floor instead.

"Let's pretend I don't. Let's pretend I'm going to let the kid off his leash if you don't clear it up."

"Booker... he lived up at the Athena. His room overlooked the farm. I guess that's how he saw my daughter out in the fields helping me. He started visiting, giving her little presents. He was a scav, so he would find toys and things. Stuff from before."

Novak thought about the little green wind-up that was in so many pieces on Booker's floor. So far, so good.

"He would hang around here. Whenever I'd come home, I'd find him on the back porch, waiting or trying to get in. It got so I didn't want to leave, ever. I chased him off one time. I thought that was the end of it. Until the night I caught him upstairs in Melissa's room."

He didn't need to say what he'd seen in there. Novak read it easily in Franklin's eyes.

"Booker went out the window. I shot, I missed. I shouldn't have missed."

Novak nodded. "He's dead now. Pulaski took his head."

Franklin calmed a bit. "I didn't send him your way, but I'm glad he went. Your man did what I couldn't do."

Robellada tried to laugh, but it didn't come out like anything was funny. "You buy this shit? Guy pimps out his kid for salvage, then tries to kill you? No, we end this piece of shit now." He racked a bullet.

Stew stepped in the way. "Put the gun down, Ricky. The man's telling the truth."

"How the fuck do you know?"

"Because we do, kid," Novak said. "I wish he was lying, but he's not." The guy was bloody, beaten, humiliated from what Novak and his men had done to him, and what they made him tell them. There wasn't much Novak could do about that and he knew it. He couldn't make it up to Franklin because Novak would be dead before that kind of thing mattered. "Stew, give the man his gun back."

Stew broke the gun and was about to remove the shells, but Novak shook his head. About a hundred things went over Stew's face in that instant, but it just looked like a shadow. He couldn't read it: dark and all-consuming. Stew snapped the barrels back in place and handed the loaded gun over to Franklin. It lay there, in his lap, like a snake.

Novak shouted: "Pulaski! We're going!"

Pulaski came out of the kitchen, followed by Mrs. Franklin. She ran to her husband as soon as she saw the hard men weren't going to stop her. She wanted to say something to them, and in the old world she probably would have. This was the new world. The only law was what you could enforce, and her husband had already failed against one man, let alone four.

Novak said: "One thing. Why didn't you go to Rippey?"

Franklin couldn't look at anything other than the shotgun. "I did. He didn't care. He said Melissa was going to need to get married sooner or later and it might as well be sooner. He said that she should be making babies."

Novak wanted to promise something, but he didn't know what. Franklin was a Townie. He had a farm, roots. Novak walked out of the man's house with his men, wishing he'd never walked in.

"Where to next, boss?" Nothing had touched Pulaski. Nothing ever did.

"Next, you guys go home. That convoy was an open fucking invite to every geek from here to San Francisco. I want you to prepare the Hill for a fight, and if you have the chance, head out and pick off any stragglers before they swarm."

Stew said: "And you?"

"I've got business at the Athena."

- 10 -

NOVAK SHIVERED IN THE SUNLIGHT as he went up the slope to the Hotel Athena. The sun shone on the east wing, turning the bricks red. He wasn't sure what he was going to say. He wasn't sure what he was planning. He only knew who he was going to talk to.

The nomads' vehicles were parked in the old roundabout, the Winnebago like a beached whale, the cars and bikes its insanely loyal pilot fish. The nomads would be inside, quarantined while Calomiris's guys looked for bite marks. The nomads had lasted. They were probably better about bite discipline than the residents of Devon were.

After all, I was about to have the run of the Athena.

The thought made him chuckle. No pain came from the arm. It brushed against his side with every step, a stranger with no sense of personal space.

Inside, Calomiris's men were on alert. They might have gotten up to stop Novak had he not headed right for them.

Marcos would be on the fifth floor, probably still sleeping with that wife of his. *Fuck it, wake him up. Wasn't like I could wait until tomorrow.*

"I need to see Marcos."

The guy on the other end, Roth, had a nice black goatee that he obviously spent a ton of time maintaining; he shot his partner a distressed look. "He's busy."

"Busy what, sleeping? Or repopulating?"

His partner, Ortiz, a big Mexican, sidled closer. This caused Roth to grow a set of balls. "Busy."

"How about you fetch him before I show your boyfriend what an inside-out asshole looks like?"

Roth blinked. Ortiz stopped in his tracks. They thought about it. There was no way his threat would end well. "Wait for him in the bar."

"Good enough."

The bar was completely empty. He'd never been there this early, and didn't like it much at other hours. Still, morning didn't mean much. Goods were the only thing that mattered. Goods, salvage, cigarettes, and drugs made the rules. Few people looked on drinking in the morning as a vice, not when Calomiris openly traded meth.

Novak picked his seat from the previous night. The stage was dark. He thought about Stacy. He wondered if she was going to listen, and go to Pulaski. Probably not. She'd be used up inside the year, die and be buried in the Athena's fields to turn to fertilizer. Novak stared at the black curtains on the other end of the room, shivering every now and then.

Finally: "What do you want, Novak?"

He hadn't heard Marcos approach. He tried to cover his surprise, but it was a poor job. "I want to talk somewhere private."

Marcos looked around. Other than the bartender surreptitiously watching with a "I hope they don't start hitting each other" look, the room was empty. "More private than this?"

"Yeah."

He shrugged, dubious: "Follow me up to five."

The walk up the stairs was easier. Novak's whole body felt like it was made from rubber bands, stretching taut and snapping back into place. He barely felt in command, as though be would suddenly career out of control. He was holding on, but he knew that hold was tenuous, a losing battle. He'd lose before the next sunrise. That thought hurt him almost more than anything else.

The fifth floor was silent. The sun was up, shining through the grimy window at the end of the passage. Maybe the rooms were empty. Maybe the denizens of the fifth had discovered sleeping in again.

Marcos led the way down the corridors, turning right and right again. He opened a door, revealing an empty room that looked out over the courtyard, but had a clear view of the Pacific from the balcony. In the old days, this would have been one of the prized rooms, probably an extra forty a night. It was almost as desirable after the end, safer than Novak's place on the Hill. Marcos motioned him in and shut the door behind them.

"Okay, Novak. What did you want?"

The room looked untouched from the old days. The bed was made in the tight-hotel fashion. The folded card that explained the cable was still on top of the TV set. The ashtray was clean. He went to the glass door. It was dusty rather than dirty, at least on the inside. He opened the sliding door and stepped out on the balcony. Ahead, the L-shape of the Athena retreated from the ocean. Below, in the courtyard, Calomiris's people worked the farm that used to be a place where rich people watched the sunset over the Pacific. Some plowed the plots of vegetables. Others tended the meth lab. Calomiris got the crops and paid them a fraction for the labor. With those goods, they could trade with Calomiris for other goods or just space in the Athena, netting even less. Nothing was free in the Athena. Nothing was free anywhere.

He turned back to Marcos, who now had his arms folded, but his left leg was a little behind his right, like he expected Novak to attack. "Something wrong?" Novak said.

"Oh, no. I've been listening to some rumors. You jumped Tigran Gamburyan last night. I heard you beat up some people in Town, too."

"You think I'm losing it?"

"If you ever had it."

"Rumors are true, you know. Something they didn't include."

"What's that?"

"The people I beat down only had that happen because I had questions they didn't answer."

"And now you want answers from me?"

Novak had seen the beginnings of fights, been in them, organized and not-so, to see that stutter, the hiccup that meant a point of no return had been reached. The body tightens, bracing for impact. That causes an almost imperceptible jump as every tendon, every muscle, pulls taut to a breaking point.

Marcos had just jumped.

Novak straightened up. He wondered how much experience Marcos had fighting men who were still breathing. "Only a couple. Real easy ones, too."

"I don't know shit."

"Sure you do. We both know Calomiris is up to something. You just know a little more than I do."

"The only thing Calomiris is up to is keeping the geeks out of Devon."

Novak nodded. "How much does he know about me and Inez?"

"Shit."

Novak raised an eyebrow. Something seemed off. He wasn't sure what. He felt the lie, but not what the truth might be, or even exactly what the lie was. Maybe Marcos had been right about the tipping point. Maybe not. Novak thought about the men and women in the fields outside. He thought about Stacy and her ribs. He thought about the nomads. He thought about Harmon and Franklin.

He had his hands on Marcos before he knew what was happening. He slammed into Marcos's chest, not trying to take him down—that would have just pushed him in to the door. Instead, he planted his feet and wrapped his hands around Marcos's back, squeezing until he linked hands, left with right, dead with alive.

Marcos tried to knee him in the groin, but Novak lifted and wrenched, spinning both of them around, landing on top.

He lifted his head and Marcos punched it, the fist spinning Novak's head partway around. It was a hit that would have dazed a less experienced man. Novak lurched forward, slamming a knee into Marcos's groin. He doubled up. That was power.

Now for control. He switched positions while Marcos was paralyzed in agony. First, he moved up, crosswise on Marcos's chest, back to Marcos's legs. Novak pinned both arms, one under his legs, the other with his right elbow, bolstered by all his weight. That left his left hand free. He could pummel Marcos all day if he wanted; and he started with five to the face. Each hit should have felt like something, but it was as though Novak had a pillow over his fist.

Marcos was bloody, cut under an eye, nose and lip bleeding.

Novak stopped for a moment. "Are we done with this shit?"

"Fuck you." He tried to buck Novak off. That earned Marcos another five hard punches. His nose gave.

"Breaking your face is just about the easiest thing I could do right now."

Marcos fought through the cotton Novak pounded into his brain.

Novak went on: "What is Calomiris up to?"

"He knows! He knows about you and Inez."

Novak wondered how much Marcos knew. "I thought so. He sent Booker to finish me off?"

"He sent Booker to kill you because you're sleeping with my cousin."

Novak got up, putting more weight on Marcos's left arm than he had to. The other man would have a nasty bruise there, maybe down to the bone.

Marcos moved into a sitting position, still a little foggy.

"Why Booker?"

"I don't know. Maybe because he could lose Booker. No one liked the guy."

He nodded. "Thanks, Marcos. You've been helpful."

He left Marcos in the room and walked to the end of the hall. This window faced south, looking out over the rest of the town, all the way to the Barricade. In the distance, he saw the glittering parking lot that the 1 Freeway had become. The antlike shapes of geeks ambled through the cars in Devon's direction. On a normal day, a hit squad, either Rippey's or Novak's, would have gone out and cleared those geeks out before they attracted more.

It wasn't a normal day.

Novak took the stairs up to the sixth floor, shivering when he reached the top. He thought the tremors would go away, but they took hold, wrapping him in ice and dragging him down. He caught the wall and put his weight on that. For a brief second, he thought of Harmon, of Nuñez and Franklin, of Marcos, of everyone he'd beaten and intimidated. He saw them one flight down, taking each step purposefully, eyes on Novak like hungry geeks. He might welcome them.

He leaned heavily and stuck his hands in his armpits. The shivers collapsed in on themselves. All his muscles were locked. One push, and he'd tip over, tumbling broken down the stairs. As long as that crucial part of his brain remained intact, he would even get back up.

He blinked stinging sweat from his eyes and made an awful revelation: *This might not go away.* He wasn't looking at a recovery. He was looking for a reprieve. Eventually, it would bring him down. He hoped for half a day. Another couple hours.

A minute more.

Suddenly, the left arm, the stranger's arm, moved. He put it against the wall. He found that the shoulder was loose. So was his neck. He turned to the right arm, flexed the hand. It was fine. He tried his legs. The shivers were gone.

He faced the door to six. It was only a matter of time before he got an attack like that again, and chances are it would be in company. He tried to forget about that, but it grew large in his belly.

He opened the door. There was no one at the door to the honeymoon suite. He thought he'd be nice. He knocked.

Inez's voice, shouting: "Not now!"

"Inez, it's me."

In a moment, he heard the chain, then the lock, and the door whipped open. She barely glanced at Novak, before storming back to the bathroom. She wore black, her clothes damp and her hair wet. He heard the splash of water.

She said: "What do you want?" More splashing.

He slowly walked toward the back. "Is Calomiris here?"

"He's on the roof."

"I just spoke with your cousin."

The splashing stopped. Strained: "Oh?"

"Yeah. Your husband knows."

Her voice was unreadable. "How can you be sure?"

"Your cousin." He was deep enough in the honeymoon suite now. One more step and he was looking into the bathroom. She had a basin of soapy water and was scrubbing her hands with a brush. In the new world, a basin of water meant someone fetched it from the pump in the courtyard. Soap meant she was using the dwindling reserves of the old world that someone had risked his life to get.

She looked up at Novak and immediately picked the basin up and dumped it into the tub. Novak could not see color in the water past the milky consistency of the soap. Her hands were pruning, raw. Almost bleeding.

She said: "What?"

"I talked to your cousin. He knows. Your husband knows that we've been fucking. Don't know how long, but he's the one that sent Booker after me."

"You came to me before Booker."

That statement was like a slap. "Booker wasn't the first try."

She frowned. In that moment, Novak saw her old face, the pretty girl that had seduced Walter Calomiris. It was an expression of innocent distrust.

He said: "Calomiris tries once, fails, tries again. No reason he wouldn't try again."

She nodded, slowly. "Makes sense."

"No, it doesn't. Not if what you told me before was true. That he didn't care about what, or who, you did."

"He doesn't."

"Then why would that provoke him? Why else would he want me dead?"

"You and I... it's an admission of weakness."

She was right. This wasn't the old world. The world was based on strength now, both the appearance and the reality. Fuck a guy's wife behind his back, and that was a declaration that he was powerless to stop it. Any weakness could and would be exploited by anyone who smelled it. If Marcos knew, maybe some of the other men knew. The more men knew, the less they would respect Calomiris. Let the respect dwindle and he was screwed. Even if he didn't care about his wife, he would need Novak gone to keep the Athena intact.

Inez searched his face. He was certain she could read through these thoughts as he had them. She said: "He sent Booker because he had to."

"Yeah. Fuck." A public apology didn't work. Then the whispers became fact and it was worse. For Novak's people too, especially if Calomiris demanded restitution. It weakened both the Hill and the Athena, which—with Rippey waiting—was not something either Calomiris or Novak needed.

"There's a simple solution," she said.

"I don't see it."

"You kill my husband."

She didn't cackle. She didn't rub her hands together. She said it matter-of-factly, near monotone. Her brown eyes were clear.

He said: "Simple as that."

"Maybe not simple, but it solves your problems, no?"

"Solves some, I guess. Creates a few more. Like the rest of his men coming for me and cutting me up."

"Kill him, take the Athena. Maybe some people are loyal enough to him that they go after you. More likely, they join up with Isador Rippey."

"The last thing we need to do is make that guy any stronger."

"That's a temporary thing. You take the Athena, and that and the Hill are yours. We can deal with Rippey after that."

Novak thought about it. Finally: "You really want him dead that badly?"

"I don't care about Rippey."

"I'm not talking about him."

"I know. Look, we all know Walter is getting weaker while Isador Rippey gets stronger. The few refugees we get, most settle in Town."

"Except for that group this morning."

Her voice caught. "A drop in the bucket. That we get lucky

one time does not reverse what's gone on for the last couple of years."

"I don't see how I change anything."

"Walter's let Rippey get as powerful as he is. Walter has been giving Rippey free rein over everything."

"Not sure how that's his fault. Rippey's the kind of man that isn't going to sit on his ass if there's power to be grabbed."

"Rippey's not a native. He showed up about sixth months after the end, and Walter just let him in. Wasn't long before Rippey owned everything in Devon that wasn't the Athena. He basically owned the Hill until you showed up. You were the first person who stood up to him."

Novak remembered that. These days, ownership was determined simply: one owned what no one else could take away. When he'd moved in and took his house on the Hill, Rippey's men had come by to inform Novak that he worked for them. They didn't expect Novak to laugh in their faces. They came back two days later to demand a portion of Novak's salvage. He said no. They came back with bats. Novak hurt a couple of them bad enough so that they were on their backs for about a month. After that, the Hill was his.

He knew how to deal with Isador Rippey because he knew what Rippey would respect. After that moment, Rippey treated Novak not as an equal, but certainly better than nearly anyone else in Devon.

Novak said: "Your husband is weak, so you replace him with someone stronger."

"Inez Novak sounds nice to me."

She would be married to a corpse. If he took out Calomiris, there was a chance for stability. It would head off the civil war that had been brewing over the past year. He would need some kind of guarantee from Rippey that he wouldn't immediately turn on

Novak's people, and enough trust to believe he'd hold to it after Novak was dead.

"You've been thinking about this a lot. Already ordered the stationery?"

"Glen, what's good for me is good for Devon. If Walter's weak, that means Devon's weak. You're strong. You could keep us safe."

"Your husband has been doing a good enough job, hasn't he?"

"You won't even say his name. You call him 'your husband.'"

"Important that someone remember that."

"But no, he hasn't been. We've had outbreaks. The population is shrinking faster than it's growing. We have this one little corner of the world and nothing else."

"One little corner is better than nothing."

"And it's a lot worse than anything else."

"You want to expand?"

She nodded.

He said: "What, to the necropolises?"

"There are other towns, up and down the coast. Far enough away, but with more resources. Probably more people, too. We could start clearing areas out."

"That's a good way to attract a swarm."

"So, we attract a swarm. We get a few just staying here, and we always beat them. So we go out to gain something rather than just sitting around here to lose."

"You're crazy."

She focused on him. "No, no, I'm not. If we could take a section of coast, maybe we could take a piece of California back. Maybe we could start up a state completely free of the undead."

"The California Republic." It sounded good. He had to remember that as good as it all sounded, it didn't matter to him. He was a dead man already. He wouldn't see a goddamn thing.

"What are you thinking?"

"That you're a fucking idiot if you think any of that is going to work."

She turned away. "Did you come up here to insult me? Or was it just to treat me like your whore?"

"No, I came up here to tell you that your husband knows about us. What you want to do after the man is dead is up to you."

She turned around. "You'll do it?"

"He tried to kill me. He has it coming."

She nodded and touched Novak's face. Concerned: "You're burning up."

"Flu or something. I'll be fine."

"I have aspirin."

"No, no. Save it. I'll be back around noon."

She nodded. "Good luck."

"Yeah."

He had to rest on the stairs on his way down. The climbing was taking its toll, but then he wouldn't have to climb very much longer. He wanted to get some food in his belly before he finished it. A couple hours to put everything in order. He thought that he should talk to his guys. He wasn't sure how these things were done, but he felt like he should pick a successor. Seeing the finish line was a strange kind of hope. Not the hope of something positive, but the hope that the condemned man feels when the hands are strapped to Old Sparky and the cap secured in place. There's only one last little bit before the pain stops.

The short rest got him down the stairs and outside into the air. The clouds were coming in hard, billowing outward, growling from gray to black.

The ocean rumbled off to his right. He walked down Hotel Street into Town and turned right on Cliffside to walk up the Hill. As the pine smell of the Hill took him, he started thinking about what he was going to eat. He had a couple cans of beef stew that he'd been saving for a special occasion. There was his stash of Butterfingers that he only touched twice a year, his birthday and Valentine's Day. He had a sixer of Bass. Put that on a layer of beef stew, thicker than mortar. All of that was going down the hatch. His stomach spurred his feet.

He caught a flicker of movement to his right, slightly downhill. He turned and pulled his hatchet. Chances were, it was a kid. There were a couple of those on the Hill—the Rodriguezes had a young son and the Sorensens had a little girl. Then again, it could be a geek that somehow threaded the needle between the Barricade and the cliff. It happened every now and then.

"Show yourself. Keep hiding, I assume you're a geek."

Nothing.

He left the road, through the drainage ditch where the pine needles rotted to mulch, to the undergrowth. He heard nothing. A geek would be closing, especially after he had yelled out like that. Then again, sometimes the bastards were strangely sneaky. He took another couple of steps.

Then he heard it: footsteps, running through the underbrush. One of his people wouldn't run from him. He chased.

Up ahead, the trees would thin out a bit. The footsteps weren't going down the Hill—that far west and downhill would lead to the open green between the Hill and the Athena, with nothing but a cliff to one side and meadow to the other, the only structures being the Dinner Bell and Bloch's office. The footsteps were going deeper into the trees.

The footsteps paused ahead. That would be the clearing. He broke through the trees. A kid stood in the middle of the clearing, terrified. His jeans were muddy, his sweatshirt sporting some new tears. Novak had never seen the kid before, but he looked familiar somehow, like a face seen in a dream. Novak opened his mouth to say something when he heard a twig break behind him.

He whirled. Nothing.

He turned back. The kid was gone.

Novak cocked his head. No sounds of footsteps this time. The kid was gone. Vanished.

If he was ever there in the first place. Inez said it: he was burning up. The bite was cooking his brain. He'd talked to a couple people who were bitten before he killed them. They saw things. Heard things. Who the hell knew if that kid was ever there?

Did it matter if he was?

Probably not. He was planning his last meal: beef stew, candy bars, beer, and a .45 caliber bullet. That sounded pretty good to him.

He turned around and headed home.

- 11 -

NOVAK SET OUT THE FOOD in front of him in a row. Three cans of stew. Eight candy bars. Six beers. Something ancient and reptile in his mind demanded the ritual. A last meal should be eaten with care and respect, even if the man eating it had none of one and demanded too much of the other.

He was in his backyard over the outdoor oven he'd built a couple years back. It started as a hole, which he then bordered in brick. It had about a foot of ash at the bottom, ash that he was adding to as he started the fire. He made sure it was low burning and stoked the embers like he was trying to piss them off.

He slid the metal grate over the pit, opened the cans and lined them up over the fire. Smoke billowed up to join the clouds. The flames tried to get a taste of the stew. He hoped to get a little sunlight, but that was done with. He figured that he might have already looked at the sun for the last time. At least he could finish it on his terms, and soon, before his body entirely gave up. They could put him in the ground. They could burn him. But he would die as he was and stay that way. He would not rise.

He would make sure of that.

The aroma of the stew brought him back. It smelled like the old world. His old life pushed in, and he pushed back, but it was too late. The memories opened the lock and flooded in, and he realized that there wasn't anything wrong with that. He only had a little while left. He didn't have to survive past noon.

He let the memories of Susan come back in and stay a while. He thought about how much smarter she was than he. He thought about how she loved him anyway. He thought about her smell, a memory he couldn't quite conjure but one that he knew he would recognize if it still existed somewhere in the world. He thought about the way she clipped *The Far Side* from the paper and taped it on her desk. He thought about the way she chewed her pens when grading papers. He skipped the part where he let her down.

The memories of her were of the old world. As they circled in his mind, he was surprised to find how dim they'd become. He groped for details: her favorite cartoon, the precise way she executed her *A*s, which hand she used to push her hair behind her ear. She had faded. Neglect—his neglect—had killed her and it had killed the last vestiges of her as ephemera. Perhaps that was better, to consign her to the old world.

Because in the new world there was only pain.

Let her memory die in that place. Let him die afterward. They could find oblivion together.

Using gloves, he took a can off the fire and moved the other two to the corner. He sat down in his lawn chair and, for a moment, soaked the moment in. The air was chilly, the stew was warm. He cracked a beer. He would have called it piss warm in the old days, the kind of beer remaining late in a barbecue after all the ice melted away. Now, it seemed cold enough.

He blew on a spoonful of stew. Not that it really needed it, but there was more ritual to that act. He savored the first bite. The beef, the carrots, the broth thick like syrup. He hadn't remembered it tasting quite so good. The first can went down nearly in one gulp. He paced himself on the second can, and took his sweet time with the third. A couple beers washed each one down, the bitterness unlocking a deeper sweetness in the meat.

With three empty cans and his mouth greasy, he unwrapped the first Butterfinger. Whoever got these would be getting the real motherlode of his salvage. He'd taken every one of them he could find and, at this point, he was fairly certain he had the largest collection in the western hemisphere and maybe the world. There was something about them that he loved. The squared off ends, like a wrapped present. The chocolate's white dust that probably meant it was low-grade stuff, but it reminded him of Halloween. Then there was whatever the hell they wrapped inside the chocolate. The flaky stuff that looked like sheets of corkboard but tasted like peanut butter crystallized in sugar. It crumbled and lodged in molars so that a half hour later, his tongue would still be digging out succulent nuggets. Ten thousand years of civilization produced the perfect candy.

He was tonsil deep in the third bar when the thumping started. His front door. Robellada's voice: "Mr. Novak! We need your help!"

He was on his feet before he could think. He kept munching as he went through the wooden side gate that led to the front of the house. His guys were in a semicircle by the door, with Sorensen and Rodriguez waiting on the street. None of them wore their packs, but all were armed. Pulaski spotted Novak a few seconds before anyone else, touching the hilt of his sword in a gesture Novak hoped was merely reflex. He clenched the left hand anyway.

"What's going on?" He half-expected to see geeks at the Barricade, but it looked quiet.

Robellada hesitated, looking to Stew, who stepped forward, pointing down through the trees toward Town. Novak followed the finger to the crowd gathered around Dr. Bloch's office. It was too far to make out exactly what they were doing, but a crowd was never a good thing, even before crowds were sometimes cannibal corpses.

Stew explained it: "Jim was in town trading for some bread from the Fords. A mob was gathering around the church, and Rippey was stirring them up with talk about Judy Bloch."

Jim Sorensen broke in. "He was saying she was keeping geeks."

Novak thought of her request the previous day. She wanted test subjects. Probably wanted *more* test subjects.

Pulaski said: "So, we going down there or what?"

He couldn't imagine Pulaski gave a shit, but he probably liked the idea of a possible fight. As soon as the thought crossed his mind, his stomach twisted in a knot. He tried not to show it. No nerves. Not now.

"Yeah. Boys, come on. Everyone else stay put."

Sorensen looked disappointed, like the kid on the bench that thinks he's going to get playing time only to be thwarted by the coach.

As they jogged down the Hill, Stew fell in step next to Novak. "What's the plan?"

"No plan."

"Oh, good," Stew grumbled.

The knot tightened.

They were in open ground. Rippey was front and center, Ford and some of his other men close by. He didn't see Finger or Gloria Wu, but there were other civilians. They didn't look like civilians any more. Judy Bloch stood in her doorway, one hand on the jamb, her other hand protectively over her belly. She was the only unarmed person.

The shouting reached him. Not words, but ragged vowels hurled like tomahawks. Dr. Bloch wasn't backing down and Rippey wasn't going away. This was going to get a hell of a lot worse before it got any better.

The knot wrung blood from his gut. He winced, stumbled, but kept going.

"You okay, Boss?" Pulaski.

"I'm fine. You worry about them."

Words resolved themselves. "Keeping the abominations within town borders!"

"That's a fucking lie!"

"Then let us see what you're hiding! The innocent man fears nothing!"

The crowd howled back its animal approval.

Novak started a head count. They were equal when it came to hardcore soldiers, but the civilians outnumbered them five to one, and anyone could cave in a skull.

It was a delicate situation. Violence could cause the whole thing to go to shit, and he'd be damned if he was going to let them at the Doc. Then again, he didn't do diplomatic.

He shoved the civilians aside. He didn't look to see if Dr. Bloch was relieved or not, he kept his attention focused on the good Reverend, forcing him to deal with Novak. The crowd had gotten quiet as Novak drew more eyes. Rippey opened his mouth for another sentence, but Novak pulled him, too. A shadow crossed his face, then he fixed Novak with a phony grin.

"Mr. Novak has come here in solidarity..."

"Shut the fuck up," Novak said.

Rippey blinked. Ford surged forward. Novak braced. Rippey put a hand on Ford's chest, no force, but Ford came to a dead stop. "Mr. Novak sometimes chooses to express himself with a lack of decorum."

"You want to explain yourself?"

Rippey said, low and even: "Were we on the Hill, I would be explaining myself. But we're in Town, aren't we? Down here, it's you that explains yourself to me."

"Bullshit. You're threatening the Doc. She's the only one we have. Doesn't matter if we're here, there, or in the fucking Athena.

Dr. Bloch's welfare is everybody's business. Not to mention the fact that you're waving weapons at a pregnant woman, which pretty much makes you lower than that shit that accumulates under my foreskin."

Pulaski said: "Smegma."

"Thanks, Pulaski."

At that moment, he wished Rippey was a white man, if only to watch the bastard change colors. As it was, his face puffed up and he grew some new veins on the side of his head. Novak didn't want to turn away to take the pulse of the mob, but he felt a little deflation. Maybe they hadn't noticed the belly. Maybe they just thought she was a heavy beer drinker.

Rippey's voice, drained of emotion: "This pregnant woman has a cellar full of the undead."

Bloch said: "He's lying, goddammit!"

Rippey brought a kid out from the crowd, a little boy who looked about nine. Novak hadn't seen him before, but he had an Okie look about him. Probably had roots in Kern County before the end. "Billy Krebs, under solemn oath on the Holy Bible, said he saw you performing foul experiments on the horrors in your basement."

Dr. Bloch turned to Billy. She was pleading, using whatever motherly aura the kid in her belly had granted. "Billy, come on. Remember when you fell in the drainage ditch? Who fixed you up? Who took care of you when you had the flu last fall?"

The little boy turned back to Rippey who smiled and said, "You care for his body, but I care for his immortal soul. You have not the authority to turn him from the truth. Now, stand aside or we will move you."

Novak said: "Touch her and I split your fucking skull."

That was the exact wrong thing to say. Rippey didn't even have to say a word or lift a finger. The mob swallowed Novak like a creature, cutting him off from their leader. He had civilians in front of him, but two soldiers were making their way through the crowd, machetes out. The knot sent fingers into Novak's guts. He felt them turning over. He nearly emptied his bowels. He clenched, sending fire up through his guts to burn the knot.

He must have shown the pain on his face, because Rippey's smile seemed to turn genuine. "No threats here, Mr. Novak." Rippey gestured to Dr. Bloch.

Ford and Louis Chu, one of Rippey's men, moved forward. To Ford's credit, he hesitated a bit. Chu grabbed Dr. Bloch's right arm, Ford her left. She screamed in rage, but both men were too big, too strong. They pulled her aside, Chu roughly, Ford merely forcefully. The mob surged inside, Rippey the cruel head.

Novak tried not to limp, but he was stiff, trying to hold his shit in. It pulsed and surged in his belly, trying to strangle him from the inside. He got in front of Ford.

"Let her go."

Ford couldn't look into Novak's eyes, but he did let her go. Chu didn't. He glared at Ford. "The Reverend wants us to hold her."

Ford said: "Let her go, Louis."

"But—"

"She's not running."

Chu threw her forward.

Novak was too stiff to catch her, but Stew quickly stepped forward.

Pulaski sidled up to Chu. "You like that? Fucking with a pregnant woman?"

"Fuck off, faggot."

Pulaski jerked a thumb at Stew. "He's the faggot. I'm just the guy that's going to cut you cock to top if you lay hands on her again."

Chu looked like he was about to come back with something, but he caught Pulaski's eye. Some people, when the blood is up, get a gleam in there. It's a promise to come back harder and crueler to the other man. Not Pulaski. He looked like he was suggesting that the two of them go get a drink, maybe watch the game or something. Because of that, Chu was scared to the bone.

Inside, crashing sounds. Rippey's men tore through Dr. Bloch's offices. Even if they found nothing, the place would be completely trashed. Whatever drugs she had would be gone or crushed to powder underfoot. Her equipment would be smashed. *The fucking idiots!*

She lunged for her door, but Novak caught her by the arm. He still couldn't control the strength in his numbed left hand and as he gripped, she let out a startled cry of pain. He forced himself to loosen the grasp but held on, saying only: "No." The pain racked through his belly. He tried not to let it show.

She whirled around. "I can't let them..."

"You're going to have to."

The frustration crumbled across her face. She looked from Novak, to Chu and Ford, to the sounds of the mob breaking things apart. She turned back: "Whatever they find, you have to understand why."

"What the fuck are you talking about?"

"It doesn't have to be what it is." She had a crazed expression now, nearly begging him, but he couldn't tell what she was begging him for. She was rambling, making him worried she was going to charge in there.

Inside: an animalistic roar. The mob was screaming now, becoming something horrible, primal, and getting closer. Novak expected Rippey marching at the head, holding some kind of token. Novak was wrong. The first thing he saw was a shambling shape, nude, gray skinned, and covered in bite marks.

A geek.

He put Dr. Bloch behind him and drew his hatchet and hammer.

Chu pulled his machete on Novak, but Ford saw the geek and stood shoulder-to-shoulder with Novak.

Pulaski, Stew, and Robellada formed up next to them, brandishing their weapons.

The bottom nearly fell out of Novak's bowels. It felt like a weight dropped, and as he clenched, it twisted his guts into burning loops.

Another geek's silhouette, then a third, appeared behind the first. One female, one male. Their backs were to the door, as though they were trying to get back inside. Something kept shoving them until it spun the female around. It saw the group outside and shambled into the light, its mouth wide open.

No, not open. Where the female's mouth should have been was a dry hole, ragged edges flapping with every step. Gray muscles worked beyond it, but without anything to anchor, it was impotent wobbling. It still had the upper jaw, but the lower jaw had been entirely removed. It lunged at the closest man—Novak—and he dropped it with a single swing of his sledge.

It fell, its bloodless skull cracked and Ford buried his machete into it, finishing it off.

Dr. Bloch screamed: "No!"

"*No?*" Stew and Novak let out the same baffled query at the same time. That nearly made him laugh, but the other two geeks were shambling out now. Both had the same mutilation.

Rippey's men were next, prodding the geeks along with poles, followed by Rippey himself, smiling in triumph. He locked eyes with Novak.

"See? You see now? She was keeping the undead inside the Barricade!"

Dr. Bloch wasn't quiet. "I removed their jaws. They're harmless!"

Even Novak saw the flaw in that argument, and it took less than a second for Rippey to voice it. "One abomination attracts another! It is not harmless until it is destroyed!"

One lunged at Pulaski. In one motion, he drew the sword and chopped the thing's head in half. Chu chopped the other into pieces before splitting the skull.

The Doc's voice was full of swallowed tears. "But we don't know why they attract each other. Find why, maybe the whole thing comes unraveled. Maybe we figure out what they are!"

"While you bring them to our doorstep!"

"I was using these for testing, I was—"

"Endangering everyone! I wish there was another way, but there is but one punishment that fits the crime."

Novak moved a little closer to Dr. Bloch in case Rippey or one of his men made a lunge.

"But I refuse to murder an innocent because of its mother's evil." Here he gestured at her belly. "'Vengeance is mine, sayeth the Lord.' Your fate is in His merciful hands. Exile."

Chu took a step toward Dr. Bloch.

Pulaski stepped forward, the sword down and said quietly: "Remember what we talked about."

Chu took a step back.

Rippey said: "Tell your men to stand down, Novak. Don't bring the same wrath upon your head."

Novak tried to ignore his roiling guts, which were trying to bring him to his knees. "Yeah. You can kick her out of Town, sure. But something about throwing our only doctor to the geeks strikes me as completely fucking stupid."

"She was harboring the undead!"

"Point of fact, so's Calomiris. Got a geek they're using for entertainment up at the Athena."

Rippey sneered: "I've heard the rumors. Nothing that man condones could shock me, but the fact remains that I don't control the Athena. Town is mine, and I will not tolerate these abominations!"

"Yeah, that's your business. Anyway, you kick her out of Town, she's got a home on the Hill if she wants it." He turned to her. "You want it?"

Dr. Bloch nodded, but her eyes were downcast, her teeth damn near tearing through her bottom lip.

"You can't do this, Novak," Rippey grated, chagrin in his tone.

"Watch me. Or better yet, try to stop me."

Rippey was silent.

Novak could see the mental wheels whirring as the mob looked to its leader. He guessed that Rippey was counting the theoretical dead. He saw Chu's head separated. He probably saw Ford take a bad hit that, without a doctor, could turn septic. He saw the butcher's bill and realized he didn't want to pay it.

Instead, Rippey said: "If she brings more into Devon, I'll come for her. Even if she's on the Hill, I'll come for her and you will be powerless to stop me."

Novak just grinned at him. "Rev, you ain't lying."

Rippey blanched. Novak and his guys escorted Dr. Bloch away from her office, toward the Hill. The mob was still surrounding the office, and probably would until Bloch was into the trees and out of sight. Dr. Bloch looked back at it, clearly longing for what she had accumulated, but everyone knew it was a lost cause.

When they were out of earshot, she said: "Thanks." Although said to Novak, it was directed at all four of them.

Stew said: "We weren't going to let them hurt you."

"Still."

They were quiet until they reached the crest of the Hill. Past the Barricade, more shapes milled through the trees.

She said, "He was right."

"Maybe," Novak said. "Some of those might be yours. Most of them are probably following those nomads."

"Rippey should have sent out his fucking guys to clean up."

"So should I." Novak turned to Stew. "Take the guys. See if you can thin out the geeks a little."

Stew nodded. "What about you?"

"I need to get the Doc settled."

Stew hesitated for a minute. Novak could tell Stew wanted to ask something else, but he just nodded. "Sure thing."

They broke off, and Novak continued to lead her up the Hill.

A cold breeze came off the ocean, stirring the clouds. They would break soon, and when they did, it wasn't going to be the light rain of the previous night. It was going to be a torrent.

The cold seemed to shrink Novak's bowels, making holding on even harder. They burned and twisted. He felt the sweat break out again on his brow, which only made the air chillier. He wanted to let go, but he couldn't. Not in front of Dr. Bloch.

"Glen, you look like shit. Are you okay?"

He nodded. He wasn't sure he could talk. His house was up ahead, and he forced himself to double his pace. The breeze turned his sweat to ice, and the shivers returned. He thought he could feel himself losing control, dropping shit into his pants.

"Hold up," she said.

He ignored her. He gestured at the unlocked door and mumbled something before running around the side of the house to the backyard. In the opposite corner of the makeshift grill, he'd had a latrine dug, shielded on two sides by a fence, with a tarp forming both wall and roof.

He barely made it inside, pants down, squatting over the hole as he shat his guts out into the earth. He didn't want to look down; he was sure he'd see a hole filled with ropes of intestines.

"Glen?" Her voice came from the side of the house. She had followed, probably with ginger steps and neck craned.

"I'm okay! I'm using the... uh... bathroom." There was more straining to evacuate, but he would be damned if she was going to hear the cloth-ripping sounds of that. He tried to close up what had been opened, and a lance burned through his guts. He emptied more, knowing and hating that she heard the wet slapping sound.

"Okay. I'll wait in the living room."

He just nodded, even though there was no way she could see that. He just crouched over that hole, letting the burning shame replace the pain in his guts. He didn't know how long he stayed in that position, but he waited until there was nothing else coming out. He wiped his ass with newspaper hanging from a nail and limped to his house.

Dr. Bloch sat on his sofa, holding her belly and staring into space. When he entered, she looked up and smiled. "Doing better?"

"A little."

"I wanted to thank you again."

He waved that off and collapsed back into his easy chair. His ass stung but he ignored it. He had a date with Walter Calomiris in a little while, but he could rest. At least for a short while.

She started up again: "So, where am I staying?"

"Here."

"You have enough space?"

"You take the bedroom."

"And you'll take the couch?"

"Sure." He looked at the inch of Jack left in the bottle on the end table. He thought of when he drank it last. He thought of the Harmons in turn, and how they'd tried to fight for one another, no matter how futile. "Does it bother you?"

"What?"

"That the father wasn't there today."

She was considering. Finally: "Who says he wasn't?"

"Who is he?"

She shrugged. "Doesn't matter."

"Yeah, it does."

"Why?"

Novak snorted. "That's not a question you should be asking."

"It could have been you."

He watched her out of the corner of his eye. Her mischievous eyes, her freckles over nose and cheeks: she seemed familiar. It would have been an easy thing to settle next to her and let her nestle in the crook of his arm. "No. It couldn't have."

She let that go. "Why the concern all of a sudden? You never asked before."

He didn't answer.

She said: "The father doesn't matter. I needed to conceive and I found someone who matched what I needed and was willing."

"Needed?"

"We're nearly extinct as a species. I felt like it was important that I reproduce, and that I do it with someone who had the right kinds of genes to survive in this world."

"You think that's me."

"You fit the bill, but you never seemed interested."

He didn't bother to lie to her. Instead: "Seems kind of a cold reason to have a kid."

"Just because one reason is cold doesn't mean there isn't another one that's warm, if that makes sense."

"Aren't you worried... bringing a kid into this world?"

"Of course. The alternative is that we die out, and I sure as shit won't be party to that."

"Don't see how one kid's gonna change that."

"As long as everyone does something, there's hope."

"You sound like Robellada when he drinks."

"Then you should start feeding him that Jack Daniels and listen up."

"Only he wouldn't do anything as stupid as bringing geeks into Devon."

"I told you why I did that. I even asked you to help me."

"I didn't think you were serious. Christ, you're supposed to be smart."

"In point of fact, I am. I'm probably the smartest fucking person in Devon, if not all of California. I took their jaws out. They weren't going to bite anyone. I kept them in my basement. If they're attracted by sight, they weren't going to be seen. The windows were shut, which cut off smell and sound. Unless you're implying they're psychic, they weren't a danger to anyone."

"You kept them around to research the cause? I don't want to piss in your Cheerios, but when the geeks first started showing up, scientists all over the world were studying them. Billions of dollars, any kind of equipment you could want. Didn't do any good. Those scientists ended up... you know... Turned."

"They didn't have time. The government collapsed too quickly. You remember that first year, after they really started swarming? There was mass panic. What they didn't have was time, something we have now."

He grinned at that. "I'd say time is in short supply."

"We have as much as we can take."

He thought about the geeks. So little was known about them, other than the bare facts. She was right. Something had been nagging him, and Judy Bloch was the one person who might discover the answer.

"Stew once told me that geeks don't use their whole brains. They only need the Medusa something."

"Medulla?"

"The reptile brain."

She nodded. "That's right. It's why you need a blow to the base of the brain to kill them. Why do you ask?"

"Do they use the rest of the brain?"

She shrugged. "I don't really know. And unless I can get one into a CAT scan, I probably never will."

The thought had him. He couldn't shake it, and he hoped that if he shared it, it might lose some of its power. "You think that when someone turns, the brain still works? That the person is *still inside* the geek? Like a passenger? Seeing and hearing and feeling everything but helpless to stop it?"

She shuddered. "I hadn't thought about it. But... I hope not... for their sake."

That was all they had. "Me, too."

They were quiet for some time.

She took her sweater off and put it next to her, revealing the old t-shirt. Novak winced when he saw the beginnings of bruises on her upper arms where he'd grabbed her. He could clearly see the imprint of his right hand on her arm. She inspected that. Then the other. He saw her take a deep breath.

She said: "When were you bitten?"

The silence that followed nearly strangled him. Eventually: "What?"

She showed her right arm, and counted his fingers on the bruises, then turned to the left. "One, two, three... nothing. When I watched you with the nomads, I saw the signs, the fever, the pallor, but I couldn't be sure. Now you've got more symptoms, and there's this."

He stood up. "You think I was bitten?"

"Glen, it's—"

"You gonna take this to someone? I save you from Rippey and this is what you're gonna do to me?"

"I won't—"

"Bullshit! Then why the fuck did you bring it up?"

"I've never gotten a chance to study someone partway through the change. A look at your blood could tell me volumes. Answer questions I didn't even know to ask."

"So I'm a fucking lab rat to you? And what if I say no? That's when you run to Rippey or Calomiris, or shit, a couple houses down to Pulaski and have them cut me up? You can take my body and pick at it like a fucking vulture?"

"Glen, wait, *no*—"

"Maybe Rippey was right. Maybe we should have thrown you and the bastard out into the woods. See how many fucking questions you can answer after you're the one who's been bitten. How does that sound? Maybe we should test it now?"

He took a step toward her, hands out, ready to sling her over his shoulder.

She quailed.

He sucked in air and imagined grabbing her. He thought about her struggles. He thought about her weight when pushing her over the Barricade. He thought about her screams.

He ran from his house.

The Barricade was slate in the growing darkness. From that distance, it was impossible to tell the living from the dead.

Both where mere spots at the edge of vision.

- 12 -

THE CLOUDS WERE CLOSE. NOVAK felt like he could reach up and touch them from the top of the Hill. The sky would open up soon, the same as the road outside. He shivered.

He felt his head. Burning up. His stomach was a lump of coal that could burst back into flame at any time. He touched his chest, and it felt like another person. He hit himself. Again. The numbness had spread from his left arm and now took up the bulk of his torso. He flexed the alien left hand. It still listened.

It would be over soon. All of it.

His guys were walking away from the Barricade. They had been refused exit. Rippey had closed Devon off entirely. His guys probably could have forced their way through, but they were already down two, and any confrontation with Rippey's people would be dangerous. What remained to be seen was why Rippey closed it off, especially from something as useful as culling the building swarm.

Beyond the Barricade, black shapes shambled across the blocked road. The trees in the wash beyond swayed, and only some of the movement wind-caused. As his gaze crawled over the trees, he seemed to fall into them. Beyond, eye-shine of a hundred geeks, swaying like plants, waiting for the moment to lunge. In those geeks, doubtless faces he recognized from his past, a roll call of his life before the world ended. They were waiting. He looked forward to disappointing them with a bullet.

The sun wasn't gone, but it was twilight before noon. Candles flickered in windows. On days like this, when the despair got thicker than snot, people stayed indoors and tried to amuse themselves in ways impossible before the end of the world.

Ahead, Novak had two choices: Town and Rippey or the Athena and Calomiris.

Rippey first, then Calomiris.

Might as well visit the guy right after humiliating him in front of his people. It's not like he had to cross that bridge for much longer. He could burn it and dance across one last time as it came tumbling down.

He passed Dr. Bloch's place. The three test geeks were gray depressions in the green grass. No one had scavenged them yet. Maybe Rippey had forbidden it. They would rot soon, as whatever reanimated them lost its hold and started to let nature take over. An earwig crawled across the crack he'd put in one. It wiggled the pincer at the end of its abdomen and disappeared into the broken skull.

Dr. Bloch's door stood open, hinting at the chaos in the dark. He passed it by, reaching the intersection of Cliffside and Hotel.

Town was silent, rather than quiet. Quiet implied incidental sounds. Birds, maybe. Kids. Distant voices, soft and even. Silence was artificial. Silence implied waiting. Silence implied a promise of violence. Silence was a threat.

The Athena loomed large on the skyline, the fire still burning on the roof of the south wing. He knew if he got closer, it would be the same feeling as Town. Both Walter Calomiris and Isador Rippey could sense the other's mood. As the smallest leg of the tripod, maybe they sensed Novak's mood as well. Maybe his downward spiral was pushing them toward their goal. Kill the other and let nature, or un-nature, take its course, and he could be the last man standing.

Right now, that last man standing would be the right Reverend.

Novak was never a religious man. He had a vague idea of God: He helped his teams win, according to them. He was kind and merciful, and when He wasn't He was mysterious. But Novak didn't bother Him and He didn't bother Novak. The end of the world changed his opinion substantially. It made him believe that not only was He real, but He was a royal cocksucker. Any desire he might have had to worship vanished.

It seemed to have the opposite effect on Isador Rippey. Before the end, Novak imagined Rippey as a holy roller, but had nothing to back that up. Novak wasn't sure who knew Rippey before, either. He arrived in Devon with Janelle and Jacen Ford, Louis Chu, and a couple others. Novak could ask them, but none of them liked him very much and the feeling was mostly mutual. For all Novak knew, Rippey was an atheist before the end, and only converted when the dead rose.

When the dead first started moving, most faiths declared it the sign of the Apocalypse. Novak remembered Susan telling him about some wall in the Middle East that was designed to stand against that very thing in the final days. In the U.S., most of the religious were some kind of Christian, and that meant the Rapture. The problem was that no one actually vanished. There were the urban legends, but most of those centered on someone disappearing without a trace. This was not exactly uncommon when there were cannibal undead wandering the wild places.

Rippey preached something else: this was not the Rapture, but another Flood, which would wipe away the wicked. They were waiting for some kind of geek-killing Noah to get wet and save them.

Novak walked to First Baptist, and as he stood in front of the doors, a raindrop hit him in the eye.

He knocked.

More raindrops.

The door opened. Jacen Ford. He didn't even bother to hide his shock.

Novak said: "I'm here to see the Reverend."

Ford was too surprised to give Novak static. "I'll see if he's seeing anyone."

The door shut. Another couple drops bounced off his head. He imagined that they turned to steam as soon as they hit. The door opened up, and this time wide.

Inside, the church. Wooden pews on either side of a central aisle. Burning candles turned the white interior gold. Rippey's men were scattered around the room along with a few civilians. A couple of the white-clad Rippettes moved from man to man with moist whispers. They were all armed. Micah Rosenberg had a black eye and a scratched cheek from when Novak stomped him. Jacob Rosenberg, the elder, stood up to lunge, but Pisspants put a restraining hand on Jacob's chest.

Ford shut the door behind them. "Follow me."

Every eye was on Novak, except Janelle Ford's. She stared down at her pew. Rippey's men held their weapons in their laps, waiting for the order to attack. He wondered how many he could take down if it came to that. He hoped that, if it did, they'd go after the head.

Jack Finger shot him a conspiratorial grin. Gloria Wu watched him with suspicion. Neither said a word.

Ford led him out of the nave to a door to the right of the altar. The hall was much darker and closer, but the openly hostile soldiers were behind them. Ford knocked at the door at the end of the hall. After a moment, the little blond Rippette, ten years old if she was a day, came out of the room, smoothing her dress. She didn't look at either man. Novak thought he caught a grimace on Ford's face, but it vanished too quickly to know for certain. Novak nodded to his escort and went through the door.

This was Rippey's office. He'd never seen it before, but other than the candlelight, it could have been something before the end. Rippey had a desk, nearly bare, but complete with blotter and Bible. There were pictures, but in the dim light, the frames only reflected candle-flame. They looked like windows to Hell.

Rippey was hanging a leather strap in the corner. His sleeves were rolled up and sweat beaded his brow.

The Reverend turned, smiling. "Glen, a pleasant surprise, especially after the unpleasantness earlier."

Novak took Rippey's hand, hiding the burning skin behind the leather glove. "Yeah, I was thinking the same thing."

"Have the clouds burst?"

A gentle tapping was at the edge of hearing. "A little."

"I fear we may be in for quite the deluge." Rippey rolled his sleeves down and buttoned them at the wrist.

"Don't sound so excited."

"Oh, I'm not." He tapped the Bible. "The literal Flood was a long time ago. We live in a more metaphorical time."

"What a relief. I was beginning to worry, but now that I know the geeks are metaphors, that makes it all better."

Rippey's smile froze. Very tight: "Do you know what the undead actually are, Mr. Novak?"

"Walking corpses with an appetite."

Rippey shook his head. "That attitude is simplistic, indicative of a dearth of true spirituality or a misunderstanding of the Lord's mysterious plan. The same problem that caused the faithful to mistake the Flood for the Rapture. There were those that believed the undead were merely bodies whose souls had ascended to Heaven. To be undead was to be one of the Righteous. Those that believed thus died out in short order. As did those who believed Satan corrupted the Rapture. The only belief that lasted was the one of the Flood."

"I don't really give a fuck, Rev."

"That would explain your absence Sundays."

"Sure does."

"But you're familiar enough with what I teach to make glib reference to it."

"As you know, one of my guys is seeing one of your people. He's been to church a couple of times."

"Enrique Robellada." He rolled his *R*s like a pro. "He seems like a good boy."

"He is."

"You see, we have some common ground after all."

"I never said we didn't. In point of fact, our common ground is everything on the breathing side of the Barricade."

"Oftentimes, the intrigues of the present obfuscate our commonality of purpose."

"Which is why I was wondering why the gate is closed."

His voice, smooth as polished shit: "The gate is always closed."

"You know what I mean. I sent my guys out there to clear out the geeks that have been gathering since the nomads showed up, and your men denied them exit."

"You seem to have answered your question already."

"What, you're worried that the nomads are going to try some shit and that outweighs a swarm?"

He laughed, but Novak didn't know what he'd said that was funny. "No, I don't think they're going to enact a putsch. But you're right, there is a swarm gathering, and I believe we're already past the tipping point."

"Why the hell didn't you send your men out immediately then?"

"We were not aware of the threat until it was past the point of no return."

And that was bullshit; Novak knew it for a fact, but calling Rippey a liar in his office wasn't going to trigger some kind of crisis of conscience. If he was willing to let a swarm build, there was a whole hell of a lot more he was willing to do, and probably already had done.

He had his hands folded over that neat salt-and-pepper beard, like he was hoping Novak wouldn't read his lips.

Novak said: "So you're worried that Calomiris will try something now that he's got those nomads. Pretty convinced they'd be willing to die for the guy, then."

"Mr. Novak, you should stop trying to think so hard."

"You're worried about Calomiris."

"Considering relative numbers, I–"

"Not what I mean. It's fine, I say something like that, and you have to show me that you're strong. I understand. It's how the game is played and God knows I played it that way for enough years. Here's the thing: I don't really care. I want to have a real discussion with you, and if you're not having it, I can go up to the Athena and try there."

He offered Novak a smile. "Yes, I am worried about Walter Calomiris."

"And he's worried about you."

"If he's half as smart as he seems to think he is."

"If one of you were gone, the other would own Devon. All of it."

"There's always you, Mr. Novak."

If only he knew. "I have the Hill. We barely have enough people to register on the radar and, after today, we have four scavs in fighting shape. That's about a fourth of what you have and much less than our friend in the hotel. If one of you took the other's land, is there really any way I could stop you from taking mine?"

Rippey didn't even try to pretend he hadn't thought about it. Novak appreciated the honesty. He couldn't help but wonder if Rippey smelled the bite. "It all depends if the victorious side remained relatively intact. Your interests are best served with

Walter and me at each other's throats. As we grow weaker, you get stronger."

"Not stronger. Just not any weaker. You know as well as I do that I never had a prayer of getting those immigrants."

Rippey chuckled, probably remembering the beating Novak threw at the head guy.

Novak went on: "Exactly. Now, even if you lost half your guys doing it, you'd still have me two to one, and we both know that Jacen Ford is worth two or three guys."

"Why are you going through so much trouble to convince me you're helpless before me? Are you asking me to take the Hill? After today, the thought crossed my mind."

"I'll bet it did. No, I'm trying to say that if you took out Calomiris, there'd be no reason to take the Hill."

"I always got the impression you were loyal to Walter."

"I'm loyal to whoever keeps my people safe."

He thought about that. "If Walter were to find his way into the ground, there would be no reprisals?"

"None at all, so long as you leave the Hill the way it is and keep the Athena open to my people when they need it."

"If you would be so easy to take, why not just do that?"

"Because easy ain't the same thing as safe."

"True."

"Look, I'll go you one better. It's just you and me here, right? Just you and me talking?"

Now they were off the beaten path. Novak could tell that Rippey suddenly wasn't sure where the conversation was going. He clasped his hands and flexed them unconsciously, eyes flicking to the strap he hung up earlier. "We are alone, yes."

"How about I give you an act of good faith. Something that says that the Hill is with you on this one."

"Such as?"

"One thing. No matter what happens, you don't try to throw Judy Bloch out. She's safe."

Something flashed in his eyes, but he gave a single, curt nod.

Novak went on: "How about I go ahead and kill Walter Calomiris for you?"

The laugh that followed was completely genuine. Novak thought others might call it warm, but he felt the chills crawling up his spine. He tensed. He couldn't handle a shiver attack, not now. He didn't bother to pray for it; a God that would have listened wouldn't have put him in the position to ask and, besides, God was only going to listen to one of the people in that room and it wasn't Novak.

Rippey said: "What an unexpected pleasure."

"Yeah, it's an early Christmas in Devon. What do you say?"

"I wish you had come to me a week ago."

"What?"

"Come with me, Mr. Novak. I want to show you something."

Rippey stood up from behind his desk and crossed to the door. He didn't look to see if Novak was following. Rippey just assumed it, and Novak was there, huddled in his jacket and shambling along behind. He entered the nave. As soon as he did, all eyes were on him. The expressions were wide-eyed, not surprised but a little scared. Lips were pressed together. Hands were tensed.

"Brothers, it's time."

Then there were smiles. No one relaxed, but tension turned to excitement. A lot of the men exchanged looks and nods, wordless whispers that said everything to them and nothing to Novak.

Rippey went on: "Mr. Novak is going to come with us to observe. He has extended an olive branch and I have accepted it."

Confusion, maybe, but barely anything could cut into the sudden good mood of the room.

Rippey led the way to the entrance where Ford handed him an umbrella and opened the door.

It was almost noon outside, but the air was thick and cold. Visibility wasn't bad, but it was through a haze of rain that cut everything into thin slashes of dulled color.

Rippey stepped outward, raising the umbrella like he was going for a stroll. It was bullshit, the kind of thing Novak had come to expect from the man. As the Reverend made his way onto the gravel path that led to the side road, he said: "There's plenty of room. No need to get wet."

"I'm fine out here."

He wasn't. The rain was hot on his skin, cutting rivulets of fire down his cheeks. He let it burn. "Where exactly are we going?"

Rippey nodded to the Athena, where the fire still burned on the roof. "The heart of our little community."

Novak wondered what Rippey would call the church. He didn't want to ask, mostly because he was certain Rippey had an answer.

Rippey's men fanned out. Their weapons weren't drawn, but their hands were nearby. They had a cordon around Novak and the Reverend, with Ford staying close to his boss. Jacob Rosenberg was closest to Novak, still glaring. He was waiting for the order to attack. He would probably get the chance.

He wondered what Rippey was planning to reveal. He had, after all, seen the Athena. Probably been inside more times than Rippey. Something in the Athena? Something behind it? Near it?

He thought about his last trip, with Finger and Gloria Wu. They were quiet this time, but both looked like they'd swallowed at least one canary. He caught Gloria shooting him glances the whole way, like she wanted to tell him something but didn't want to spoil the surprise.

Novak started to plan his run.

There were two guys between him and the side of the road. Rosenberg was watching him closely, so going through him was a foregone conclusion. He'd be ready, so taking him out first made the most sense. Beyond him, one more. From there, the steep slope into farmland and Town. That was Rippey's neighborhood, but Novak could take cover in the houses and circle around to the Hill. He'd have to cross Hotel Street eventually, but that could wait. More would pursue. He'd have to drop them one by one until the cost of catching him was just too high.

His best bet was going over the side at its steepest. That meant waiting until they were almost all the way up the street. He could tackle Rosenberg and use him as a sled. That would break some of the fall. He didn't know why Rippey would want to execute him in front of the Athena, but it was looking like that was the plan. Maybe the joke was on him. Maybe Rippey had planned Novak's murder with Calomiris. They wanted to get rid of the asshole on the Hill who kept them from owning the whole town.

Rippey stopped just shy of where Novak wanted to make his break. The Reverend stared up at the Athena.

Novak took as subtle a look around as he could. Everyone was focused squarely on the hotel. Only Rosenberg returned his look, and he had to yank his eyes off the Athena to do it. No one was going for his weapon.

The Athena had nothing to say.

Rippey made a motion with his hand. Finger scampered over to him, and they put their heads together under the shadow of the umbrella. Novak didn't catch anything of what they said over the drumming of rain. Then Finger jogged over to the hotel and disappeared inside.

A moment later, he came running out. He went right to Rippey and they had another conversation that Novak missed.

Finally, Rippey turned around. His eyes looked haunted through the sheets of water coming down in front of him. "Mr. Novak, may I speak with you a moment?"

Novak nodded, beckoning Rippey over to the shade. He made Novak walk, and he was going to make Rippey do the same. He dearly wanted to get away from the tapping razorblades on his skull. His clothes were glued to his skin, and the shivers were starting up yet again. At least his bowels were empty.

When they were under the roof, Rippey said: "Were you serious?"

"Serious about what?" He knew what. He wanted to make Rippey say it.

"Were you serious about killing Walter Calomiris?"

"Why the change of heart?"

He didn't have the energy to flash that politician's smile. He was trembling in the cold, drawing short, nervous breaths. "I'll pay."

"You were very eager to show me something, Reverend. I kind of want to see it."

"There's nothing!" he shouted. He glanced nervously at his men. They milled and murmured in the rain. He turned back to Novak. Quieter: "There's nothing to show you. Will you kill Walter Calomiris?"

"Hold on. I want a witness." He didn't trust anyone in Rippey's camp, but there were degrees. "Ford! Come here, please."

Frowning, Ford walked over from the rain. He gave Rippey a questioning look.

Rippey was annoyed, but he nodded.

Novak said: "Okay, Reverend. Say what you said again."

"Mr. Novak, I want you to kill Walter Calomiris. If you do it, I'll pay you."

Ford's head whipped around to stare at Rippey.

Novak said: "Pay me what?"

"The Athena."

That stunned him. "I thought you'd want that."

"The Athena is yours. Your people will have their shelter from the swarm. But Devon is mine. All of it. You report to me."

Terms were pretty useless to Novak, but he thought he could give the Athena to Stew.

"Deal."

Rippey took Novak's hand but not his eyes.

- 13 -

NOVAK WAS DRIPPING WET WHEN he walked into the lobby. Roth waited there, holding his baseball bat in one hand and staring past Novak, past the silent hulks of the nomads' vehicles, out into the rain. He only focused on Novak for a second, ascertaining that he wasn't a Townie, then went back to watching the rain. Novak glanced through the sliding metal gate that now made up the front.

The rain had turned Rippey and his men into ghosts. If not for the Reverend's umbrella, they would have looked like a group of geeks waiting for the sight of living flesh to bring them to life.

Footsteps pounded closer from the east wing, muffled only slightly against the rug. It was a detail of Calomiris men. No Marcos, but Sakimoto was amongst them, shelling out orders in his soft and clipped tone.

The revenants in the rain turned, one by one, following their leader down Hotel Street. Sakimoto would be smart enough to know that Novak's presence wasn't a good thing, especially if he arrived with Rippey's men. Novak had to move before Roth thought to inform his boss.

Calomiris would be on the roof of the south wing, probably tending that fire that burned in the rain. Novak was going to murder this man in cold blood. He'd killed humans before. They were always bitten, and then he thought of it as an act of mercy. This time it would be someone living and breathing, someone with many more years left. Someone who had killed him. He had to keep that in mind. Whatever life Calomiris had was spent when he put that head in Novak's locker.

The bar was packed, standing room only. The rain, the geeks, the foreboding had pushed everyone inside. They didn't know about Rippey's men outside consciously, but they knew it somewhere deeper in their guts. Something was coming and they didn't know what.

Tanner and Pink Snapper were onstage, the chain leash pulled tight. The geek had its legs spread, and was alternately trying to bite Tanner and something that was behind the heads of the crowd.

After a moment, the crowd applauded, and Stacy stood up in front of the geek, turned, wiped her mouth, and bowed.

Novak's stomach turned over.

Stacy faced straight ahead. She seemed to stare right in Novak's eyes. He tried to tell himself that was impossible, with the lights shining in her face. He dropped his gaze. Her pelvic bones rippled under her skin. He turned away from the door and found the staircase.

The stairs were dark. There was maybe a candle every two floors, already guttering. The air was chill and heavy. He shivered. Goddamn staircase hit him every time. He could take comfort in the fact that it would be his last time going up or down it.

A faint hit him across the head. He caught the wall. Something moved under his hand. He turned. The wall was a mass of earwigs, crawling across a huge crack that spiderwebbed the wall. He took two steps up the stairs. The fissures radiated from a central point where the wall seemed to be peeled away. Something was in there. Still, dry, but somehow still vital. The walls had finally come away to reveal the Athena's innards. It—she—was alive. They had known it all along. She had protected them and they had bled in her. Something had taken root and there she was.

And now she was food for the bugs.

The shivers cascaded over Novak. He took each step painfully. He had made it to the second floor when he heard the ground floor door open.

Sakimoto's voice: "Follow me. He can't have gotten far."

The shivers got worse. The air seemed to have turned to ice. Novak opened the second floor door as quietly as he could. He looked to the crack in the wall, but it had healed over. He went through the door into the hall beyond.

The pattern in the rug flowed downstream at a good clip, swirling into arabesque whirlpools. A shiver dropped him to his knees. He couldn't let it take him. Not this soon. He was close to the end. Let it cripple him later. He needed a little more time.

Sakimoto and his men were coming up the staircase fast.

Novak lurched down the hall to the first closed door and shouldered it open and shut it behind him. The room was empty, but it was clearly lived in. The bed was unmade, filthy. There was a paperback on the bedside table, creased and water-damaged. He ducked between the bed and closet and pulled his gun.

Sakimoto's footfalls got closer, the sounds eaten by the balding rug. He wondered how many men Sakimoto had with him. Seven rounds in the gun, seven more in the spare clip in his belt. That had to be enough. He might have to use all fourteen.

The cold swept over him. The bottom fell out and he collapsed into a shivering ball.

Sakimoto was outside, getting closer.

Novak couldn't move. His whole body was nothing more than a mass of shakes. He lay there, helpless, hearing the footfalls getting closer. His gun lay inches in front of his face, but there was no force on earth that could get him to reach out and pick it up.

Footfalls were right outside the door. He tried to remember if he heard opening doors. He couldn't. In his head, he heard it both ways. Sometimes he heard Sakimoto kicking each one in. Sometimes he only heard those dead footfalls coming closer.

He shut his eyes and tried to will his body into directed motion. Every joint was locked into its cycle of weakness.

The footfalls seemed to stop.

He wanted to scream in frustration.

His heartbeat pounded his eardrums. Deafening. It hammered in syncopation, getting softer and softer until...

Not his heart. The footsteps.

He flexed his hand, blinking, staring. He brought it in front of his face and did it again. He planted his hands on the floor and boosted himself into a standing position. The shakes were gone.

He crept to the door and put his ear against it.

Sakimoto was talking to his guys by the window at the end of the hall. The voices disappeared around the corner shortly afterwards.

He opened the door and peeked out. The hall was clear. He took a few steps into it. Paused.

Sakimoto was around the other side of the wing.

Novak lurched to the stairs as quickly as he could. It was a long several flights up. After the shaking fit, his legs felt like rubber. He wasn't going to be able to make it up the whole way in one try, and the one place he could be found easily was the stairwell. But he had to put some distance between him and Sakimoto's dogs.

He took the stairs gingerly. His left arm couldn't feel the railing, but it could haul him up when he wanted it to. The arm was stronger, or maybe he only believed it was. Maybe every time he used the thing he was tearing muscles, ripping tendons from the bone. The body was far more powerful than most people believe because to push it farther than it can go makes it fail. His was already failing, and maybe the bumpers had been removed. Best enjoy that.

He made it to the third floor.

His breath came easily, but his legs weren't cooperating. He hadn't been this bad since the Olympic tryouts when he was twenty. Because of his height, he wrestled at 163. Problem was, though he was short, he was solid muscle. He'd had to cut nearly fifteen pounds of water weight to make his class. This meant wrapping himself in garbage bags and jogging a couple miles. It meant chewing gum and spitting every five chews to get rid of the saliva. It mean sitting in a sauna for a couple hours. At the weigh-in, his legs were noodles and his hands were palsied. He'd barely made it.

The next day, his opponent threw him around like he was made of Styrofoam.

At least this time, there wouldn't be a next day. His legs went out around the fourth floor. That might be the worst place to lose them. The fourth floor was for Calomiris men, his twenty-odd hard cases. At least half of them should be elsewhere, and maybe half of those looking for Novak. He wasn't up to doing math, but as long as that number was greater than one, he was still outnumbered. At least they weren't looking for him on that floor. They wouldn't want him on it, but he'd be asked to leave rather than whatever Sakimoto had planned.

Novak opened that door and nearly collapsed right there in the hall. The hotel swam for a moment, but he blinked that away. The carpet on four hadn't yet been stomped into baldness. It was dirty, but the worst was tracked into the first few floors.

A few of the doors were open. Sounds reached from each room. Individually, they meant nothing but, in the hall, they wove together and Novak began to hear something he could understand. He heard names that he knew, the living and the dead. He heard threats. He heard dark things.

He lurched down that hall, looking for a place to wait Sakimoto out. Let him check the Athena and come to the conclusion that

Novak had gone. Better yet, give him a place to catch his breath and put some strength back in his legs.

Novak staggered past the first door. He saw: a boy, maybe ten years old and shirtless, his back to him. The boy stared out the window toward the Barricade, completely motionless. He watched the bones on the boy's back ripple like a pond, and moved on from there.

Now he heard voices. The muted clatter of plastic on cardboard. He heard a giggle, then a groan. He crept to the next door and peeked in. It was probably a Monopoly board, but it was hard to tell. Three guys, Calomiris hard cases that he barely recognized, were crowded around the board.

A man moved his pawn and shot the man across from him an expectant stare. There was a metallic whisper and the man held a Bowie knife into the light. He sliced three parallel cuts into his arm. The blood tapped the board. "That's three more," he said.

Novak moved on.

Metal sounds poked into him from the next room. He expected an arsenal being checked, but he was wrong. He saw a young man, nude, crouched over an old television, the thing's guts arrayed around him. He was reaching into the box itself, maybe trying to repair it, maybe just picking it apart. These clanks merged with the slaps from the bed. One set of feet, probably male, bare, and another in boots. From the position: fucking. The kid ignored them in favor of the TV.

Novak made it to the end of the hall. The grimy window was melting with rain. Beyond, the Barricade. No one was on the rampart; probably one of Rippey's guys was crouched miserably in the blockhouse, if anywhere at all. Past that, the road was dotted with black shapes, more than he could count. Farther, the plants swayed. It was a swarm all right, and it would hit as soon as it saw something to eat.

Not my problem. Not any more.

He made it around the back, where the rooms faced the Pacific. There was actual dust in that section, and not just in the corners. He picked a door at random and found the lock broken, opened and then shut it behind him.

The room had been altered since the end of the world. Someone had scavenged a whole library's worth of pornography, clipped it, and wallpapered the room, so that no single bit of wall showed. The women stared at Novak in blank amazement, displaying themselves submissively. Over and over, he felt he could have reached into the wall and found a never-ending garden of these nymphs. They would turn and with hungry mouths tear him apart.

He picked one of the women, a blonde whose hair was teased out to ridiculous proportions. He locked his dying eyes into her dead ones. He could not ignore those white teeth poking from her glittering lip. Absurdly, he thought of Pulaski; he had the same shade of lipstick. The thought made Novak laugh. If Pulaski didn't, this sweaty sex goddess would behead Novak. She could keep it on the wall of her... Novak couldn't figure where she was, but placing her in context was missing the point. That thought made him laugh again.

He collapsed into the corner between bed and closet. The door was off to his left, around a corner. He put his pistol in his lap and waited and trusted his security to the blonde with the big hair and dead eyes.

He shut his eyes and leaned back. Something pulsed in his left shoulder, but everything around it was completely dead. His heart thudded underneath a layer of flesh, distant and fast. He wanted to shrug his jacket off and let the sweat steam off of him. Instead, he mustered his strength.

Sleep pulls downward, but he drifted upward. He never lost consciousness, but he lost himself. He felt his mind merge with the Athena. He saw the game of cut Monopoly. He saw Sakimoto emerge onto the fifth floor. He saw little Stacy doing her listless show downstairs. He even saw Rippey and his people making the slow march down Hotel Street, ignoring the massing bodies beyond the Barricade.

Novak felt himself rising into the clouds, but they weren't soft and welcoming. They were cold and damp, like a seaside shack at the edge of a hurricane. He kept going upward, never once losing consciousness.

Until he fell. His eyes snapped open and he sucked air.

He expected Sakimoto or one of his goons above him, but the room was empty.

He had no idea how long he sat there. With any luck, Sakimoto's search was done. They'd chalk it up to paranoia. Glen Novak was spotted, but he'd left somehow, or if he hadn't, he wasn't causing any trouble.

That thought gave his legs some strength again. He felt the chills, but kept them at bay with the simple thought that he only had one more thing left to do. After that, the five years he spent in the bones of the world could finish up. And if there was any justice, he could forget them entirely.

He got to his feet and went to the door. He thanked the blonde for doing her job and let her get back to her naked aerobics.

The hall wasn't swaying. The hotel wasn't breathing. He turned the corner. The sounds had stopped, but he never looked into a single doorway on his way past. He went right to the stairwell and climbed two more flights. At the top: the metal door that led to the roof. Calomiris might have a man on the roof with him. If so, Novak had to be ready for that. He checked his pistol. Loaded.

He opened the door.

The roof was covered in pearlescent gravel, since turned into a tideland by the rain. The landscape was dotted with electrical boxes, air conditioning units, all of which were softly rusting in the salt air. Ahead, there was an open section, maybe twenty feet on a side that led to the lip in front of the hotel. If he walked to the edge, he could look down across the entirety of Devon. This high, he could probably see all the way to the highway. He turned away.

The rain seemed lighter, as though it hadn't fallen far enough to get any punch. A tarp flapped in the wind behind him and off to his left.

He turned.

Just ahead was the old sign, spray-painted directly onto the gravel in huge block letters. Those signs were on rooftops all over the country. "ALIVE HERE."

Not all of us.

Past that, through the islands that bled rust, the fire. It was the fire Novak had seen burning up here before, a flickering orange on a makeshift barbecue pit. It sat under an improvised tent, just that tarp that cracked like cheap thunder, pinioned with some aluminum poles.

Novak damn near threw up when he got a little closer. Calomiris, in his shirtsleeves, stood next to the grill. He sliced a strip of meat from the young woman on the fire.

Novak could identify gender, but that was about it. The skin had wrinkled into plastic, but she still had her shape. Most of the meat was carved off her ass and left thigh. Calomiris sliced a piece from the thigh and dangled it into his mouth.

The rain felt greasy on Novak's skin.

He stepped out into the open.

Calomiris was chewing when he saw Novak. Some part of the girl popped and sizzled on the fire. He looked ready to bolt.

Novak held up the pistol. "Don't move."

"Glen, wait."

"Wait? For what? This isn't something you can explain."

Calomiris relaxed, even though Novak still had the pistol pointing where Calomiris's heart should have been. He nearly smiled. "I know this doesn't look good."

"No shit, Walt."

"I'm unarmed. You can put the gun down."

He gestured at the knife in Calomiris's hand. It was greasy rather than bloody, and that made Novak gag. Calomiris put the knife on the side of the pit, next to a cleaver and a few other blades. He snorted, swallowed. He then backed away, palms out. "Good now?"

Novak lowered the gun, but kept a good several paces away from Calomiris. "What the fuck is this?"

"It's nothing. It's just something I do."

"That covers jerking off to old ladies or wearing heels on Sundays. It doesn't cover this."

In response to the hysteria in Novak's voice Calomiris slowed and evened his cadence: "No, maybe it doesn't. If it helps, no one was hurt."

Novak nearly laughed. "What about her?"

He gestured to her. "May I?"

Novak shrugged. *Why the hell not?*

Calomiris picked up a knife, slow and easy as he could, and speared her left arm. He showed Novak the bite mark on the outside of her hand. "She was bitten. I had her killed." He put the knife down and backed away to his earlier position.

"Who is... who was she?"

"One of the nomads from today. She was already turning. I did the only humane thing." His voice was speeding up a little.

"The only humane thing. Cook and eat her?"

He tapped the back of his head. "She didn't feel a thing."

"Was she... was this the first?" Novak knew damn well she wasn't, but he wanted to hear Calomiris say it. He wanted Calomiris to try to lie.

"No."

Novak took in the rest of the little set up. Calomiris had a nice table and chair he'd dragged up here. Tablecloth even. "How long have you been doing this?"

"A couple years. It's mostly geek meat."

"You eat geek? How haven't you turned?"

He shrugged. "Maybe it's the killing. Maybe it's the cooking, I don't really know. Hell, maybe I'm immune."

"I always wondered what you did."

Calomiris frowned, on uncertain ground, but letting his guard down the longer violence was allayed. "What do you mean?"

"Since the end. Everyone does something. Your wife washes her hands. My guy Pulaski wears make up. That farmer, Robert Franklin, collects flags. You fucking eat people."

"Geeks. Mostly. Sometimes someone has to be executed. Then it's not."

"Why?"

"It's the sweetest meat you'll ever taste. The juices running down your chin and knowing they were inside someone. They were what kept a person going, and after that, they were what animated a geek."

"That's fucked."

"They're trying to kill and eat us. Why not return the favor?"

"You're disgusting."

"Maybe. But I'm the only one getting fat off this thing. Everyone else is getting worn down to little nubs. We're all on starvation rations. Everyone but me. I'm thriving and part of that is because I'm the only one willing to look at the geek as a resource. It's a food source. More than that. It's a delicacy."

"Every fucking word you say makes this easier."

Calomiris's eyes widened. "Wait. I thought..."

Novak holstered the gun. "Yeah."

Calomiris relaxed again, but tensed as soon as Novak brought out the hatchet and hammer. "I'm not wasting a bullet when I put you down."

"Glen, wait! It's not as bad as it looks."

"Can you answer me one thing? If this was really how you get your rocks off, why the fuck did you care about me and Inez?"

"I didn't! I mean, I don't! I've known about you and Inez for years. I don't care, Glen. She's yours. She's all yours!"

Novak tried a smile. He was pretty sure it didn't look right. "She's nobody's. But if she didn't matter, why did you put that head in my footlocker?"

"Glen, I swear, I don't know what you're talking about."

"The hell you don't. The geek head in my footlocker! Why did you have it put there?"

"I didn't! I wouldn't! We're allies! We're friends!" He shrieked in terror as Novak lunged. "Glen, no!" Calomiris backpedaled, out from the shade of his tarp into the rain. Then, the inevitable: he slipped and tumbled to the gravel with a splash. "I didn't do anything to you! I promise! Glen, please!"

"Don't think of this as a kill. Think of it as your check."

Novak swung the hammer low. Calomiris skittered backward, throwing up a wake of rainwater. The impact ran up Novak's left arm, but he only barely felt it in his lats. The crunch of Calomiris's kneecap merged with his howl of pain. Novak wanted it to get swallowed up by the storm, but it didn't. It wasn't raining hard enough.

Calomiris tried to back away, but he was dragging his broken right leg.

Novak caught up and stood over Calomiris. "You brought me here, you son of a bitch. Know that."

Calomiris's mouth was open. His eyes were filled with water. The rain plastered his thin hair to his skull. "I promise you, it wasn't—"

Novak swung the hatchet. First a crunch, then a hot spray. Calomiris's body seized, then twitched. He braced his leg on the dead man's chest and shoved. The hatchet came free.

Blood flowed from the crown of Calomiris's head into the layer of water like ink. He'd killed Novak. Now Novak returned the favor.

Calomiris's leg twitched.

Novak sat down maybe three feet distant, leaning against the wall. Above him, the gray sky kept pissing.

He put the hatchet and the hammer down into the cold water. Calomiris's blood blossomed outward from corpse and murder weapon. In a little while, it would touch Novak. He wouldn't notice it by the time it did.

He removed the .45 from its holster. It was cold, wet. He cocked it.

He put it in his mouth.

He shut his eyes.

He saw Susan's face, broken, bloody.

At least it was the end.

And then the Dinner Bell started to ring.

- 14 -

NOVAK RESTED HIS FINGER ON the trigger.

The Dinner Bell kept ringing. He heard shouts from the front of the Athena, and panicked footfalls on the slick road. Every resident of Devon knew the protocol. The Dinner Bell rings and they answer. Able-bodied men and a few of the crazier women go to the Barricade and get to cracking skulls.

Calling him able-bodied might have been stretching it, he knew. He was at the end. His murderer was next to him, dead. Glen Novak was finished.

The Dinner Bell kept ringing.

Fuck.

He took the gun from his mouth.

He holstered his weapons and pulled himself to his feet.

Thunder cracked from the Pacific, momentarily drowning the Dinner Bell. He ignored the storm, instead looking out over Devon. At the Barricade, stiff shapes were clambering over the side. Two defenders were on the ramparts, swinging clubs. More men were pouring in from Town, and a thin stream was charging over from the Hill. Novak couldn't recognize individuals from this distance through the weather, but he knew his guys were at the front.

His guys: Stew, Pulaski, and Robellada. Good guys who were always there for him. Behind them would be a few of the men from the Hill, guys like Sorensen and Rodriguez. The others, some fathers, all the women and kids, would be up in their homes, praying.

Novak lurched to the stairs. The rain turned to steam on his skin. He wondered if they would fetch Calomiris. Probably not. He never manned the Barricade. He probably demanded privacy when he was on the roof.

Novak nearly fell into the stairwell.

Calomiris was dead. That could keep him strong for a little while. At least long enough to deal with the swarm. Every step put some more mortar back into his legs. By the second flight, he was at full speed. When he burst through the door onto the ground floor, he was going faster. He felt as though the fever had turned into a furnace and he was pissing gasoline all over it. He was running for the wave of geeks and when they'd meet, they'd both disappear into something white hot.

The lobby was empty of Calomiris men. Families would be hiding in their rooms and the soldiers had better be running for the Barricade. Novak burst out the front doors into the dank air, ran past the dark Winnebago and bikes.

The rain came down in littering sheets like fish scales. The Dinner Bell continued its insane call, threatening to crack Novak's mind wide open.

Men ran down Hotel Street full tilt. Novak expected someone to trip and get a mouthful of asphalt, but they didn't. He ran after them. Even at his best, he was never that fast. Short legs and a barrel chest worked wonders for power and leverage, but killed foot speed. But that day, the last of his life, the fire burned from his insides, turning joints to thudding pistons. He overtook the last of Calomiris's guys, and soon he was amongst them. Ahead, he dimly saw Sakimoto, suit plastered to his body, vaulting up onto the Barricade and taking a swing with some kind of club. A geek lunged for him and he grabbed it, using its momentum to fling it into the metal wall of the Barricade. The metal rang out in counterpoint to the Dinner Bell's maddening toll.

The geeks weren't over the Barricade, but they were trying. Head and shoulders would appear, and someone would swing. Full contact Whack-A-Mole.

The sky let out another roar. Far down on the Barricade, a geek pulled itself over, falling onto the narrow ledge of the rampart. No one saw it. Novak tried to yell, but the thunder and the Dinner Bell ate his voice. He was twenty feet off.

His guys had been separated. Stew was far to the right, closest to the Hill, Pulaski ranged in the middle, looking relaxed as he beheaded the cresting geeks. Robellada was near the gate, fighting side by side alongside both Rosenbergs and Louis Chu.

Novak blinked the rain away. The ladder was clogged with men. He found a section of the Barricade, made from an overturned car that formed a treacherous ramp to the ledge on the inside. Novak's foot hit the transmission and propelled him up the side. He caught the ledge and pulled himself the rest of the way. The freezing metal turned his fingers blue, but he only felt that in one hand.

Stew had turned around. He saw the geeks that had made it over. More were coming over that section of the Barricade. The way they swarmed and lunged, they had already knocked some off the battlement onto the wet grass—inside Devon. Stew advanced, shield up and machete down and out, ready for that overhand swing that split skulls like cordwood.

The geeks lunged for him, knocking one another aside to get to fresh meat. Novak pulled himself onto the rampart and shouted: "One side!"

Stew heard. He didn't bother to look—he didn't have to—he just gave Novak enough room to pass him, using that clear riot shield to herd the fuckers right in front of Novak's charge.

Six milky eyes focused on Novak. The fingers of one made wet plastic sounds on Stew's shield. Novak barreled into them. They fell backward, clutching at him. He brained one with the hammer.

The head cracked inward. The thing was still reaching, but Novak moved past it. Then, the chopping sound of Stew finishing it off.

Novak smashed the others. The geeks were struggling on top of one another on the Barricade, trying to make it over. They had effectively neutralized each other with their scrabbling. As Novak crushed their skulls, he shouted to Stew: "Get the ones that passed!"

Stew jumped from the Barricade, slipping in the mud as he landed. Two geeks that had fallen inside already turned to him. Two more were stumbling toward the blockhouse and a few of Rippey's guys.

Novak looked out over the Barricade. It was a swarm. He could barely see the ground from the base of the Barricade to the swaying woods and roads where the things staggered out in an endless tide. Their mouths were open, the rain on their lips like slobber. Their milky eyes were empty, but all were focused on someone on the Barricade. Every geek that had fixed on prey had claw-like arms outstretched.

Back toward the gate, the geeks had made a ramp out of their own, like army ants. It wasn't intentional. They just kept climbing over one another, the ones on the bottom falling to be trampled by the others. They didn't notice. They didn't care. Even the ones at the bottom only wanted to get up to make it over the Barricade to the warm flesh on the other side.

Novak ran toward that unliving ramp. The battlement was mostly made from dented metal, but in places it gave way to wood, smashed together in some Frankenstein thing. It was solid enough, and he only registered the change in the sounds his feet made as he pounded back to the trouble zone.

Ford got there first. He pulled himself up, scaling the underside of a tipped-over Bronco. He made it up in time to cut a new smile in a geek's head that went all the way around the skull. His attention was to the left, toward the main gateway. There were two points where the geeks had formed their undead ramp. He stood between them, tensed, trying to gauge the bigger threat in that moment.

Novak called over to Ford: "I'll take right!"

He glanced at Novak and threw a nod. Between them, they hammered the geeks back down into the writhing mass of bodies below. The storm roared back.

Ford turned to Novak: "This is getting bad, quick."

"Yeah. You okay here?"

Ford hacked a geek's head and shoulders apart. "For now."

Novak knew what Ford meant. This was a bad one. Maybe the worst they had ever seen. He wondered when the furnace in his chest would go cold. How long did he have and how many of the fuckers could he put down before he died? *Only one way to find out.*

The entire Barricade shuddered. Off to the right, a hundred feet down the barricade, Louis Chu slipped right off his feet. A geek pulled itself over the side and landed right on him. In a minute, Chu's scream cut off and the side of the Barricade was washed in arterial spray.

Stew was on it. He beheaded the geek and did the same to Chu before turning on the rest of the bastards climbing up and over.

Novak turned to the left. The Barricade shook again. Ford nearly fell. Suddenly Novak noticed that the Dinner Bell had gone silent.

The gate bowed inward. The geeks had found the weak point. They had pressed forward and whichever area gave kept giving and became their point of entry. The gate was buckling and a gap had formed between each side. A few pasty white geek hands groped through this, trying to get something to eat.

Five men, including Robellada, strained against the gate, trying to push it shut. They weren't fighting muscle with muscle. They were pushing against geology. That the geeks would break through wasn't a question. It was a timeframe. Novak had to accept what was going to happen and work with it. He hopped off the Barricade near the side of the road and rushed to the men on Hotel Street.

Novak grabbed Robellada's shoulder. He yelped and reached for his fire axe.

"It's me!"

"Mr. Novak?" He sounded confused.

"We're fucked, son. I need you to evac our people to the Athena!"

"We're fucked?" Robellada's eyes were empty. Behind him, the slit in the gates sprouted more and more arms: a horrible, carnivorous birth. He tried to turn around, but Novak's fingers sank deep into Robellada's shoulders like clay. "They're coming in!"

"I know! Whether we like it or not! I need you to get our people to the Athena before the Barricade breaks!"

Robellada had always lived with the Barricade. Since he lived in Devon, he hadn't experienced a swarm they couldn't break. He wasn't there for the two times they had to fall back to the Athena. To Robellada, the Barricade was a constant. It was bedrock. It didn't give, because that would defeat the whole reason for its existence.

He was wrong, of course. The wall wasn't a constant because, on a long enough timeframe, nothing was. The wall existed not because it would save a life forever, but because it would buy time.

His eyes said Novak was crazy. Robellada wanted to struggle, but Novak's fingers bit too deep and the boy was doing all he could not to flinch from his old teacher. "Just. Fucking. GO!"

Novak threw Robellada aside, toward the Hill, and he staggered backward, nearly falling into the muddy drainage ditch at the edge of the road. The rain plastered his hair to his head. Drops fell from his eyes and lips. His nose was running. He sniffed. Glared at Novak. In those eyes was pure hatred. Novak saw that fear that he had seen in Robellada's eyes that Thursday when he left his class on his pointless errand. There was more. *The kid's blood is up.* But Novak saw something else, the weakness in Robellada, wrapping the boy up like a snake, whispering horrible things in his ear. In that moment, Ricky Robellada was the most dangerous person Novak had ever seen.

Then, just like that, the kid ran for the Hill.

Novak turned back to the gate. Thunder cracked across the sky again.

Sakimoto stood on the bowed gate above, geeks surrounding him. He looked to be a dead man. There were three of the undead ramps that led all the way to the top, the weight of them partially responsible for the collapsing gate.

On each side, a press of bodies blocked Sakimoto from either of the ladders back down. He could jump, but it was fifteen feet to the asphalt or seventeen into either of the muddy drainage ditches. Either option risked a sprained ankle, which in the new world meant death. The geeks had so taken over that they were falling from the sides into the street where the Rosenberg brothers bludgeoned them with frantic speed.

Novak ran for the ladder, really just rungs of bent rebar welded to the side of the Barricade. The geeks up top saw Novak before he was halfway home.

"Are you crazy? Don't go up there!" It was one of the Rosenbergs. Probably Jacob, but they sounded identical to him. In any case, he had some information that they didn't.

Two geeks had seen him. They dropped to their knees. Novak felt their fingers on the top of his head, scrabbling for purchase. "Heads up!" he shouted.

He grabbed one arm and yanked. The geek fell past him. He heard it land, then the crunch of one of the Rosenbergs cracking the skull. The second geek followed the first.

He pulled himself onto the rampart into the waiting arms of the geeks up top. He felt hands on his left arm. He twisted the arm and felt the chomp come down on the plastic armor. He wanted to pull the thing to him and split it open, but the hands were all around. He knew that this was the last thing that most people felt. In a second, it would be the teeth on him, and once that happened, in full view of Devon, he was a dead man. They'd kill him just like he'd killed others in the past.

The instinct was panic. That was wrong. He fought it. He forced his will on himself, pulling strength from the fire in his belly. His limbs were his for the time being. He was going to use them.

He dropped, dug in, and pushed.

There were a lot of them, but they were not acting together. They had a single purpose, a single motivation, but they were no longer human. Each one existed utterly alone, even within the larger swarm. As he pushed back, every muscle straining, he felt the weight fall away one body at a time. They tumbled back over the side, even as others tried to struggle with smashed fingers over the Barricade.

Novak was free. He pulled hatchet and hammer. The rampart was still covered. They were coming at him, and as soon as he gave up ground, there was no guarantee he'd make it back to the ladder. In any case, climbing down a ladder with ten geeks trying to gnaw him to the bone was just about impossible.

Below him, the gate bowed further. It was a parabola at this point, held in the center by bolts that were nearing their breaking point. When they broke—and they would—the gate would split open, and Novak would fall, along with a heap of geeks on the hard asphalt of Hotel Street. That would be the end of him.

Well, not the end of all of me. There would still be something with my face.

He advanced over the rocking surface as the rain soaked in. The geeks ahead hadn't seen him. The ones behind were shambling, but he was faster. He couldn't see Sakimoto through the bodies of the geeks going for him, but they looked to be at least fifteen deep. The first one would be the only easy kill.

He lined up the shot and slammed the hatchet through the top of the head, then knocked it off with the hammer. That would obliterate the Medusa-whatever. The motionless geek tipped over and fell onto the wet road.

Novak launched into the next geek before it knew he was there. His good hand was going numb. He hoped it was freezing in place from the rain. He hoped he could ignore it until the work was done.

He was on the fourth geek in before they noticed him. The one ahead, a female whose cheeks had been chewed to ribbons, turned on him. Its mouth was open, eyes milky and wide, hands ready for a grapple. He put the hammer on its forehead and split its skull with the hatchet.

Slow footfalls behind him told him that the geeks were getting too close. He pushed ahead, swinging his weapons like a windmill. The crunching sounds turned into background noise, like the hollow rain drumming on the Barricade, like the screams of the defenders, like the blood buzzing in his ears.

Sakimoto was visible, past swaying backs of the undead. He was in a bad place. Another ramp had formed at his back, and there was no one beyond him on the Barricade, so he was getting all of them from one side. He caught Novak's eye through it and nodded, a thanks for pulling the bastards off one side at least. He spun then, throwing another one to the asphalt below, where its face caved in from the impact. It was getting to its feet when Micah Rosenberg smashed the rest of its head flat.

Sakimoto's balance was amazing. His legs were planted wide, but he moved easily, even though he was fifteen feet in the air on wet metal. When a geek would lunge, he would either take its momentum and swing it into others or the wall of the Barricade, or he would crush the face with a sawed-off baseball bat he held in his left hand.

Novak dropped the last one between them.

Sakimoto said: "What the hell are you doing up here?"

"Looked like you could use the help."

"Appreciated, but you've managed to get yourself royally fucked."

Novak glanced behind him. More ramps had been created and the geeks were clawing over. From far away, they might have possessed a distant beauty, the swarm taking the soft green-gray of deep water, moving with a pulsing pattern, cresting like a wave. Maybe everything was horrible close up. Maybe beauty was something that could only be seen from far away.

"Not exactly news."

Sakimoto clubbed a geek. "We need a plan."

The gate shuddered and creaked. "It's gonna give!" Down the Barricade, on the far side of Hotel, Novak saw it. Gino's. Geeks had fallen off the Barricade on that side and were already shambling through the alley, or else reaching up toward the ramparts with mouths open. There was about an eight-foot distance from the top of the Barricade and the sloped roof of Gino's. Miss it and fall into the depressed ground, twenty feet down. Earth was wet, that meant sink into it a couple of inches and while he was pulling his boots free, about ten geeks would be trying to chew him up.

Still, it was the best bet. He started running. "One side!"

Sakimoto knocked a geek backward and hugged the bad side of the Barricade. Novak charged past. He wasn't even trying to put the geeks down any more. He was just trying to knock them aside. He was no football player, but he'd do in a pinch. The furnace was still blazing in him; even the rain couldn't put it out. He knocked them into Town. He knocked them back down their undead ramps.

Behind him: the roar of steel. The entire Barricade shuddered. Geeks reached for Novak on both sides as the floor threatened to drop away entirely and dump him into the waiting arms of the dead.

Gino's was just ahead. He couldn't get parallel.

Another roar, louder this time, and the Barricade cracked like a whip. He was too far. He jumped anyway.

As he was in the air, time slowed to a crawl. He could see the individual raindrops that he smashed apart like geek skulls. He could see the claw of lightning over the Pacific. He could see the dead below him, seeming to groan with frustration as they reached. He could see the roof, coming up to meet him.

Suddenly, it hit him.

The air went out of his lungs in a rush. The shingles were slick with rain. He slid down. It was ready to dunk him into the alley. In desperation, he slammed the hatchet down. It bit through the roof, and he jerked to a stop. There was a thump next to him. He brought the hammer up, but it was Sakimoto, now unarmed.

He got to his feet and offered Novak a hand. "That was your plan?"

Novak coughed. "Worked, didn't it?"

"Sort of." Sakimoto pointed.

Novak turned to see what he already feared was there. The gate had broken inward, spilling the swarm into Devon. The defenders were backing off, trying not to get surrounded. They were not running, if only to give the people behind them time. He looked toward the Hill. A group was making its way across the fields toward the Athena. It looked to be everyone, but there was no way to tell from here.

The swarm advanced, flooding the gaps between buildings like water, arms out, mouths open.

Sakimoto and Novak stood on the roof of Gino's, looking back toward the Athena.

Novak wondered how he'd get there.
And part of him wondered if he should even try.

- 15 -

STEW STOOD IN THE CENTER of the road, closer to the oncoming swarm than anyone. He had the shield up, machete back, shouting to the exodus. Rippey's people were in full rout, panic tearing through them. It was the end, they all thought as one. This was the final swarm, the apocalypse finally come to Devon. Novak couldn't make out Stew's words, but his voice was low and calm. The panic didn't stop close to him, but it slowed, moving from wildfire to controlled burn.

The gate hung off of the Barricade as the swarm shambled through.

Pulaski cut a head off and joined Stew. Pulaski was grinning.

Sakimoto stood near the edge of the roof. "Geeks below us!"

He was right, geeks had made it through the alleys in the southeast part of Town. They were spilling over the Barricade at a decreased rate, if only because Hotel Street was now wide open. Geeks staggered through the grass below, tramping it into the mud. They hadn't seen Sakimoto and Novak, or else they'd forgotten the living morsels on the roof.

In the old days, Gino's would have been the first thing people would see coming into Devon, a welcome sight for road-trippers. The parking lot butted right up against the eastern hills. To the north was a section of gift shops that had lately become home to some of Rippey's people. Still, they were across a short street—Beach Avenue—from Gino's.

Directly below, there was a short section of dirt, then a sidewalk, then the street, one car wide, then the collection of shops. Either way, it was looking like a jump down from Gino's before they could leave the dead for the living.

Sakimoto came to the same conclusion. "You ready?"

"As I'm ever gonna be."

Neither bothered counting down. They jumped.

Sakimoto landed on his feet as graceful as you please. Novak landed badly, toppling over onto his left shoulder, but he only felt the impact when it rattled his teeth.

The geeks spotted them quickly. The intersection of Beach and Hotel was already clogged with the dead, shambling north for the Athena. At least their attention seemed to be on something else for the time being.

Sakimoto grunted, and a metal ringing sound exploded near Novak. He got up and saw that Sakimoto had just thrown a geek face-first into the rusted No Parking sign. More geeks slapped milky eyes on them.

The shops were probably supposed to be rustic and charming, all wood with lots of alcoves and stairs. They might have been, back in the world, but they had become a maze that no sane person wanted to get stuck in. Unfortunately, both ends of Beach had swarms, and the one to the right had seen Novak and Sakimoto.

Sakimoto raced up the outside stairs, and Novak followed. The slow-moving geeks had just started after them while the one Sakimoto introduced to the sign was struggling to get up.

The west side of the shops faced Ocean, a road that ran parallel to Hotel, staying level while Hotel climbed to its terminus at the Athena. The east side faced Reef, which started in Gino's parking lot, traced the hills for two blocks before disappearing into houses and trees.

They ran along the balcony in front of the second-floor shops.

For the time being, they were out of the rain. Didn't feel like it; the wind on Novak's face was a constant mist of ice. The storm continued its hammering. The geeks seemed to be pacing them. He knew that was his imagination, but every look to the right showed one or more shambling up Reef after some kind of prey. He couldn't tell if they were the same ones or not. At this point, they all looked the same. He wondered how deep they'd penetrated into Devon.

He stumbled, caught himself, but his legs gave. *Christ!* The furnace in his belly was going out. He should have just stopped right here. Wasn't like he was going to make it out alive. Sakimoto could look back, questioningly, and Novak would hold up this ruined left hand. Sakimoto would see the missing finger. He'd nod, and Novak could pull his gun and get some fucking sleep.

Calomiris had killed him, and he'd killed Calomiris. The scales were balanced. It was time to give up.

But he couldn't. He kept moving. He forced the power into his legs, moving them with conscious effort.

Sakimoto was rapidly outdistancing him: half a block ahead, right in front of an abandoned toffee maker, with the lead growing. Sakimoto would make it to the stairs before Novak was halfway there.

Sakimoto turned. Novak must have been obviously ailing, because the other man suddenly looked concerned. Weird look on him. Or maybe it wasn't. The fact was, he'd never seen it on Sakimoto's face before, but it wasn't as though there was much time they spent together. He waved Sakimoto off, using the pristine right hand. The other man hesitated for an instant at the top of the stairs, and then he turned back and rushed down.

Then, a sound like a baseball bat hitting a log.

He glanced toward Reef. Right below was the parking lot. A few geeks staggered through it. None of them had eyes up at him. On Reef, a larger swarm was poised to plunge deep into Town. They were only two blocks south of First Baptist. Losing the church to the dead wouldn't be good for Rippey, but then, it wouldn't be good for anyone.

Novak coughed into his hand. It came out red. *Great.*

He pulled himself to his feet. His legs might be rubber, but they would run. He'd make them. He lurched to the stairs.

It was a one-story descent, with a small landing in the middle where a geek lay, its head split open and some gray matter dripping off the wood railing. The stairs led to Cliffside. For a moment, Cliffside roiled like a river. He blinked. It was just the gutters.

Sakimoto stepped out of a copse of trees and waved Novak down. He would never know why Sakimoto waited.

He hoped Sakimoto wasn't going to start making Novak like him.

He stumbled down the stairs. Cliffside was mostly clear. Sakimoto had maybe a minute more before he'd have to leave, and Novak would have been stuck on the second floor, alone and cut off by the swarms on Reef and Hotel.

"Come on," Sakimoto said. "I think we have a window to cut over to Hotel."

Novak nodded.

Sakimoto moved at a brisk jog.

Novak tried to keep up, but every step left him a half-step behind. There were few geeks this far north. Must have been the early arrivals, the ones that found breaks in the lines before the breaks were detected. Their attention was on the herd of meat that fell back on Hotel. They didn't seem to notice two stragglers. At least not yet.

Sakimoto made it to the corner of Ocean and Cliffside. He glanced back toward Beach and his eyes widened. By the time Novak could see around the corner, he knew why. The swarm coming up Ocean—that had been blocked from them by the shops—was bigger than he thought it was. It was a little silly, thinking of these as separate swarms. They were just fingers, each geek a single cell in the cancerous mass beyond. The mass that would devour Devon.

The swarm noticed both men. Eyes got bigger, mouths opened, hands outstretched. All of them sported some bite damage: fingers chewed to bone, flesh stripped away in the soft midsection, chunks of neck simply missing, all showing the bloodless tissue underneath.

Novak thought about standing and fighting. Just to see how many he could put down before they helped the rain pummel him to the ground.

To the west, where Cliffside linked up with Hotel over a small incline, the swarm was thin. Some of the defenders were still falling back. He could just hear Stew shouting orders in a reassuring cadence over the rain and thunder. If he didn't know better, he'd have thought Stew was a military man. The shouts stopped for a second, then resumed, only slightly winded. This time Stew was yelling at Pulaski, calling him by his Christian name. Pulaski would be the very last, in the thick of the geeks, killing as many as he could.

"We can make it." The rain dripped off Sakimoto's eyelids like tears.

"You got some big balls, my friend." There were maybe ten geeks between them and Hotel Street, with the massive swarm gaining to their left.

Sakimoto shrugged. "I don't see another choice. It's go now or try to scale the muddy hill at Shoal."

"Yeah. Let's be fucked now."

Sakimoto grinned at that. He looked like he was about to say something, but had a second thought about it. Instead, he just started to run. Novak had never seen an unarmed man run at a bunch of geeks. He got to the first one and threw the lunging creature face first into asphalt. It struggled to get up with a skinned face and broken incisors.

The second and third he reached, he was able to throw aside just as easily, but the other seven had converged and Sakimoto had no way out of the trap he'd just marched into.

He had Novak, at least for the time being. Novak felt he was a pretty shitty backup. The fire was out, but maybe he could fake it. He tried to charge, but it wasn't any faster than a jog. Still, he hit the closest geek fairly hard. He didn't have much strength left, but he still knew how to use every last bit of it. Three toppled over, giving Sakimoto some breathing room/space.

Novak wanted to fall onto them and finish them off, but he didn't have that kind of time. Instead, he took a wild swing at one of the others and caved in the left side of its skull.

Sakimoto added more geeks to the pile, letting them get tangled up in their eagerness to kill the living.

Through the pounding rain, Novak looked up at Hotel. A familiar face was at the apex, looking down. Stew. "Come on!" Stew shouted. "Move your asses! You can make it!"

Sakimoto sprinted for the incline.

Novak followed, as fast as he could make his legs go.

The swarm had made it to Cliffside, boiling into the street behind him.

He made it to the incline. His legs wobbled, tried to give out. He couldn't let them.

He felt a hand on his shoulder, bunched up on the cloth.

Stew again. He dragged Novak the last few feet up the incline to Hotel. He glanced to the left and nearly stopped moving.

The gate was smashed open. The Barricade sagged in the middle, forming a nice ramp for the geeks. The swarm was less than half a block behind. The only man between Novak and the geeks was Pulaski.

"He's insane," Stew said. "I'm trying to get him to fall back faster, but he wants to be a hero."

"That's not why he's lagging."

Pulaski dropped a geek with a slash, then another. Every step he took, he stopped one of them, but even as he did, the swarm was closing like enormous ravening jaws.

This time Novak shouted: "Pulaski!"

Pulaski didn't turn. He was smarter than that, but the shrug in his shoulders said he'd heard.

"Get your ass back here before the fuckers surround you!"

Pulaski couldn't resist: he dropped three more before backing up, then turning and joining Stew and Novak. He was grinning ear-to-ear, his mascara running into Tammy Faye tears. "It's endless," he said.

"Don't sound so happy about it," Stew said.

They sped up, providing a buffer of thirty feet between them and the vanguard of the swarm. There were a few other people in back: Micah Rosenberg, Jacen Ford, and one or two more guys. Ahead, Barrett Cheeseman desperately dragged a cooler that was probably stuffed with soda.

Abruptly, the rain stopped falling on Novak's head. He was under the Athena's shelter.

"Get inside!" Sakimoto's voice.

They turned—Novak grabbed Pulaski and dragged him—and ran for the Athena. They threaded through the silent vehicles the nomads left and hurried to the front door.

Calomiris men, with Sakimoto in the center, were just inside, ready to drop the three barricades on the lobby entrance. Novak and his men were through.

Sakimoto's guys slammed the black iron fence down and locked it into place.

The geeks were maybe twenty-five feet from the door.

Sakimoto's guys shut the doors with the sheet metal welded over them. The doors looked like they were covered in the scales of some giant fish.

The geeks were out of the rain.

Sakimoto's guys put the iron bars in place, fully locking the doors down.

On the other side, the geeks clawed at the iron.

They were safe, if there was such a thing. The Barricade was broken because there was so much of it. The swarm could bring its fractured strength to bear on it. Now, there was a smaller place, and they would be distracting the geeks from the second floor. It would be harder for them to concentrate on one point. The downside was, if the geeks ever got in, everyone was dead.

The lobby was stuffed with people from the Hill and Town. Novak didn't see Rippey—he was probably already in his section of rooms in the east wing. Finger looked shaken, and Gloria Wu was nowhere to be found. The lowing sounds of the Athena's herds echoed from the east wing where they'd been pulled inside.

Novak raised his voice: "People of the Hill! Our rooms are waiting for us! Let's move over there, get situated, then anyone that wants can join in with the defense."

He nearly swooned with that effort, but kept his feet. His eyes swept the crowd. He saw the Harmons, Dr. Bloch, and a quick headcount said everyone got out. Robellada had done well. Novak pushed through the crowd toward the east wing. Their section was on the ground floor, toward the northern corner of the hotel.

Just as he had given rooms to the Athena's residents, he had given places to those people who chose to live on the Hill or in Town. Granted, they were less comfortable, but it wasn't like anyone was complaining. They paid for the rooms with crops or salvage, Novak buying the rooms for those few who couldn't pay Calomiris's prices. Novak's prices were cheaper. The place marked for the Hill was the old indoor pool, long since drained, and the locker and shower rooms. Novak had no idea what the Athena's guests needed with an indoor pool, what with having an outdoor one and a small beach, but that choice had given him someplace to put his people, even if it still stank a little of chlorine. Better than the smell of animal shit that would blossom in the coming hours.

He led his people into the main chamber. Some of them had brought things from their houses, whatever they grabbed on the way out when Robellada told them that the Barricade was falling. He was pleased to see that they had picked functional things: sleeping bags and food.

Stew and his husband embraced, Stew comforting the smaller man. Robellada lit the candlesticks in the corners of the room. Even this deep in the Athena, they could hear the drumming of the rain, the intermittent rumble of thunder and the clawing of the undead. And all this by candlelight: he supposed it was a good room to die in.

They spread out, the thirty or so of them, forming into their loose family groups, neighbors close by, like they were recreating the layout of the Hill in that room, as though some part of their consciousness wanted to spite the geeks.

Novak realized he had settled in close to the Harmons. Karen held her daughter, but no one was crying. They'd been through an incursion before and hoped they would again. It would take someone like Novak to make them cry. When he looked over at Harmon with his eye nearly swollen shut and split lip, Novak wanted to shoot himself right then.

His time was running out. He realized he had something to say and he needed to say it. He approached the Harmons and watched them go tense like a kicked dog.

Novak spoke to Harmon: "Can I talk to you?"

Karen Harmon trembled. "If you—"

"I won't."

She looked like she had something else to say. Maybe she saw Novak's pallor. Maybe she saw the chunks of geek flesh on his weapons. Maybe she was too tired to fight. She shut her mouth and looked to her husband.

Harmon nodded and stood.

He led Harmon to the inner doorway of the locker room. Harmon didn't speak; it was Novak's right to speak first, since he ran the Hill and called the meeting. Maybe also the fact that Harmon could probably read the contrition in Novak's shoulders and wasn't going to make it easy.

"Thanks for talking to me," Novak said.

"Did I have a choice?"

Novak's cheeks burned. Part of him, the irrational part, wanted to hit Harmon for that. He fought that part. "Look, Harmon, I wanted to tell you that I shouldn't have come into your house like that. I... shouldn't have hit you. Not in front of your kid." He tried to look at the other man, but couldn't bring himself.

"So you're sorry."

"Yeah."

"Then say it."

Novak ground his teeth. In the old world, commit a wrong, seek absolution. In the new world, there was no wrong except for what one couldn't get away with. "I'm sorry."

Harmon sucked in a quick gust. "Why did you do it?"

"I thought you'd done something that you didn't do."

"Like what?"

Novak shook his head. "What I did, I didn't have the right. I thought I did, but that's not the case."

There was silence as Harmon considered. "I figured you thought you had the right to do whatever you wanted."

"I wanted to deal with everyone the right way. You pay your way, but you buy something."

"You know, when we first came to Devon, Walter Calomiris took us in at the Athena. Did you remember that?"

He nodded. A week later, the Harmons had shown up at his doorstep. They had fresh bruises, but the kid was unmarked.

Harmon went on. "I checked around. Anyone would give you a place to live, but Calomiris put you to work in the fields and Rippey made every man leave Devon to scavenge. You were the only one that didn't ask that kind of sacrifice. Everyone I talked to said that you would deal fairly as long as we were willing to meet your price. I wanted to be alive to see Michelle grow up. We moved in and you gave us what we needed."

"Are you trying to thank me?" Novak put some levity in his voice and immediately regretted it.

Harmon's voice was cold. "No. You know why? Because it wasn't charity. Karen paid for everything we got, and she paid a whole hell of a lot."

"Yeah, I guess she did." There was no hole for Novak to crawl into, which was probably a good thing. Harmon deserved to be heard.

"I don't have to tell you that it hurt, do I? Every time she went to your place and came back with food, it hurt."

Novak wasn't sure what to say. He decided on the truth. "It's not going to happen again. After tonight, you make a new deal with Stew. He'll treat you better than I did." He reached into his pack and pulled out Booker's bloody wrench. "Here. Take it." Harmon hesitated, but accepted it. "I'm... you know." Novak didn't wait for a response, but felt Harmon's eyes as he retreated. He didn't feel Harmon's gaze burning, just the faint flicker of pity. That made it worse.

He tried not to collapse. He put his back against a wall and slid down it to a sitting position.

For a moment, the pool was full of pink water, but a blink got rid of that.

Dr. Bloch was looking around, not sure where to go. She seemed even bigger in the dim light of the room, one hand on her lower back, the other protectively over the bump. It appeared like she was trying to make up her mind. She did, moving toward Novak with a purpose. The gold light polished her skin and turned her eyes into coal.

"May I sit?" she said.

Part of Novak wanted to respond with a little sarcasm. Something along the lines of: "It's a free country" or maybe "I'm not Rippey; you sit where you like." But they both knew that she wasn't asking Novak's permission and he couldn't stomach acting like a child in front of her again. Instead, he gestured to the floor next to him.

She gingerly settled in. "This is hell on my back."

"Sorry. My bag is back at my house."

"No, it's fine. I didn't mean to complain. We're all in the same boat."

"Not the *same* boat."

She glanced around the room for eavesdroppers. "About earlier. I didn't tell anyone."

He shut his eyes. He tried not to think about the things he'd said to her and what he'd fantasized in that moment. She didn't deserve that. Maybe he did.

She said: "How are you feeling?"

"Not good."

"Fever? Aches?"

"The aches are gone. I've got numbness. But fever, yeah. Definitely have that."

"How long has it been?"

"I don't know. Twelve hours, maybe? Maybe more."

She didn't answer but he sensed her nod. She didn't have to tell him how long he had. Anyone who had lasted this long knew. He heard a rattle. He opened his eyes. She was rummaging through her bag. She found a bottle, shook out some pills and offered them. "Maybe I can treat some of the symptoms. Make you more comfortable?"

He took the pills. "What are these?"

"Amphetamines. Uppers."

He frowned. "Why?"

"I like to think I sort of know you a little. You're the kind of guy that would have ended it. You don't want to turn and you know there's nothing to be done. So you would have ended it. Unless you had something else to do."

He gave her a tired smile. "Already done. Right before the Dinner Bell rang." He told her, in stark whispers, about the head in his footlocker and about Calomiris on the roof and the motive for the murder.

She thought about it. "I don't think you're done yet."

"Why not?"

"You're describing a pretty advanced paraphilia." Adding, after his confused look: "A fetish. A kink. If he was that fucking far gone, I seriously doubt that he had any sexual desire for his wife any more. Unless they were doing some kind of eating... play." She shuddered.

"Inez probably would have mentioned that."

"Then he was telling you the truth. He didn't care that you were fucking his wife. It was probably a pretty convenient arrangement for him. It kept her from bothering him for something he couldn't provide."

"Fuck."

"Yeah. Whoever..." she had trouble with the next word, but she did get it out: "killed you is still out there—or rather, in here..."

He looked at her face, at the wide mouth, the dark eyes, the regal arch of her brows. He wanted to kiss her, give her some kind of heroic one-liner, and get a Hollywood ending where his infection died in his bloodstream. But that was bullshit. Hollywood was gone.

Instead, he palmed the pills and waited to get some strength back.

- 16 -

JIM SORENSEN WAS THE FIRST to leave the room. He settled his wife and young son and was out the door. Robellada was next. He fairly scampered out of the room, probably to make sure Janelle Ford had made it to the Athena. Novak didn't want to think what would happen if she hadn't—they'd have to tie the kid down to keep him from going out there. Beto Rodriguez was next. Sorensen and Rodriguez were good men. Not scavs, but they could be trusted to man the Barricade to combat swarms and would be upstairs with the rest of the defenders.

Robellada came back in with saucer eyes just after Rodriguez left. Janelle Ford was with him. She was a pretty girl, even if her frame needed another fifteen pounds to look right. He looked around for Stew and found him sitting with Michelle Harmon, a D&D book opened between them. She was noting something down on a sheet of paper while Stew had a professorial look on his face.

Robellada went right over to Stew and whispered something. Stew excused himself from Michelle and he and Robellada put their heads together. Novak made out tones: Robellada's panic and Stew's measured calm. He glanced over to Pulaski, who was fixing his makeup in a compact, but he too had paused and was watching the other guys.

When Stew led Robellada to Novak, Pulaski got up and joined them.

He didn't like the idea of talking with Janelle Ford so close, but she had already heard everything so it wasn't like she was getting any new information.

Stew said: "Ricky has some disturbing news. He... you tell him, Ricky."

Robellada looked to Stew for encouragement, then to Pulaski. Finally: "Yeah, disturbing news. Reverend Rippey is in the lobby. He's, ah, he's stirring something up. He's asking everyone why Calomiris wasn't at the Barricade."

Novak knew the answer to that one. So did Rippey, which was worrying.

Pulaski said: "Calomiris hasn't manned the Barricade since... I don't know, never."

Stew said: "Not the point. Ricky says it's like Rippey is trying to lead a coup. Right now. In the middle of a swarm."

Robellada went on: "He's threatening to go upstairs to the penthouse. Craig Sakimoto and some of the others are blocking the way."

Janelle, worried: "My brother is with them. If something happens..."

"Where is Calomiris? He should just come down so we can get to fighting the geeks!"

Novak grunted: "You're talking like Rippey." He thought about it. He was going to need the energy. He popped the uppers in his mouth and crunched them.

Stew said: "I think we should try to calm things down."

Novak said, "More of us in the lobby, might make things worse."

"Not if we side with Walter's people."

Robellada said: "Side with Walter's people? The only sides are the breathing and the dead, right? Should we be siding with anybody?"

Stew said: "Not what I meant."

Pulaski yawned. "If Rippey's shitting where we eat, I say we cut his fucking head off."

Janelle's eyes got wide. Stew very quickly said: "He's joking."

Pulaski might turn things violent, but then, they might go that way with or without him. If that was the case, they'd need him. Stew would give Novak the advice he needed. He wished Martinez were still alive; Martinez would have been the perfect person to place in charge. All Novak had was Robellada. He was going to have to lose the cherry eventually. Besides, Dr. Bloch wouldn't let him do anything too stupid, and Novak couldn't have Robellada and his girl gumming the works. Novak said: "We need a lay of the land first. Robellada, I need you here to take care of our people." He was about to bitch, but Novak cut him off: "It's important, kid. We protect these people. End of story. Stew, Pulaski, you're with me."

He thought it was the uppers, but whatever the cause, his legs felt a little stronger.

The hall looked longer than he remembered, but he didn't worry about that too much. His world was the Athena, so the bigger it got, the better for him.

The lobby was clogged with people. He didn't like that. In a siege situation, the lobby should have a couple guys, no more, just in case the gate gave. Everyone else should be up on two.

Rippey was in the middle of the room, surrounded, the Rippettes flanking him like a choir. Most of the people were Townies, but some of the lower-level Athena residents were sprinkled in the crowd. He was winning hearts and minds, apparently. Beneath it all, the drumming of the rain outside, and under that, clawing to the surface, the undead.

Novak and his guys entered just in time to see Inez come down from the south wing with Sakimoto, Marcos and a few other soldiers at her back. She looked small with them, but her back was straight, and she didn't blink.

Rippey was in the middle of grandstanding: "Where is Walter Calomiris? While the rest of Devon's citizens were fighting, where is her supposed first citizen? Is he too important to tempt the ultimate sacrifice?

Inez saw the flaw in Rippey's argument immediately. "And I suppose you were on the Barricade, then?"

She let Rippey gasp in indignation as he groped for a response before she bulled on. "We both know the closest you got was Shoal Road. Maybe Cliffside if you were feeling tough."

Rippey recovered. "Mrs. Calomiris. I'm pleased you chose to join us, but I am calling for your husband. No one expects you on the Barricade."

"No, they don't." Inez knew her husband was dead. She responded too quickly. Novak couldn't tell if she'd seen the body, and if she had, the remains of the feast.

His eyes flickered to Marcos, nose taped and bandaged, both eyes black. He knew as well. His attention was on Rippey. Something was strange about Marcos. It took Novak a moment, but he realized that the man wasn't carrying his customary axe. He had a large metal club that Novak could not quite see clearly through the crowd.

He looked at Sakimoto, his brief ally on the Barricade. He was ready for a fight.

Inez kept talking: "Anything you want to say to Walter, you can say to me."

"We have the right to hear it from his lips. Mr. Sakimoto was on the Barricade. Many of Walter's men were there, valiantly defending our town, but Walter was not among them. I want to ask him why he ignored the bell's tolling."

Because he was dead. Because I killed him, like you hired me to do. Both Inez and Rippey knew that Calomiris was dead. They were just trying to gain something from it now, picking over the corpse in public without actually producing the body.

"So you're asking Walter why he didn't do what you didn't do? Seems strange to me. Why not talk to the one town father who actually was on the Barricade?" Her eyes found Novak. "Glen? Glen Novak, from the Hill."

Now the crowd's attention was on him. He felt the fever's cold flames crawling across his body. He knew he was pale as death. He wondered if his eyes had a milky cast. He balled his ruined left hand into a fist.

"Yeah. I'm here."

The crowd let him breathe. Stew was at his right shoulder, Pulaski on the left. He knew Pulaski's hand would be on his sword and Stew would have his shield in his hand. He couldn't help it: he did the math. The three of them could probably take everyone in the room, except Sakimoto and Ford. Short answer: he and his men weren't taking everyone without getting torn apart.

Inez went for formality. Novak wondered how many people knew he was fucking her. Probably more than he'd like, but less than he was afraid of. "Mr. Novak, you own the Hill, but you were on the Barricade today. In fact, Craig Sakimoto said you saved his life."

Other way around. Novak caught Sakimoto's look. He was mad, that much was clear, but Novak thought he saw the tiniest nod, as though to say, "Take credit for it. Both of us know that I'm the real man, and once you lie about it, you owe me even more."

Sakimoto was right. He'd risked his life to save something that wasn't going to see tomorrow. Novak kind of wanted to say something just to give both of them a good laugh.

He said: "I was on the Barricade. Lot of life saving up there. Didn't really keep a tally."

Inez said: "Did you see my husband up there?" That choice of words was probably for Novak's benefit.

"No."

"How about Reverend Rippey? Was he up there?"

"No. A lot of his boys were, though."

Rippey had that smile plastered on his face. "This is unimportant. I want to speak to Walter Calomiris. Why this resistance? What could he possibly be doing that's more important than planning the shared defense of our Jericho?"

Inez paused. To her credit, she didn't look up or down, for a lie or uncertainty. She kept her gaze fixed on Rippey, her face stone. "My husband is very ill, Reverend. He's been battling a flu and isn't up to seeing anyone."

"He seemed fine this morning," Rippey said.

"He's not now. If you need to plan with someone, I have the authority to speak on his behalf. And you have Mr. Novak here. Anything that needs to be done can be done with us and us alone. You don't need to disturb Walter with any of this."

Rippey knew he was beaten for the time being. He was smart enough to lose a battle if it meant the war later on. "Of course. Let me get my people to their places and we can get to work defending the Athena. By the Lord's grace, your husband will recover soon."

Inez said: "I'll be on two, leading the defense."

Rippey nodded and gestured, his people following him into the east wing like ducklings.

Novak tried to unclench his left fist, but the fingers weren't listening.

Inez found him. He wasn't sure what to do with himself. Jitters flopped through his numb body, like a dying wasp on a block of ice. She whispered: "You did it."

He pulled her aside. Everyone was out of earshot, but Sakimoto was trying to lip-read. Suddenly, he turned and disappeared into the east wing, the new location of the Hill and Town.

"What does Sakimoto know?"

"He knows. Not that you did it, but he suspects. You didn't cover your tracks very well."

Novak didn't tell her that he nearly covered them much worse. He opted for a slightly more diplomatic approach that was almost the truth: "The Dinner Bell interrupted me."

"Craig found the body." She tried to nod at him, but only then noticed he was gone. A frown creased her face, but she moved on. "He got me. He, Rudolfo, and I have seen it." Rudolfo Marcos, her cousin. They could trust him in the sense that he wouldn't stab Inez in the back, and Novak only had to convince her that she needed him for less than half a day.

"How many know?"

"I told them to keep it quiet."

"Are they going to listen?"

"I hope so. I hope they realize what's going on outside."

Maybe he had been blocking it, or maybe it had faded into background noise, or maybe the geeks still had their sense of humor, because as soon as she said that, the clawing and rattling from outside got much louder.

She misinterpreted his face. "It's okay, Glen. We just have to make it through the swarm. We do that, you're in charge."

"I know." Neither one of them was being honest about that. "I want to check on the bombers. They might need my help."

She nodded. She looked like she wanted to kiss him on the cheek, one of those comforting pecks, but she didn't. That would have damned them both.

He left her and passed the hotel bar, but that was dark. He wondered where Stacy was. Maybe she was waiting for Pulaski at his house. Maybe Novak had turned her into geek-bait.

Novak's body was light. He moved quicker than he had in hours. The stairs were easy, even if he couldn't feel the footfalls. The wallpaper hid veins, but he could ignore those. His head pounded.

Briefly, he shut his eyes, but the pounding stretched through his body. It collected in his knees and elbows, turned those into red knots. Then he noticed something that almost made him smile. His left hand throbbed. He felt something in it. Nothing good, of course, but he'd take it.

He opened the door onto the second floor. The sounds of siege flowed in to greet him: grunts, laughs, catcalls. All the things that people used to convince themselves they weren't terrified. Under it all, he heard the same desperation that was in Tom Martinez's voice right before Pulaski gave him the chop.

Every door along the front wall was open. Every room had at least two people in a miniature bucket brigade. One person picked up a rock, a chunk of engine block, an old television, and would hand it to the person at the window. There wasn't much aiming involved: just a slight pause, then a release. Below, the slick sound of a geek falling to the wet ground and a whoop from the bomber. The air was chill and wet. Gusts blew raindrops nearly to the doors.

Novak picked a room. It stank: oil, mildew, smells that should be in a garage. The two guys were Townies, Borassi the candlemaker and Wang, a guy who had a small pig farm pushed up against the east hill. The operative word was "had." Those pigs were geek food as soon as the Barricade fell.

Borassi saw Novak when he came in. Out of breath, passing a TV over to his partner, he said, "Hey, Glen. Come to help? I think they could use you a couple doors down."

"I'll be sending some people up in a little bit."

"Jim's already here. Saw him when I came in."

Novak nodded. He went to the window and craned his neck. His coaches always told him never to look at a wound. They said it made it hurt more, like the act of seeing snapped the body out of its protective shock. Novak never listened. He always preferred to know how bad things were.

The answer was bad. Maybe not as bad as he thought, or maybe worse because he couldn't see everything. From the vantage of the window, he looked out into the green field sweeping all the way to Cliffside. On the left side, he could see Hotel Street and a very little bit of Town. Farther out, the ruined Barricade, and beyond that, the road and the interstate.

He wasn't looking at Devon. He was looking at what infected it.

The Athena's south side was surrounded maybe twenty deep. He couldn't see how far around the hotel they'd made it, but then, he couldn't see the end of the press. Beyond that, geeks were still coming up Hotel and through the fields, dotting it. A swarm of them were around the shops that Novak had used to escape over, the ones between Ocean and Reef. Probably someone had holed up there and been spotted. Another swarm, much smaller, was disappearing into the trees of the Hill. Robellada had gotten everyone out, hadn't he? They hadn't left anyone?

Borassi said: "Looks bad, huh?"

"Looks like you're gonna be in business for a hundred years."

Borassi snorted. "We make it outta here, yeah."

"That's the first trick."

"You seen Walter Calomiris? Usually by now, he's roaming around calling for water and stuff for us."

"His wife said he's sick."

He couldn't tell from Borassi's face if he knew about Inez and him. They didn't know Walter Calomiris was a freak. They didn't know he was dead. They knew he was a comforting presence when the fuckers surrounded the Athena, and now he wasn't around.

Novak said: "I'll send my guys up. If I hear anything else about Calomiris, I'll let you know."

He got a curt nod for that, but that was it.

He spent a little while up there, but it was the same story in every room. There wasn't enough ammo to kill all of the geeks. They'd have to do what they'd done twice before. Thin the swarms, then lead sorties outside, killing as many as possible before retreating to do it all again. They'd do it in shifts, only this time Novak wasn't going to be up to it. And this time, the swarm was much larger. At least, it seemed that way. He hoped the fever was making him see things, but he knew he wasn't that lucky.

Everyone who talked to him asked about where Walter Calomiris was.

On the roof, with rainwater collecting in his brainpan.

He was going to fetch the rest of his men. He returned to the staircase, to find Barrett Cheeseman sitting on his cooler and drinking one of his sodas. His gnomish face wrinkled with disgust at the sight of Novak. "Hey, you faggot. Somehow made it out with your pussy intact."

"Not now, Cheeseman."

"That other piece of shit Sakimoto saved your ass. Wonder why he did that."

"Essential goodness of man."

Cheeseman sucked the rest of the Coke down. "Fuck that. Fear."

In spite of himself: "What?"

"Fear. If you died, like you should have, he'd have been alone. You two are such Marys you couldn't handle being alone." He got up, opened the cooler and took out another Coke.

"You gonna help with the siege?"

Cheeseman snorted. "Fuck you. A Coke ain't gonna break a geek's skull."

"They could always throw you out."

"If I turn, I'll bite your three-inch tadger off at the root, shitbird."

Novak left the dwarf to his soda, and went downstairs.

The clawing was beginning to drown out the rain. The lobby was peppered with Rippey's people, including Jack Finger. They had formed into clumps of twos and threes, including the occasional

Calomiris man. They spoke in hushed tones and when they put their eyes on Novak, their mouths shut. The only one that didn't shut up was Finger, who hissed in Micah Rosenberg's ear, making him scamper off toward the east wing.

Novak had a few options.

Actually, he only had one. He wasn't going to run away from a toad like Finger, even if he could count his remaining breaths on one hand.

Finger had one guy with him, a tough named Kramer or Kramden or something. Finger flinched as soon as Novak got close. Maybe Finger saw the caffeine shakes in his hand. Maybe Finger realized that Novak already lost everything he had.

"Glen Novak, you're uh..."

He grabbed Finger's tie and swung him. Hard. His back hit the wall and the lobby went completely silent except for the faint drumming and the scrabbling of dead hands.

"I'm what, Finger? Want to tell me what everyone else seems to know?"

Kramer or Kramden put his hand on Novak. He grabbed it, stuck a leg behind Kramer's and with a push, sent him sprawling over a big silver trashcan.

Novak turned on Finger.

Then Finger gave Novak the punchline: "You're under arrest."

"You're fucking joking."

"You killed Walter Calomiris."

At least he had his facts straight.

Novak glanced around the lobby. There were only two of Rippey's hard cases, but neither of them was Ford. They were unsure. The hyenas could see the lion was hurt, but they knew that he was still a lion and someone was going to end up dead. They had fanned out so Novak could hold only two of them in his gaze at one time. They didn't want to close.

"Mr. Novak? The ruse is over. Your malfeasance is apparent." The voice was Rippey's, coming out of the hall.

The hyenas grew some balls when they heard their alpha. They rushed Novak.

He turned to the south wing and caught one of them with a palm to the nose. He felt something give.

One of them grabbed him from behind, but an elbow to the face proved convincing. For a second, Novak was free.

Then he ran.

- 17 -

NOVAK WAS CERTAIN THAT ALL of Rippey's hard cases were on his ass. He cursed Rippey. Not because Rippey had stabbed him in the back; that was to be expected. The contract murder of Calomiris left a loose end, no matter that he was going to do it for free. Rippey wasn't planning to pin a medal on Novak for it. There were two men who knew about the hit firsthand. One was loyal. The other was only a liability.

He charged up the stairs, hoping the pills would carry him through. It might have been stupid to run, but he wasn't exactly anticipating a fair trial. Maybe that's exactly what he was expecting. He *had* killed Calomiris. Admitting a motive other than the promise Rippey gave would expose the bite and Novak was a dead man sooner than he would like.

And there was still the matter of the son of a bitch who'd killed him.

The men were maybe a flight below and they weren't getting any further behind.

He'd been chased hours before, but that was slower. There wasn't as much at stake. They might have thrown him out. This time, same penalty, different meaning.

He passed the second floor. Nothing here for him. The pills had stoked his false furnace, but he knew that they'd burn through the fuel faster. Every movement was pushing the inevitable deadline closer. He couldn't take any chances. He had to buy time.

He pulled his pistol. Fourteen shots total. He'd held onto them as long as he could. Time to spend some.

The guys rounded the flight of stairs just below, Jacob Rosenberg in front, with that little fuck Pisspants right behind him.

Novak fired twice, not at them but at the wall behind. He wondered if someone outside the stairwell mistook it for thunder. Rosenberg backpedaled right into Pisspants, and both men nearly fell to the floor.

Novak put another bullet a little closer to them and they hit the ground before the chipped plaster settled out of the air. His nose and throat burned from the coal miner's tattoo in his lungs, but he ran anyway.

The footsteps behind took a little longer to get started and when they did, they were now much more cautious.

Three would be the safest floor. Too high for the defenders and too low to run into the real hard cases. He burst out of the door into the hall beyond. Empty. This far up and he couldn't hear the geeks scrabbling at the doors any more. The footsteps in the stairwell sped up: they knew he'd put a door between them.

Novak broke to the right. He was in the south wing, two floors up from the mezzanine. He ran to the end of the hall, and didn't glance out the window: he knew what was there already. He turned the corner, and maybe a half-second later, heard the door burst outward. Jacob Rosenberg barked orders. They were going to surround him. He'd done the same when the last of Gautreaux's bite victims holed up in the gas station on Ocean.

The hall was a long one, leading all the way down the southern face of the Athena, where it would terminate at the short, Pacific-facing edge. He ran, ignoring the dissolving muscles in his legs, ignoring the burning blood under his tongue, ignoring the axe-wound in his side. Let the drugs run him, like he was a sled dog, whipped by a maniacal master.

The hall was a hundred miles long. The carpet's pattern danced under him like a kaleidoscope and washed up over his ankles.

A shout echoed behind him.

He chanced a look: Pisspants. He stood at the corridor's elbow, far too close, pointing and shouting. Pisspants unslung his rifle and Novak barely managed to swear before the crack of the gun nearly brought him down. He threw himself to the side, feeling the wash of the bullet across his side. He stumbled against the wall and kept running. There was no way he'd make it to the corner before Pisspants racked another round and fired it. He might be a pussy, but he wasn't going to miss again.

Novak pulled his gun and shot back blindly. Two shots. Pisspants's gun cracked again. Plaster sprayed across Novak's face. Pisspants swore. Novak had some time. And only nine rounds left.

He hit the corner and glanced back. Pisspants was picking himself up, and Jacob Rosenberg just came around the corner. He wouldn't miss.

Novak had to take Rosenberg's shot away.

He rebounded off the wall and ran down the western hallway. It was far shorter and probably completely empty of tenants. He picked a room and kicked the door in. Empty. He shut the door behind him. Dust had grayed everything in the room until it looked like a town after a volcano. Absurdly, he thought of Judy Bloch's story about the Toba Event and let out a braying laugh. This was the final sign of the extinction of man. Room 346. No one else would ever see it. He went to the glass door on the other side and tore it open.

The rattle of the rain turned into a roar as the wind numbed his face. Salt worked into the crevices of his face. He slid the glass door shut behind him. He was three stories up. Below, on the cliff, a couple geeks wandered, looking for prey. There was maybe fifteen feet of open ground before the old fence and, beyond that, the cliff. Then it was a hundred feet down to the rocky beach and the gray ocean. He briefly thought about jumping to the ground. Maybe a geek would break his fall. That high meant a sprained ankle was a best case scenario, and something broken was the most likely.

In his mind, he heard the footsteps up the hall like a heartbeat, but he knew he was imagining it over the howling wind. He holstered the pistol and hoisted himself up onto the stucco decorated lip of the balcony. He looked down and over. He had no other option, or if he did, he knew he wouldn't think of it before Rosenberg's hit squad came in with rifles blazing.

He jumped.

The second-floor balcony came up faster than he'd expected. He hit the side and wrapped both arms around it. His lungs crumpled. The wind tried to push air through him, but he could catch nothing. He held on, somehow, wrestling the sticky air into his lungs.

Finally, he inhaled, catching an inch of rainwater in the process. He hauled himself up, body burning, and fell into the balcony of the room one floor down and one over. He gasped for a second, then rolled across the floor and managed to get to his feet and forced the door. It gave, and he stumbled into the room beyond. He wanted to lie there and gasp, but he needed to hide. He shut the glass door.

He felt the rain running down his body, leaving rivers of ice. He sucked air and waited. They needed to find the room, find that he was gone, and move on. He couldn't use the hallway. That wing would be swarming with guys—both the hit squad and the defenders. And there was no way he could move along the second floor without being spotted.

The walls were bare. He wished it was the room he'd hidden in earlier, if only so the blonde could have looked after him. He berated himself: that was the kind of superstitious fatalism that developed as death moved into focus.

When he could stand up, he went to the glass door and pressed the side of his face to it, trying to see up and over to the balcony he'd jumped from. He couldn't. He would have to go and hope that Pisspants wasn't waiting above with his rifle trained. He moved his head away; he'd left a large red splotch, dripping sluggishly down the fogged glass.

He went to the mirror. The stucco balcony had torn his chin apart. He would have a good scar, if he'd had a life beyond tonight. The blood was flowing, trying to clot over the thinning rainwater. He grabbed a dusty towel and turned it red, pressing it against the cut.

His stomach turned upside down. He sank to his knees and emptied his guts onto the carpet. It came out with what fire there was in him, dark and red with chunks of things he didn't want to name. The stench hit him in the face, like he'd just opened the belly of a corpse. He realized then that he had actually done just that. He gagged. Something rose into his throat. He forced himself to swallow it.

He didn't want to look at what he'd vomited. God knew what was in there. When he tried to rise, his arms and legs were rubber. The pills.

He'd vomited up those helpful little pills. Among other things.

No way to know how much he had managed to absorb before he disgorged them. He needed them. His strength was jumping ship. There was still someone who needed to die. He couldn't let the murderer live.

He looked down at the dark red that spread across the carpet. A commercial popped into his head from the world: paper towels, mopping up blue liquid. They sucked it up. Now the carpet was doing that to his guts, his life.

He leaned down to the carpet. He picked one of the clumps of meat, shutting his eyes and ducking down like a dog to eat it. It snapped under his teeth and tasted like a broken nose. His throat closed when he tried to swallow. He forced it, fighting the urge to drop it, wet and mashed, back into the soaked carpet.

He swallowed.

And then he found another.

With each clump, it went down easier. By the fourth, he was craving it, his stomach roaring for more.

Five minutes later, he forced himself to his feet. He couldn't look at the stain below.

He stumbled to the glass and forced it open.

Back out in the rain, he tried to pretend it was washing away the memory of what he'd just done, but he couldn't. It would be there until the end. Fortunately, that was close.

He glanced up. His pursuers weren't there.

Below him, more geeks milled around, looking for a way into the Athena.

He shakily clambered up on the stucco barrier. The scrape of his feet alerted a geek directly below. It reached up, fishbelly mouth wide. Novak recognized it. Same filthy robe, flapping open obscenely. Same dark hair, hanging like swamp vines. Same partly-eaten face. It was the geek he hadn't killed the day earlier, staggering out and reaching for him from behind the scavenged house where Tom Martinez died. He felt the same urge as before, but the time had come to conserve his bullets.

Five feet from the next balcony over. Standing jump.

He hoped that he had enough of the drugs in his system to power his legs. If he fell, at least it wouldn't be fatal. No more fatal than living for the next several hours anyway. He tried to smile at that, but the razor in his chin made that impossible.

He jumped.

This time, he hit the target better. His toes gripped the edge and for a moment, his weight nearly sent him backwards into the arms of the geek below. But he wind-milled his arms and lunged forward, and with one step he was steady.

The jump over to the next balcony was even easier.

The one after that was easier still. He got his timing down, measured the force and went. Practice made perfect.

He got to the corner of the south wing. Below him, the fence would have once closed off this area, but it had collapsed a long while ago, when a geek swarm pulled it down. This little bit of land between the Athena and the cliff face led into the courtyard. The problem was that he was at the corner of the tower. There was no way to jump to the next balcony.

He had a choice. He glanced down: there were few geeks from what he could see, but that didn't mean much. If there was a gathering in the courtyard, he couldn't see it from his present position. He could chance it and jump down, hoping he landed well, or he could gamble that the room he was outside of was empty and sneak back in for at least a moment.

His friend from the farmhouse was directly below. It had tracked him, staggering along with each jump, hoping that he'd fall. He thought about ending it again, but he couldn't justify it. Not to feel marginally better for five seconds.

He forced the glass door. A quicksilver line opened from handle to halfway down the pane, but it didn't shatter.

The room was empty. It didn't look as unused as the others. The graying of the dust was subtler, and it seemed like there were darker splotches: the remnants of touches. He knew he could have been imagining that. The television was gone. So was the phone. Both scavenged to serve a use: to be dropped on heads.

He went to the door and pressed his ear to it.

Down the hall: shouts, some laughs. The sounds of the siege.

Nothing close.

He opened the door.

The hall was empty. It was a quick walk to the closest room whose balcony would border the courtyard. The problem would be that the corridor would lead straight to the front of the hotel. That hall, the one that bordered the front of the Athena, would be swarming with people. He had to chance it.

He went to the door and shouldered it open without bothering to look. Better pretend that he belonged. Maybe someone would even believe it.

The room was empty, but someone clearly lived in here. The bed was filthy. There was a precious bit of scavenge, some canned goods, a flashlight, and some tools, on the shelves. The heavy things were gone. No weapon, no person. The Bible was on the mantle with the ribbon stuck somewhere close to the back. He wondered if they were reading Revelation when the swarm came. He doubted God had much of a sense of humor, even an asshole one.

The sliding glass door to the balcony was open. The journey across these balconies was going to be worse. The second floor was fairly densely populated, with only the Pacific-facing rooms being predominantly empty. The geeks were spread fairly thin along the rain-soaked ground, though his friend had found him, reaching up with ragged fingers. Visibility was getting worse, partly from the mists blowing off the ocean to die in the cul-de-sac.

He started moving. His legs were numb. His fingers were numb. His head steamed. His stomach snarled.

As he jumped from balcony to balcony, the geek below paced him. His dead bride, calling him home.

He moved fast. In some of the rooms, he heard people moving around inside. The trip across this wall was two and a half times farther than the last, but his body had learned the motions. It was on autopilot, leeching the energy from Dr. Bloch's drugs. He was running on fumes and he knew it. Maybe Bloch had more. Probably didn't matter. Even if he somehow got to her, there was no way he could keep the pills down any more.

He jumped onto the last balcony. The room on the other side of the glass door was silent, but the corridor beyond was loud. The door was wide open, and he could just see the corner that led to the front hallway. He got up on the lip of the balcony and jumped.

He hit the roof of the lobby hard, barely managing to roll across the white stones, throwing up a wake of icy water. His head stung. He hauled himself to his feet and sloshed over to the east wing. The wind buffeted him from the Pacific, trying to push him into the front of the Athena, where the swarm waited impatiently. He heard the crashes and wet sounds of things being dropped onto the geeks. Part of him wanted to go over to the driveway's roof and look down. The swarm would be directly below. He could get an idea of their number.

That was pointless. The swarm wasn't really his problem. He was dead anyway, whether or not those bastards made it in. No sense in counting them.

Windows looked out from either wing, nearly head-level. He ran in a crouch, fighting the gusts of wind that pushed against him. He stood on tiptoes, peeked through the window into the hall of the east wing. It looked empty, but there was no way to tell. There would be geeks under it, but far less because of the steep and now muddy slope that emptied into the farmlands beyond. A geek took a wrong step, it would find itself tumbling into Franklin's cornfields. Geeks took a lot of wrong steps.

He went to the inner side of the tower. He jumped to the first balcony. He glanced into the room.

Occupied.

Damn.

He forced the glass door open. The pills, the adrenaline, all of it was wearing off. The wet and the cold and the infection swirled together in his body, pulling him to darkness. He wasn't going to let it.

In the room: two women and a man. He recognized one: Stacy. They all had the lean and hungry look of Athena people, scratching out a living, trading themselves.

She pulled the blanket closer around her skinny shoulders: "Mr. Novak?"

He tried to grin at her. "Glad you didn't listen to me."

She looked at the floor. He wasn't good at joking, at comforting. He was good at scaring, and that's what he'd done without trying.

"Stacy. I need you to do me a favor."

Her voice came out thin and reedy. "You need something from me?" He hated the hope in it. It came back to him, what he snapped to her when she lay on the floor.

He tried to keep the shiver from his voice. "You didn't see me."

Stacy offered him a pathetic smile. "We didn't see you."

Novak lurched outward and made an immediate right. The stairwell was where he left it. He passed it and made his way down the inner wall.

Toward the end, he listened at a door. Nothing. He forced it.

He nearly collapsed as soon as the door was open. His breath was ragged. His ruined hand had gotten some feeling back, but none of it was good. It was the slow rend of a recent burn. He barely managed to shut the door and put his back on a wall before his legs gave out.

The wallpaper swirled in front of him, so he shut his eyes. He heard geeks scratching at the walls, so he closed his ears. He pulled the blankets from the bed and made himself a wet and miserable cocoon.

Rippey had sent them after me. He had to have been the one who told them what was what. Probably phrased it like a rumor and planted it around. Thing was, he was right. They didn't know that it was both Rippey and Inez Calomiris who sent Novak up there with death in his hands. Novak didn't mind fucking Rippey right back, but Inez seemed innocent in the whole thing.

Was she? Dr. Bloch was damn sure Calomiris was telling the truth, and Novak knew she was a lot smarter than he was. So if it wasn't Calomiris, then Isador Rippey? Then why bother spilling the beans about killing Calomiris? Much easier to just tell everyone Novak had been bitten. No questions, just a quick execution. And he knew his own guys would help out with that. Couldn't be Rippey. Then who?

Inez? Why set him up if she was going to take over? Wouldn't she want Novak to take out Rippey?

Like I was preparing to do. If Rippey came after him, he kills Rippey, and the problem goes away. It was possible. Inez would eliminate all three town fathers in one day, leaving her running all of Devon. It didn't fit, though. It was entirely too ruthless for Inez. He would believe it of Calomiris, especially in light of his phrenalia—whatever Dr. Bloch called it. He would even believe Rippey would do it. Inez wasn't a monster yet, or at least that's what he had to believe.

That left—God knew! Closer to the end, but no closer to cutting the Gordian knot. Susan told Novak that story once. He'd heard the expression, but of course he didn't use it right. She chuckled gently but not cruelly, told him the story, about Alexander finding the impossible solution by simply being destructive. Can't untie a knot? Just cut it in half. Same endgame.

That was exactly what he was doing. He might not know his murderer's name, but if he took enough people out, he'd eventually get the right person.

The shiver worked its way into his nose. He sneezed.

"Bless you."

He looked up. Craig Sakimoto and three of his guys stood in the doorway. Only Sakimoto's hands were empty; the others carried guns and hammers.

Novak hauled himself up, shedding the now damp blankets. Only Sakimoto didn't tense.

"Jesus, Glen. You look like shit."

Novak coughed. "The fuck do you want?"

"You killed Walter Calomiris."

"Don't suppose it'll help if I say I didn't."

Sakimoto's eyes glittered. "Maybe if you weren't such a shitty liar."

"Gotta be bad at something, I guess."

"You coming quietly?"

Novak lunged. Sakimoto caught Novak's clumsy punch and spun him. He hit the far wall. The man closest had a pistol and Novak grabbed the man's gun arm and guided it past his body. The gun went off. The man behind Novak cried out. He head-butted the man he was holding. There was a crunch and the man went down.

Novak turned. Sakimoto punched him in the face once, twice, three times. He'd get a good shiner if Sakimoto kept that up. He needed to get his hands on Sakimoto. Sure, he was fast, but get control and the fight would be his.

At the end of the hall, Novak heard a shout. He couldn't look at it. No time.

He felt a crunch in his side, right below his short ribs. He stumbled away to see the last man bringing his hammer back for another crack. Novak leaped at him. Sakimoto's swing glanced off Novak's shoulder as he landed on the other man.

He was pinned under Novak. His first punch broke the man's

nose. The third cracked his left eye socket. Novak felt part of the man's cheek give under the fourth and the sixth dropped pieces of his teeth back into his throat. The man belonged to Novak. Arms pulled Novak up.

He whirled: Sakimoto.

Novak swung, but Sakimoto was already somewhere else.

Suddenly, the infection sunk its shivering claws into Novak. He wanted to curl up. He wanted to cry out, but he couldn't. The infection wrenched the fight from him, sending him helpless into the abyss.

Novak blinked. More Calomiris men were coming down the hall. He was cornered. He could try the balcony trick again. He only had to get past Sakimoto and through the bite.

He hauled to his feet the man he'd head butted. He groaned. Novak dragged him into the room, trying not to collapse under the weight of ice. Sakimoto punched Novak, but he put his head down, letting Sakimoto connect with the hardest part of Novak's forehead. The knuckles popped. The second punch staggered him. Black crept into his vision.

Novak pulled some strength from the infection's claws and threw the man through the glass door. It shattered. The man hit the balcony, still as death.

Sakimoto punched Novak again.

At the doorway, more of Sakimoto's men were trying to get inside, but something was distracting them.

Novak swung at Sakimoto again, but he ducked aside. Too fast. He punched Novak in the kidney. If he had been feeling better, that would have hurt. He smiled at that.

Sakimoto stood just before the threshold, in front the still body of his friend. The rain blew in around his shoulders. His face, deadly serious.

"Boss!"

Novak glanced.

Pulaski knocked a man aside to get into the room. His sword was still sheathed; he was using the whole thing as a club. A mixture of terror and relief mainlined into Novak's heart. Pulaski would defend him right up to the point that he saw the missing finger.

Novak lunged at Sakimoto. He would pin Sakimoto down and open him up. Control him, break him, own him. The claws dug deep and Novak stumbled, his body constricting.

Sakimoto was impossibly light, dancing aside, grabbing the outstretched arm and putting his body in the way. Novak lost his feet. The world spun.

He was airborne, breaking through rain. He saw the balcony shoot upward.

He reached for something, anything. He found nothing.

Then, Pulaski was jumping off the balcony above him, the sword naked now, crazy grin plastered all over his face. For a second, Novak was certain Pulaski knew. This was the end.

The ground slammed into his back, pushing the air out of his lungs in a frosty plume.

Pulaski landed in a crouch a few feet away.

The rain filled Novak's eye sockets as he waited for the sword to come down.

"Might want to get up, boss. Shit's about to hit the fan."

Novak wiped away the water, like tears.

The geeks had spotted them.

- 18 -

THERE WERE JUST NORTH OF thirty of them. Heads turned, mouths open, eyes empty. Among them was his rotting valentine, just turned from where it had been probing the back wall of the Athena.

He tried to pretend that the fall hadn't stunned him. His back felt like it had been skinned. His joints burned in time with his pulse. His head pounded with the twin howls of storm and blood.

And there was still the closing swarm.

Pulaski let out a little laugh. "They look hungry."

Above them, Sakimoto looked down from the balcony. He looked like he wanted to say something, but he just shook his head and got out of the rain. *Fuck him.*

Novak was finally on his feet.

Pulaski decapitated the closest geek, then advanced two steps through the shit-smelling mud and cut the next one up. On a good day, the two of them could carve through every geek in the courtyard, but with Novak in the shape he was in, the geeks could surround and overwhelm with ease. Not that Pulaski thought about that for an instant.

Novak felt a hand on his collar, cold skin, strangely dry even as it was soaked through. He turned on the geek as it dipped its head in for a carnivorous kiss. The hammer broke its forehead and the hatchet finished it off.

Pulaski had advanced to the edge of the cornfield that used to be the swimming pool. Six geeks were about two drunken steps from him. The rest were moving in for the kill, cutting off avenues of escape without even knowing they were doing it.

The rain tried to pound Novak back into the mud; the wind tried to throw him back into the Athena.

"Pulaski!"

"Yeah, boss?" He split one.

"Make for the south side!" He lurched forward, back to the corner of the Athena he had navigated during his trip over the balconies. The geeks weren't fast; but then, neither was he. The infection dragged on him, worse than the mud, worse than the rain, worse than the wind.

Pulaski was first. Novak wished Pulaski were Stew. Stew always fought smart; taking geeks on one at a time whenever he could, sprinting from geek to geek to keep from getting outnumbered. Not Pulaski. He wanted the long odds. He stepped into empty spots between two geeks and let them come to him. Slow as hell, daring the ones behind them to catch up. At least with his attention on the geeks, he might not notice Novak's missing finger.

"Move your ass!" Novak shouted.

"Not with you dragging yours." Pulaski cut into two more.

For a second, Novak thought about being in the lobby, when he was the lion and Rippey's men the hyenas. It didn't work under the sky. Pulaski and Novak might be lions, but the geeks didn't know about things like fear. They didn't even know how not to be hungry. They were closer to locusts, fires, or floods. The utterly inhuman that only has death inside it.

He was twenty feet from the corner of the Athena, where the collapsed fence formed a ramp out into the rolling green hills. There were only three geeks between that goal and the two living men. He didn't want to look around to see what was behind them.

The sloshing doom-laden drag was enough.

Pulaski stepped between all three geeks. Just then, he slipped on the slick mud. Just a little stumble, but sometimes that was enough. They were all ready to fall on him and get to work.

Novak forced himself into the wind, throwing himself at the closest.

Novak liked to think the geek was confused. It was wearing an old business suit, stained brown from mud and blood, tattered at wrist and ankle. He grabbed it by the lapels and threw. It never left the ground, staggering back, before slipping and falling against the outer fence.

He turned back. One of the bastards gripped Pulaski's arm, and he barely fended off the other one.

Novak grabbed the one attached to Pulaski and yanked it backward. It lost its grip and hit the wall of the Athena.

Pulaski killed the third.

"Come on!"

Pulaski didn't even look rattled. The shit-eating grin stretched across his face and, for a moment, Novak thought he was going back for seconds. He stepped on the collapsed fence and stumbled over it. There was nothing between them and the cliff now, except some stubborn scrub. A single geek probed the defenses. It attacked, but Pulaski and Novak dropped it with one swing each.

Ahead, the slope was steep and the rain had pounded the grass into a single, slick surface.

"Looks like a water slide," Pulaski said.

Novak wished he hadn't been thinking the same thing, but he took some comfort that he wasn't happy about it. He'd been hanging out with Pulaski entirely too long. He chanced a look back; the geeks were having trouble with the collapsed fence. One had made it over but immediately fell, and was trying to get up on the other side. The others hadn't figured out to step on the thing.

Only a matter of time before they created one of their army ant structures of undead bodies. Along the Athena's south wall, there were a few geeks, but most were trying to join the swarm at the gates.

Novak turned back to Devon. The place was dotted with them.

Pulaski's water slide was a risk, but Hotel Street was clogged with the bastards. No way Novak and Pulaski could make it more than fifty feet down.

"Boss?"

"Down the hill."

"Hoping you'd say that."

Pulaski went first. At least this section of the grass was clean of the undead: too steep for the clumsy bastards. They waited at the bottom of the hill, stepping onto the slope only to slide right back down.

Some of the geeks at the top had seen Novak. They were already coming, arms out. No time like the present. Novak took a step onto the slope and nearly went tumbling down it. The grass formed a mat, somehow woven by the wind and glued by the rain. He picked his way down it, three steps, then four. He could see the halfway point. A geek tumbled past him; it would be waiting at the bottom with the others who had started lining up.

"Pulaski! Hug the cliff!"

Pulaski nodded and moved laterally ahead of Novak. The terrain was flatter next to the cliff, forming a lip that dropped to oblivion. Of course, a single gust of wind, a bad step, and they were memories. Not that Pulaski gave a fuck.

The geeks were restless. Behind him, some had predicted the move, or else they knew to stick with the flatter ground. They'd traced the lip of the slope and were moving toward the cliff.

Pulaski and Novak made it to the side. The wind wanted to push them into the bowl of Devon. They were maybe two steps from the edge. The slope ran downward, then back up over more rolling hills until it hit the tree-covered Hill. There was nowhere else he could think to go.

Farther down the slope, where it was gentler, some of the geeks were already picking their way up it. Worst case scenario, a dozen of them would make it to the lip, and both men would have to fight them while they fought the wind and rain. *No reason to think about that yet. Just think about taking another step.*

Pulaski ranged ahead.

Another geek tumbled past Novak into the grassy dell below. He tried to be optimistic that they were pulling a couple away from the Athena, but optimism didn't suit him now.

The first of the geeks stumbled toward Pulaski, but took a wrong step and fell off the cliff. With any luck, its skull would be shattered. Pulaski beheaded the next one, sending the body into Devon and the head into the Pacific.

Two more and the path was clear. Pulaski didn't bother looking back to him. The slope moved down into the bowl, where the geeks who couldn't make it up the slope had collected, hungry arms outstretched. Pulaski knew where he was going as soon as he saw it.

He sat down on his ass and slid down the slope.

Novak swore.

Pulaski crashed into the geeks at a good clip, sending them sprawling like tenpins. He bounced up to his feet, either unhurt or deep enough in shock that it didn't matter. He cut apart the two closest, and backed off until the other four had him dead to rights. Novak swore he heard the fucker laugh.

He tried to keep his feet on the way down. For a little while, he managed it, looking like he was surfing the hill. Then he tipped forward, overcompensated and landed hard on his ass. After that, he wasn't in control any more, if he ever was. He shouted a warning to Pulaski.

Pulaski glanced and stepped aside, slicing another geek up.

Novak bowled two of them over, coming to rest partway up the gentler slope ahead. There were a few more geeks on that, shambling forward for the fallen meal. He clambered to his feet, but three were on him by the time he stood up. He swore again. *Fucking Pulaski.*

He reared back to smash one in the forehead, but Pulaski's sword flashed in front, dropping that one. Novak turned, used the hatchet to take one off its feet and bashed the other in the forehead with the hammer. The one on the ground groped for Novak, trying to get some calf meat. He brained it.

"Where to, boss?" Pulaski said.

"Home."

"L.A.'s a bit of a walk!"

"Up the Hill, wiseass."

Pulaski grinned. His mascara was almost washed away entirely. Even the black tears were gone. He was just an ear-to-ear grin, having the time of his life. He nodded his head to some beat that only he could hear and ripped apart the two remaining geeks in the bowl.

A smallish swarm next to Hotel Street spotted Pulaski and Novak and stepped into the green fields. There were a few between them and the Hill. If Novak had been at full strength, they could have run past with no trouble, even putting a couple down as a bonus. As it was, they would be lucky if the thirty or so crossing from Hotel Street didn't catch up.

Above them, the clouds kept pissing rain. He looked up. For a moment, he saw faces, clear as day. Susan. Karen Harmon. Judy Bloch. Walter Calomiris and Robert Franklin. Angry, sad, disappointed. Eyes bored into him. He spat blood and turned his attention back to ground level.

Pulaski led the way up the slope. There was a small dip

downward, then an open area, and finally the Hill. "Okay, you showboat, think you can carve a path to the Hill without jumping around like an asshole?"

Pulaski grinned. "You gotta embrace this shit, boss."

"Little late for that," Novak muttered.

Pulaski didn't hear, or if he did, he pretended he didn't. He did obey, though, for the most part. Pulaski was a guy who would never find the lock step. He was a guy that leaned on instinct and talent, and couldn't be told differently. After all, it worked. And it would work, right up until the moment it didn't. If he was lucky, he'd die in that moment. If not, he'd end up like Novak. He would have hated coaching Pulaski but, he had to admit, Pulaski was the perfect man for his day and age.

He hacked them a path to the base of the Hill. They had maybe forty geeks on their asses, staggering across the green.

Novak lurched as fast as he could. He felt the drugs bleeding from his system. Every step was harder. Pretty soon, it was like walking through snot.

On the Hill, they could get lost in the trees. Maybe the geeks would lose interest if they saw something else. They'd fan out aimlessly in the absence of something to eat. Pulaski could pick them off on the way back, one by one. They wouldn't have to fight the swarm at once. He didn't give a fuck if that disappointed Pulaski.

At last, they slipped into the trees. The misting rain turned the carpet of pine needles into a polished floor. No crinkles, at least none that could he heard over the rattle of the rain. They could see shapes in the trees, just silhouettes in the twilight of the Hill. Up ahead, terrified bleating cut through the storm's racket. The Sorensen place.

They broke the tree line. Six geeks had descended on Jim Sorensen's house, battering at the back gate. The flock of goats was pinned against the back wall, unaware that their bleats drew the geeks.

Pulaski didn't wait. He dropped all six. The moves were simple, like he was trying to placate Novak. Pulaski sprung the latch on the gate. The goats could get out then, the geeks could get in. There was no good solution. At least this way the goats could run. Let Sorensen find them later. They didn't thank Pulaski. They shied from him as well. Not that Novak blamed them.

They both moved on.

Fifty feet from the Sorensen place was Pulaski's house. They made it to the back door without any other geeks spotting them. Pulaski opened the door and was inside.

Novak followed.

Pulaski ruffled his blond hair, spraying the hall a bit with raindrops, leading the way through the living room and into his bedroom. His bed was a mess. He checked the blinds. They were drawn tight. He sat down at a makeup table and lit two candles. The scent of the candles, made from rendered geek fat, infected the room.

Novak collapsed in a chair. It would be wet, but he couldn't feel it.

In the quiet gold light of the room, Novak curled his bad hand into a fist, wincing as the bite gnawed into him anew. This was the time Pulaski would notice, and when he did, there'd be a quicksilver flash and the end.

Pulaski wiped his face with a towel and blinked, then fixed his eyes on Novak's.

Novak tensed, ready to fight his man.

Then, Pulaski rummaged around on the table, selected some lipstick and got to work.

After a moment, Novak said: "Why do you do that?"

Pulaski pursed his lips. "Do what?"

"Wear makeup."

"Just something I always did."

"Bullshit. You did that back in the world, you'd have gotten your ass kicked."

Pulaski finished with the lipstick and carefully blotted it with a tissue. He looked around the table, at all the little metal tubes they'd scavenged over the years and selected one. "I did. I had three older sisters. They used to do this to me when I was little. Make me up, put me in their clothes kind of thing. Pissed my dad off, but it made Mom laugh. It was the only time my sisters paid attention to me. I was the little brat who was underfoot until they dressed me up. Then I was... I don't know. I was somebody."

He went to work on his eyes expertly. "I wore makeup to school one time. Got my ass kicked like you said. Then it was just at home, alone. I hid it through junior high and high school. Didn't tell my girlfriends about it. Probably get my ass dumped. Then this shit happened, and I figured that I might as well feel good."

Made about as much sense as anything else. "Fair enough."

Pulaski painted his eyelids purple and blue. The lipstick was a subtle pink that looked shot through with glitter.

Pulaski said: "So what about you?"

"Don't wear makeup."

"Not what I meant. Why do you break things?"

It was true. Novak liked to collect things: fine stemware, electronic appliances, models and figurines. Anything that was a relic of the old world. He threw them from the cliff onto the rocks. He had started it the first year they arrived in Devon and never stopped.

He smiled. The wound on his chin burned, and he reflexively touched it. No blood. That was something. "It feels right."

"Exactly. I figure we all got something like that, and now nobody can tell us not to. So we do it."

Novak thought about Calomiris on the roof. "Yeah. Gotta go a little crazy."

"Not about that. It's about being who we are."

Novak nodded. He let the silence fill the room along with the geek stink. He knew he had to tell the guy. Pulaski had saved his worthless life and had taken him to the Hill. Pulaski was one of his guys. If Pulaski came after Novak, he'd deal with that when it happened. Not before. He owed it to Pulaski to trust him that far.

Novak's voice broke, rusty: "I've been bitten."

The pause could have fit the whole Athena between them.

Pulaski said: "Yeah, I thought so."

"You knew?"

"Not exactly. But I thought maybe. I was hoping you had the flu or something."

"When? When I was dogging it over here?"

"Nah. When you didn't hand Craig Sakimoto his ass, I figured something was up."

Novak snorted. "That confident?"

"Fuck, yeah. At a hundred percent? You'd fuck that guy up."

"Maybe."

Pulaski considered his next question, but said it anyway. "When did it happen?"

Novak told the story. He left nothing out. Pulaski listened while he fixed his makeup, making the same faces Susan used to when she put hers on. Occasionally he'd catch Novak's eye in the mirror and nod.

When Novak was done, Pulaski said simply: "That's pretty fucked up."

"So where's that leave us?"

"You still haven't found the fucker that killed you. That's where it leaves us. We find that person and we put the hurt on him."

"And when I turn?"

"I give you the shortest fucking haircut of your life."

Novak nodded. Pulaski fluttered his eyelids at the mirror and stood. He picked up his sword, and Novak tensed, but Pulaski didn't draw.

Novak pulled himself to his feet.

Pulaski blew out the candles.

Novak lurched into Pulaski's kitchen.

"You hungry boss?"

Novak shook his head.

Pulaski went to his cupboard and stuffed his pack full of granola bars.

Novak glanced up at his house, up the Hill.

Pulaski said: "So, back to the Athena? Try to fight our way in?"

"First, I want to stop by my place."

"Why?"

Novak nodded up to it. "Because Dr. Bloch wouldn't have left a candle burning."

Pulaski followed Novak's gesture and saw the diffuse light barely peeking through the curtains.

- 19 -

THEY WENT OUT PULASKI'S FRONT door. Through the trees, shapes moved in the rainy twilight. Pulaski and Novak ran furtively, sticking close to the trees whenever they could.

The path was clear, paralleling the winding road that led up to the shelf where Novak's house stood. From here, the candlelight was more apparent, finding the cracks in Novak's blackout curtains to suck them in. The geeks hadn't spotted the light yet, it seemed. No idea why, but then no one was a hundred percent sure what attracted them or what their priorities were. Novak remembered Susan telling him that dogs prioritize scent over hearing and hearing over sight, the exact opposite of the way humans behave. Maybe geeks were like dogs, attracted to the scent of living humans: sweat, piss and blood, so that they ignored the smell of their own dead fat burning.

Crossing the street would be the most dangerous. Away from the cover of the trees for that ten foot stretch, then the short walkway to the house. He wished he'd been like some of his people and planted the front yard more densely. As it was, there were only the scrubby cannabis. He always figured he could scavenge what he needed and anyplace he could hide one of them could. It never dawned on him that he would fall on the other side of that debate.

He waited expectantly for the candlelight to suddenly go out. It didn't. He reckoned it was in the living room.

They raced through the rain to the door. Novak unlocked it quickly, picking speed over silence. Pulaski pushed past to be the first one in.

There was a scramble in the living room. Pulaski swore. Then a high-pitched and terrified groan erupted behind. Novak shut the door against it. Hopefully the rain would drown that out.

For some reason, the first thing he saw in the dim yellow light was the whiskey bottle next to his chair. The second thing was the kid that Pulaski held by the shoulders. The kid looked maybe twelve years old. Novak blinked. He knew that kid. He'd seen him hours before, but he'd vanished. At the time, he'd thought he was seeing things. "Holy shit. It's you." Not the smartest thing he'd ever said.

Pulaski said: "You know this boy?"

The kid's face and clothes were streaked with mud. His hands and mouth boasted patches of lighter brown, and one look at the candy bar wrappers next to the chair told Novak what that was. The kid's eyes were as big as softballs, going from Pulaski to Novak and back again. Novak moved his hands away from his weapons.

"It's okay. We're not gonna hurt you."

Pulaski put his body between the kid and the door to the kitchen, and only then did he let go of the kid's collar. The kid's eyes flicked back and forth between them.

Novak said: "You gonna run?"

The kid thought about it, then shook his head.

"Good. The Hill's crawling with geeks. You wouldn't make it five feet." Novak settled down on the sofa and Pulaski took a step back. For a moment, Novak thought he could smell Judy Bloch's scent, woman cut with iodine, on the couch. That was probably wishful thinking. "Sit down. Finish your candy bar." There was a half-finished Butterfinger on the end table. Novak's saliva faucet turned on, but an angry stomach clenched.

The kid reached toward the candy bar, stopped and checked on the strangers. They hadn't moved. He grabbed the candy bar and tore into it. He'd taste the chocolate first, then the peanut butter part that'd get lodged in his molars. Novak turned away, briefly, then faced him again.

"I'm Mr. Novak. That's Mr. Pulaski."

"Dave," Pulaski said.

The kid took that in.

Novak said: "Kid, I don't know you. Where do you live? Town? The Athena?"

The kid's face was blank.

"The Athena. The hotel up on top of the hill."

The kid stopped, frozen in some imaginary headlights.

"The Athena?" Novak persisted.

The kid shook his head.

"Okay, enough with the mute routine. What's your name?"

The kid swallowed. Thought about it. Managed a whisper that Novak scarcely believe was real: "Skyler."

"Skyler, okay." Poor kid. "Where are you from?"

"I... I came in today."

"You're one of the nomads? What the hell are you doing in my house? Why aren't you with them?"

The kid tensed to run, but Pulaski grabbed his collar. The kid freaked out, flailing at Pulaski like in a tantrum.

Pulaski said: "What the fuck?"

Novak had some experience. The kid was younger than those he used to corral, but he could give it a shot. He grabbed the kid by the shoulders and received two weak roundhouses to the side of the head. He dropped his voice to a harsh whisper. "Skyler! Calm down, son! It's okay! You're safe here. You're safe as long as you stay with us. As long as you're quiet, you're safe. Got me?"

Novak earned two more swings that thudded off his head.

After the fall from the Athena and the hammer in his side, he could take Skyler's flailing all day. With each swing, they got softer. The boy was coming to his senses, drawn in on the tether of Novak's voice. He kept up the promises until Skyler's eyes were open and his arms were at his sides. The kid was small, smaller than he would have been in the old days. All kids were. In a generation or three, everyone would be the size of Barrett Cheeseman.

"You understand, Skyler? Safe. I'm not going to let anything happen to you."

Finally, the kid nodded.

"Tell me what's going on. You don't tell me, I can't help you."

Skyler glanced from Novak to Pulaski.

Novak wished Pulaski wasn't wearing makeup like a freak. Of course, he realized he was clammy and pale and probably a little more desperate than he should have been. He took a breath and got ready to be hit again.

"Did something happen in the hotel?"

The kid was a statue. He could see the gears whirring past Skyler's eyes. Skyler would have to come to Novak on his own. Push too hard and the kid would shatter. Neither one of them really had the time for it, but this kid was a blank slate. He had the chance not to hurt the boy.

Finally, a nod. Really just the ghost of a nod. Like he had to push it through a haze of memory, knowing it was there without going back.

Novak said: "What?"

Skyler just pointed. One finger, crusted in dirt and chocolate, at his belly. He wore a windbreaker, zipped up, still covered in barely dried mud.

Novak waited.

Skyler pulled the zipper down to reveal a white shirt with the Incredible Hulk on the front, smashing both meaty fists into the ground. As the zipper parted over his belly, right where Hulk was pounding a fissure into the ground: blood.

It blossomed over Skyler in an impact flower. Novak didn't recoil. The shirt wasn't torn, so the blood wasn't the kid's. Novak tried to see the whole thing. The stains on the thighs of his blue jeans: they looked like mud. Had they been there when Novak saw Skyler on the Hill? He thought so. Maybe. They were streaked, dripped and spattered. Not mud, blood. A closer look at his hands, at his arms, showed Novak more streaks of brownish red.

Walter fucking Calomiris. There was something there. Novak wasn't sure what. His mind picked at the edges of the thing, not quite able to take it all in. He remembered when the nomads arrived; he was at Franklin's place with Ford and Pisspants. They'd heard the engines, then they had...

No. Novak found the memory and wrung it. Pisspants had reacted as soon as the sun got up over the eastern hills. He had reacted, and then they had heard the sounds of the engines. Pisspants knew the nomads would arrive around sunrise.

Which meant that Rippey knew. It fit with the grandstanding that seemed fake. They had a deal. But Calomiris had taken them in.

And Rippey had barely put up a fight.

Had that been the plan all along? Had the nomads been a fifth column that Calomiris sniffed out?

Another memory fell into place. Rippey had wanted to show Novak something. He'd been surprised when Calomiris was still alive. That was it. The nomads, probably that big bastard Novak had taken down, were to kill Walter Calomiris. They had failed. Maybe slowed down by the hurt Novak had put on him.

Calomiris butchered them. But he hadn't stopped with the ones who had done it. He tried to kill them all, including this boy, but the boy had escaped.

The worst part was that Novak knew Calomiris had help.

There were people in the Athena who were party to that slaughter.

Pulaski said, "What's up, boss? You got a look like you know."

"I do. I wish I didn't."

"You gonna give me a primer?"

"With the rest of the guys." Novak stood. The room swam under him.

The only light in the dim place was the single candle. It seemed to collapse into that single point of gold. Novak fell into it. Warm. Safe.

He blinked. Pulaski's voice, bubbling up from the depths. Novak ignored it, staggered to the kitchen window. He parted the curtains slightly. From here, through the trees, he could look out into Town. A few geeks were in his field of vision, but all backs were to him, wandering downhill. He looked beyond them, squinting. A swarm had surrounded Gino's, already pulling in the few geeks that weren't around the Athena.

He closed the curtains before one of the geeks figured out that there was meat inside.

Skyler was trying to zip up his jacket to hide the pain. People trapped in Gino's versus Novak, Pulaski, and the kid. Getting them meant risking three lives. Meant risking the kid that Novak had already promised safety. Gino's wasn't equipped for a swarm that size. Novak knew that much. They were dead if they stayed in there. One hundred percent.

We might die. Easy equation when put like that.

Novak said: "Get your bike."

Pulaski grinned. "Gonna pull the fuckers to us? Take 'em that way? Hell, yeah, boss."

"Partly. People are trapped in Gino's. We should try to get them back to safety."

There were geeks to kill. Pulaski didn't care why. "How's this work, then?"

This old riddle popped into Novak's head. It was the one where a guy has a dog, a chicken, and a bag of grain and he needs to cross a river in a boat that only holds one at a time. The trick is to get across without the dog eating the chicken or the chicken eating the grain. Send Pulaski on distraction duty meant the kid couldn't go with him. Send Pulaski on the Gino's run meant he could get distracted and just start hunting geek. Whether Novak liked it or not, he had to move his sick ass.

"We go into Town. We split up at Hotel. You gun your engine and get every geek you can on your ass. I go into Gino's and get those people out and up to the Athena."

"Sounds like fun."

Yeah.

Pulaski slipped out the door.

Novak turned to Skyler. "It's not safe here, kid. It's not really safe anywhere, but it's safer with me. For now, anyway."

The kid watched him.

"Take as many candy bars as you want."

Not like Novak needed them.

The kid followed him out to the front, pockets stuffed with Butterfingers.

The sun was getting low beyond its cloud cover. Novak's bike rested against the side of the house. He pulled it up and mounted, motioning to Skyler. The kid climbed on and wrapped too skinny arms around Novak's waist.

Novak waited. Pulaski should be at his place. Novak waited a little longer. Pulaski should have been on his bike already.

He was about to do something he knew full well was stupid when he heard it: first a rumble, then a buzzsaw. Pulaski caught air before swooping down the Hill.

Novak started his and gunned it, following Pulaski on his suicide run. Skyler held on tighter.

The geeks on the road were turning, and Pulaski took a head off, laughing while he did it.

They broke the treeline and the rain pummeled them in the face. Geeks in Town turned their stupid ravenous heads and took the first drunken steps toward the bikes. They zoomed past Dr. Bloch's empty office. In front, the dead corpses of her pet geeks lay in the rain. One of the brainpans had filled with water that dribbled down the front of its fishbelly face.

Past that, and the bikes barreled into the intersection of Cliffside and Hotel. To the right, Hotel went toward the Barricade. First left was Beach and Gino's. Geeks were lightly dotted between the two swarms, pulled lightly in either direction by stimulus unknown. As soon as they heard the buzzing of the bikes, the geeks had their prey. Novak streaked past as Pulaski spun his bike in a circle and chundered partway into the muddy field near the Dinner Bell.

Novak burned down Cliffside, passing the still corpses of the geeks he and Sakimoto took out on the way up. Novak killed the engine at the corner of Reef and Cliffside. He had five geeks in his wake, and three more between him and Gino's that hadn't seen him yet. He hopped off and turned to Skyler.

"Stay close, kid."

Suddenly, the chainsaw buzzing of Pulaski's bike stopped. Novak swore under his breath. Had Pulaski already forgotten the plan? Then, Novak heard it.

He nearly burst out laughing.

"Thriller."

He remembered the day he and Stew found Pulaski. Like a dancing blender. He'd chop two up, pause do some dance moves and get two more.

That's why he took so long at the house. He was getting his fucking stereo.

Novak turned back to Skyler and nearly burst out laughing again. He didn't think the kid was ever so confused in his life. He looked like a dog hearing his master's voice on an answering machine. He thought about trying to explain to Skyler, but explaining Pulaski would take too goddamn long.

"Come on, kid. That's our distraction."

They slipped around the corner from the five that were following them. Novak hoped for an out of sight out of lack of mind situation. Maybe the dulcet tones of Michael Jackson would keep the geeks busy. The three that were joining the swarm had turned toward Hotel and Pulaski. Novak dropped two without trouble before the third saw him and lunged. Novak crunched its head with the hammer. A look toward Skyler assured him he was okay. He even seemed to like watching Novak kill geeks. That boded well for their relationship, brief though it would be.

The swarm around Gino's was four deep at the doors and windows, but only one deep in other spots. With geeks, everything was the snowball effect. "Thriller" pulled one away, then two, two more, then they were leaving in threes and fours. They thinned out on the Hotel Street side of Gino's faster than those on the parking lot. Novak tried to will the people inside to stay quiet. *Don't give the geeks a reason to stick around.* Let them go try and chew on Pulaski for a while.

By the time the swarm thinned out to a point where Novak thought he had a fifty-fifty chance to make it through, Pulaski's radio was playing Duran Duran. Apparently, it was a mix tape.

Novak brained the geek in front of the door. Another turned. It took the hatchet to the forehead. He yanked. The hatchet was stuck. He bashed another across the face, planted a foot on the head of the axed one and pulled. The hatchet came free with chunks of bloodless flesh.

He whispered as loud as he dared: "It's me! Open up!"

The geeks along the wall had forgotten all about Pulaski. Now they had eyes on a ready food source: Novak and the kid.

He banged on the door. "I'm breathing goddamn it, open up!"

If all the geeks surrounded them, they didn't have a prayer.

Novak banged on the door again. He might as well have opened a vein and put his arm to the wind. The first one got to him. After that, it'd be in twos, then more, then more, and then nothing at all. He felt Skyler's hand on his belt, holding on like that would help. He hated himself for bringing the kid. He wouldn't have lasted in Novak's house, but he wouldn't have gone this way.

He smashed the skull of the first geek.

Skyler's hand pulled away. Novak turned, ready to break a head, and saw the door open. Nuñez was inside and pulled Skyler into the darkness. Nuñez said: "Glen, come on!"

Novak slipped through the door and helped Nuñez slam and barricade it. The room was dark except for a few candles that burned their rank scent. Skyler was in the arms of Gloria Wu. Nuñez held a bloody axe handle. Robert Franklin was slumped by the door, the slick blood down his cracked face turned gold in the candlelight.

They were the only ones in the room. *Fuck.* For two people, Novak had risked three. Two, actually, and one of those was a kid. Not a fair trade at all.

Gloria Wu, confused: "Novak?"

"Yeah. What the hell are you doing here?"

She grit her teeth. "Jack sent me in here. To get the Reverend."

"Rippey's not in here."

"I know that. Now. The little..." She paused, worked up to it and spat it out, "*effer* was trying to get me killed!"

"Nice to have some company." Novak turned to Nuñez. "What about you?"

"Went back for my pack. Found Gloria and Rob already in here. Rob'd been bitten."

"Sorry to hear it." He was. Another person he couldn't possibly make anything up to.

"What are you doing here? You didn't make it to the Athena either?"

"I made it. Then I came back out."

Nuñez shook his head. "You got *cojones*, man, but they're gonna get chewed off."

"Bullshit. We're going to the Athena." He checked the room. The shuttered windows were letting in a little light from where the geeks had pounded through. Gino's would be a cracked egg soon enough.

Gloria said: "What, now? We're surrounded."

"We have some support."

His eyes drifted toward the bar where the bullet had marked its futile furrow. He stood where Booker had stood in the wee hours. Novak marked his seat, Pulaski's seat. He marked the path of the bullet. Booker was a shitty shot. A really shitty shot.

Nuñez said: "Something wrong?"

"Yeah. I mean, no. No, nothing important. We have to get out of here."

"What makes you think we can make it?" Gloria said.

"Not a whole hell of a lot. Just that I know if we stay, we're dead. I'll take the chance over the certainty, right? Maybe you could drop a prayer to what's-his-name if you don't like the odds."

Gloria scowled, but she nodded.

Nuñez went behind the bar and lifted up a pack. He looked to the collection of Donald Ducks. After careful consideration, he selected one and put it in his pack. Novak considered asking, but didn't. Nuñez nodded. "Lead on."

"When that door opens, we have to blitz through. Like a defensive line. If we get hung up, we're meat."

The two men took point. They lifted the barricade on a whispered three count, and then shoved the doors.

A geek backpedaled, but two more surged forward. Novak dropped his shoulder and hit his geek square in the gut, while Nuñez swung his axe handle in a wide arc, dropping the other geek with sheer leverage. Gloria and Skyler ran between them to the open ground of the parking lot.

Novak staggered to keep up with them, limping on a suddenly bad ankle. The rain cut visibility some, but he could still see the Athena looming large at the apex of Hotel Street.

As they ran down Reef, Gloria said: "What's that?"

Novak listened. The sounds of Pulaski's music drifted through the rain. "Toto, I think."

He wished he had a Polaroid of her expression.

"Go north. Do you know where Franklin's farm is?"

She said: "We're taking that slope? It's going to be slippery!"

"No geeks that way. We'll be clear up to the east side of the Athena, and which should have less geeks than all the others. Get to Franklin's farm as quick as you can. I need to get my guy."

Skyler reached for Novak. He gently disengaged from the kid. "Stay with them for now. Trust me, kid."

Gloria folded her arms over Skyler's skinny chest. The rain seemed to mold them together into one miserable creature.

Novak turned away and tried to run. He made it to the short hill he'd taken earlier on his first retreat to the Athena.

The street was free of moving geeks. When he hit Hotel Street, he gasped.

Pulaski was thirty feet from his bike and boom box. A trail of dead geeks marked the path. The swarm reached for him like a single living organism. He had even pulled a few geeks from the Athena that were cutting off his fighting retreat. It didn't look like he was aware of them at all.

Even from that distance, Novak could see the huge smile on Pulaski's face. He couldn't win this fight and he knew it, but he was still fighting. He wasn't fighting because Novak had told him to. Pulaski wasn't fighting because he wanted to save anyone. He was fighting because that's what he loved. He would happily stay there, ankle deep in mud and grass, sending the undead back to the dirt until they dragged him down.

"Pulaski!"

He didn't hear. Novak was pretty sure Pulaski was singing along to the blasting music. He called Pulaski's name again. This time, he did hear, along with some of his friends. He waved Pulaski over. But Pulaski shook the wave off. Novak waved again and cursed under his breath.

Pulaski sighed. He cut the head from a geek almost as an afterthought and started to run. Of course, running through that field was closer to running through syrup, but he was game. Novak turned and started his own loping stagger, like he was a relay runner ready to get the hand off. Pulaski made it to Novak before he was even down the hill.

"Where's the others?"

"Franklin's farm," Novak gasped out.

The first of the geeks appeared at the apex of the short hill leading down to Cliffside as Pulaski and Novak disappeared into Town.

Novak tried to concentrate on the run, but his breath had razors in it. The whole time, they were drawing the geeks along with them like a trawler's net. As they ran, he reflected that, from a distance, the roles would appear reversed. The living humans ran with bent backs and loping strides like animals, while the geeks would appear human.

The small swarm that was still following was only a few streets behind. Novak dipped into Grant Duman's vineyards. The grapes would hide them, but that probably wouldn't stop the swarm. From there, Novak and Pulaski ducked through the necrosculptures in Borassi's yard. He couldn't stop the thought: *Will my bones be here tomorrow?*

It felt like hours before Franklin's farm was in sight. The fields looked empty, the soaking flags sputtering in the wind.

The Town buildings ended. They were in farmland, following the curve of the hill on the left. As soon as they reached the edge of Franklin's corn, they saw movement at the farmhouse. Pulaski had the sword out, but it was Nuñez, Gloria, and Skyler, advancing out of the porch, backs hunched against the rain.

"You made it," Nuñez said.

"Not quite. Still got the hill. And there's that." Novak pointed. The swarm boiled out of Town. If they stayed, they'd be hemmed in the bowl formed by the hills on all three sides. The small valley was already thrown into shadow, the sun falling behind the hotel.

The hill to the Athena was the steepest part. It wasn't vertical, but it looked it. He hoped they could use the grass to haul themselves up. Maybe they'd end up falling backward into the swarm with a handful of ripped green.

Had to chance it.

Pulaski took one look at the slope and knelt, back to the kid. "Get on." Skyler obeyed, and Pulaski started climbing, using the smaller of his swords as a piton.

Novak followed, with Nuñez and Gloria close behind.

The swarm entered the field.

Novak's fingers bit into the slick hill. He was getting sharp handfuls of something. He didn't want to think about what it was or what it was doing to his hands. He slammed his feet into the side of the hill. He had some purchase.

The swarm had gotten to the base of the hill, ten feet below him and Nuñez, twenty below Pulaski. Cracked hands reached upward. Rain splattered in open mouths. He thought about how turkeys supposedly drown in the rain because they look up and are too dumb to close their mouths. No such luck here.

They were halfway up the slope.

Below, the geeks tried to climb after them. One step, slide back down. One step, slide back down.

He turned to Nuñez. He smiled as they struggled up the hill. He allowed himself to think that they might actually make it. They were three quarters of the way up.

Then the sky opened up. The rain turned from a trickle to a goddamn downpour.

He clenched fingers in the mud. He started to slide.

He looked up. Pulaski hung off his sword, buried in the cliff. Somehow, Gloria Wu was stuck in place like a gecko. They were moving up and away.

Novak swore.

Nuñez turned, reached a hand out.

Novak tried to grab it, failed.

Below, the geeks reached for him.

The rain kicked up more. A mudslide tore down the slope to his left, right at Nuñez. He didn't see it. Novak shouted a warning, but it was too late. The mud hit Nuñez in the face and he toppled backward as it tore him from the hill.

The rain didn't drown out the ripping sounds.

Novak hacked into the slope. He had no strength in his arms or legs. He forced them to move. One at a time, slam a limb into the slope and pull himself up.

He didn't know he was at the summit until he reached up and found nothing. He collapsed into the mud.

Hands hauled at his collar. He nearly attacked, but saw it was Pulaski. "Come on, boss. We still need a way in."

The ledge along the east side of the Athena was narrow. One

person could walk it, maybe two if they were midgets. There were few geeks—they were swarming creatures, like insects. Most would join the swarm at the gates or would be headed to Franklin's farm. The few that were on the ledge turned to the small group of humans, but Pulaski sent their headless bodies back down to the swarm that claimed Nuñez.

The windows were shut on this side of the hotel. His people would be on the other side of the wall. Might as well have been in the heart of a swarm.

He lurched toward the northern end. On that side, it was a series of cliffs, finally leading down into the Pacific. Another wall ran along the few parts of the cliff that weren't completely impassable. Every now and then, a geek would get stuck in some elbow of the wall, but before long it would find its way onto the rocks below.

Gloria Wu and Skyler were just behind him. Pulaski kept up the rear. They hugged the side of the hotel, out of the wind and rain for a short time.

"Novak! Are you all right?" If he didn't know better, he would have thought there was concern on Gloria's face.

"Been better." He tried the same lie he'd been trying all day. "Got the flu."

He didn't know if she believed him. Even if she didn't, there wasn't anything she could do. They couldn't stop. He couldn't get rest and plenty of fluids. And if it was a bite, she didn't have a weapon. She held Skyler close to her, fear perhaps endowing her with some maternal instincts.

The corner loomed ahead. He knew it was going to be bad. He turned left and the full force of the storm slammed into him. He dug his feet into the mud and leaned into it, the individual raindrops as sharp and cold as diamonds. Ahead, the gray clouds strangled the dying sun. The ocean tossed, angry. He saw limbs in the water, reaching upward, white mouths gaping. The cliff shelves seemed to stretch to infinity below. If he fell, he would keep falling—perhaps forever. He'd be cold and wet and half-dead forever.

Half-dead! I've finally become an optimist.

He felt a hand on his shoulder. He almost swung round to bash a geek, but it was Gloria. The hand was too gentle to be anything else. She held on, using Novak as a windbreak. He didn't have to look. He knew she'd have Skyler between them. The north wall was short; from there, they would make another left and find themselves on the edge of the courtyard.

The fence that once guarded the guests from the cliff had collapsed and now dangled over the edge. Geeks staggered through the courtyard on the other side where Novak had made his escape earlier. Some seemed lost. Hunger and the wind had pressed the others against the wall of the Athena. There were doors on the ground floor, but they were effectively barricaded, and in some cases welded shut.

The balconies on the second floor were empty, the sliding glass doors closed.

In the courtyard: maybe fifty geeks in all. He laughed as he spotted his "girl" immediately. Its back was to him, as it scratched its fingers on the hotel bar door. She was too far to end. Good thing, too. Waste of a precious bullet.

A look at Pulaski said he wanted to take them on. It was possible he'd dropped that many outside, but he had a place to back up. Here, in the courtyard, there was only a cliff and a hundred feet below, the ocean. Fighting them was suicide.

Novak didn't know what did it, but one of the geeks turned. It was his rotting valentine, of course. That one knew him, and wouldn't rest until it chewed his soft parts into mush. It fixed its good eye on him, and took a wobbly baby step forward.

After the first one turned, then the second one did. Then the third, the fourth, the fifth. It was now only a matter of time.

He looked up to the second floor. Might as well. They'd already been seen. Fifty geeks were coming whether they liked it or not.

"Hey! Anybody! Help! Come on!"

Gloria whispered harshly: "What the hell do you think you're doing?"

"We're already spotted. Keeping mum isn't going to get us less spotted."

Pulaski laughed. "The lesser spotted humans!" Then he shouted: "Come and get some!"

Gloria shouted: "Anyone! Help! Please!"

The geeks were twenty feet off.

He and Gloria kept yelling.

Then ten.

A sliding glass door on the second floor opened, just visible through the first wall of geeks. It was Jackson Harmon.

Fuck.

Gloria kept screaming. Novak swallowed his voice for a moment, then spat it out with his pride. "Harmon! Help!"

Harmon disappeared back inside.

Novak cursed him.

"Where's he going?" Gloria said.

He didn't have time to explain his history with the man. Instead, he braced for the first wave of geeks.

Pulaski stepped in, a huge grin on his face, the rain tapping off his sword.

"I think we can take 'em," he said.

- 20 -

THE SWARM STAGGERED CLOSER, BLINDLY intent on consuming the living.

"Novak!" It was Harmon voice, above and behind them.

Novak turned.

Harmon was on the balcony of the room closest to the corner. He threw a comforter over the side, holding onto one end. That was a tough piece of fabric. No question it could hold one person.

Gloria ran to it. He thought she was going to grab it, but instead she held Skyler up as high as she could. She whispered something, but he couldn't make it out. The kid's little hands grabbed hold of the comforter. Harmon hauled Skyler up and in, shouting into the room. Karen and Michelle, his wife and daughter, joined him at the window. Karen took Skyler in her arms as Harmon threw the blanket down again.

Gloria was next. They hauled her in without trouble.

The geeks had made it to him and Pulaski.

Pulaski hacked into them.

Novak looked for his "friend" in the bathrobe, but it had vanished into the press of bodies.

He told Pulaski: "Go on!"

"Fuck that, boss. You first!"

"I'm dying, you dumb fuck!"

"We're all dying. You're just gettin' it done quicker."

"Asshole." He grabbed the comforter and tried to haul himself up, but his arms were rubber. He heard Harmon grunting at the top. He looked up: Gloria and Michelle had joined him, straining against the comforter, hauling him in inch by aching inch.

At the top, Harmon grabbed the back of Novak's belt and heaved him in. He tumbled onto his head, breathing into the rain. "That was close," he gasped.

Ignoring him, Harmon shouted down to Pulaski: "Now you! Let's go!"

Novak got to his feet, forced his hands on the comforter.

Pulaski grabbed hold with one hand.

They pulled.

The geeks grabbed for him. Hands snaked around Pulaski's ankles. Mouths went to take a bite. The dumb bastard was about to die.

Novak pulled his gun and put the last two bullets of his clip into a pair of geeks.

Harmon got his hand on Pulaski, and they were all on the balcony.

Below, fifty geeks reached upward for food and went hungry.

Pulaski grabbed his crotch. "Next time, pig-fuckers!" He turned back, slapped Harmon's hand and ruffled Michelle's hair. "You want me to go back out later? I'll pick up some shit from my place for you guys."

Michelle mumbled, turning bright red. "It's cool."

Harmon said: "Rain check. If we make it out of this."

"We'll make it," Pulaski said. "Not all of us. Most, though."

Gloria Wu stood in the room, just out of the rain. "Thank you. All of you." She said this with eyes on Novak, face unreadable.

He nodded to her.

She said: "I need to have a word with Jack Finger."

"Give him one for me, too."

She smiled at that, and was gone.

Novak couldn't avoid it: "Thanks," he said. He kept his head so low that the top of his spine might have been his tallest point. He didn't want to picture Harmon's face in his head, but he did. He went through the gamut. He saw Harmon smug, saintly, and seething. Then he saw the worst one of all: blank. Not caring whether he lived or died. Harmon hauled Novak up because that's just what people are supposed to do. They don't demand rewards. They don't assume the rules changed just because everything else did.

He hated Harmon. He owned Novak now. Save a life, own a life. Part of Novak wanted to throw the other man over the side. At least then, he wouldn't have to deal with the facts. If he hadn't been so weak, he might have surrendered to that base instinct and fed a good man to the swarm.

He lurched through the glass door, coughing into his bad hand. It stank like it had been dead for days. *But it was not even a day...* The rainwater fell off him in waves. He might have been carrying another ten pounds in water alone. He smiled at that: water weight was what you cut before wrestling matches. He wouldn't have time to sweat it off, he couldn't run it off. It was a little late for all of that.

He heard Karen speaking. He thought it was directed to him, but it was far away and he couldn't really hear her. He made it out into the hall before his legs decided they were done with him. He fell back into the wall and forced wind into his lungs.

"Fuck me, boss, you looked like burned shit." Pulaski would have looked concerned if he was capable of that kind of thing.

"Go get the guys. And Dr. Bloch. I'm going in there." Novak pointed to a room to his left, one of those on the north-westernmost point of the Athena.

"Okay, boss."

After a moment, Karen Harmon and Skyler stepped into the hall. Skyler immediately disengaged from her and took cover behind Novak. The old story about the little boy who brought a baby bird home: *Sorry, Mom, I handled him and now his real mother won't take him back.*

"He wants to go with you," Karen said.

"Yeah, I know."

"You don't look so good."

"Don't sound so happy."

She was silent for a moment. Finally: "I'm not."

He looked into her tired face. He didn't know what he expected to see, or even hoped to. Love was out of the question. Stockholm Syndrome was the closest he and she would ever get to that. Affection, maybe. In the new world, that might have been possible. Hatred. Disgust. Pity. Acceptance. There were no easy answers in her eyes. Everything overlaid one another until they were full of so many things battling for dominance. Maybe she felt all of those things at once for Novak, for her, for the world. He didn't know. He couldn't know. He wanted something clean and easy, but that died with the world.

Instead: "Take care of him," she said.

"I will."

She disappeared back inside. No forgiveness, no rage.

He strode unsteadily to the door he'd indicated to Pulaski, mustered some strength from somewhere and kicked it in.

The room was empty. The door hung askew on its hinges. It creaked half-shut. He settled down on the bed and let the rain turn to mildew under him.

Skyler settled down between wall and bed.

Novak lost track of time in the swimming ceiling but, sometime later, the door creaked open. He half-heartedly put his hand on his gun before remembering the stupid thing was empty.

It was Stew, Robellada, Pulaski, and Dr. Bloch. Everyone was concerned, except Robellada who just looked scared. Novak guessed how he must appear to them, and didn't want to think about it. He touched the wound on his chin and didn't find a scab, just a loose flap of skin, tacky with rain. Pain bloomed along his face.

He winced and made himself sit up. The room bled around him. He heard the geeks scratching below. His vision swam, blurred. He saw them reaching for him out of the Pacific. He saw the rain turn to pus.

Dr. Bloch set a stinking geek candle on the bedside table.

Stew said: "Oh, God."

Dr. Bloch sat on the bed on his left. She made a noise.

He looked at his hand. Pus, greenish and dead, had wept through the bandage, out of the leather glove, and had stained the coverlet.

She didn't touch his hand. The damn thing weighed five tons.

"Hey, boys," he said. "This is Skyler."

Skyler watched them with the hunted suspicion of a cat that has seen the kitty carrier. He didn't bolt. He knew the two men who protected him on the way to the Athena, and there was something coded deep into human DNA about pregnant women. Dr. Bloch smiled at him. Skyler seemed to calm.

Novak tried to hear his heart slow down. He couldn't hear it at all.

"Glen? What did you want to tell us?" Stew's voice was tender. He knew. Hell, they all knew. Still, he felt he had to say it.

They had arrayed themselves at the foot of the bed, Stew in the middle, Pulaski on the right, Robellada on the left.

"I've been bitten."

Stew and Robellada didn't look surprised. Stew's eyes crinkled. Robellada studied the floor.

He told them how it happened. He told them what he had done. He told them what he had left to do. They took it in silently.

When he was done, Stew said, "What now?"

"I find out who killed me. Kill them. Then... you know."

"You shouldn't go anywhere. Glen, you can't see yourself right now. We can do what has to be done. We'll finish it for you."

"Come on, Stew. You know I can't let you do that."

Stew chuckled, but a sob thickened it. "You know I had to say it."

He looked at his guys. "One way or another, I'm dead before sunrise. When that happens, I know you'll all do the right thing."

They all nodded, even if Robellada couldn't look at Novak. He felt bad for the kid. He probably thought of Novak as a constant like the Barricade. Good a way as any to learn there's no such thing.

"When I go, Stew's in charge. No ifs, ands, or buts, got it? Stew, Pulaski's your number one."

Pulaski and Stew sized each other up. Maybe they would argue when Novak was in the ground, but not at that moment. Stew stuck his hand out first and Pulaski took it.

Novak said: "Pulaski, give me your word."

"You got it, boss. Chris is the man. I know." He turned to Stew. "My word on it."

"Thanks, Dave," Stew said.

Novak forced a laugh. "You two don't have to make out or nothing."

Pulaski grinned and Stew wiped his left eye. He gestured at Skyler. "Who's he? Kind of young for a notary."

"This is where it gets fucked up," Novak said.

"Oh, *this* is where it gets fucked up." Dr. Bloch laughed from her position at his bedside.

"Skyler arrived with the nomads this afternoon."

Stew nodded. "Right, the ones Calomiris settled in the Athena. Where are they, anyway? Oh... goddamn." The realization pinned him and he looked at Skyler in horror. "Please tell me I'm wrong."

Novak said: "You're not. Calomiris and Inez, maybe both of them, had all the nomads killed."

Dr. Bloch said: "Motherfuck. Why? We're fucking dying out. If nothing else, they could have added to our gene pool, which is gonna get really shallow."

"Rippey was using them to assassinate Calomiris. But he figured it out, killed them all. Women and children, too."

Stew said: "Why fight to get them if he was just going to kill them?"

"Best way to get them where he wanted them. Plus, he was crazy." He told them how.

Stew showed disgust and shook his head. "He couldn't have done it alone."

"His guys. Maybe Inez. I was thinking about her too. For all of it. The head in the footlocker, pitting me against Calomiris, like this is all part of some fucked-up power play."

Stew said: "For her or Reverend Rippey?"

"Looks like I have to talk to both of them." Novak tried to sit up, but the walls melted and the bed fell away. He nearly screamed, but swallowed it.

Dr. Bloch put her hand on his chest. "Get some rest at least."

"No time for that. We both know it."

She closed her eyes.

"You got any more of those pills?"

She nodded.

"I'll trade you my house."

She smiled. "Yeah? You gonna bring it in here?"

"Sure I will. I just have a couple errands to run first."

She rummaged in her pack and gave him another handful of pills. "Here."

He managed to sit up. Stew put his arm out to help him. "Fuck off, Stew." He backed off. Novak got to his feet. The ground swam under him. He sat down at the table across from Pulaski and put the pills in front of him. He took the sledgehammer in hand. Old geek flesh was caked on the scarred head. He carefully crushed the pills into dust.

Pulaski handed him a dollar bill. The George Washington had been defaced into Zorro, wearing a domino mask, a sombrero, and a dirt 'stache. Novak rolled it into a tube.

"You shouldn't do that," Dr. Bloch said.

"I can't eat any more."

The sound she nearly swallowed was pure despair.

He inhaled through the tube. The powder hit his brain like a heavyweight punch.

He hoped that was enough juice for the endgame.

- 21 -

HE LET THE PILLS FLOOD his limbs with phony fire. The candle had turned the window into a burning mirror. He didn't want to look into it. His guys watched everything except him. Even Pulaski fiddled with the short sword in his hands to avoid looking at him.

The room seemed darker than it should. The borders of the candle's fitful light turned to black. He was in a tunnel with only the burning geek fat to give him guidance.

He knew he couldn't ask his guys to come with him. He hoped they would come without his asking. He hoped he deserved that much loyalty.

He got to his feet. His knees ached and stabbed at his vitals and nearly gave out. He took an experimental step. He felt like he was walking on jagged ice. He tried not to show the pain.

He smiled at those assembled. He guessed he probably looked like a grinning skull. "Showtime."

Then a sound, down the hall. It was the same sound that had bored into his mind before, that desperate, failed muffling of footsteps. He turned, tried to say something, but nothing came out.

Then, eclipsing the doorway at the far end of the hall, silhouettes. At first, they were just shadows, but he started to make out faces. Micah Rosenberg was in the lead, face still bruised from when Novak stomped him that morning, with Pisspants and Gray Hervey behind. "Come with us, Glen," Rosenberg said.

He took a step forward over the protests of his knees. "What, no 'please' any more?"

"If it'd make you feel better."

"Rippey wants to see me?"

"The Reverend needs you to answer for Walter Calomiris's murder."

"Maybe he should answer for his fucking self. Thought about that?"

Rosenberg was serene. "Come on, Glen. Let's not get violent. You don't look like you're in any shape to put up a fight."

That got him. There was too little space between them for a simple takedown. He took another step, played possum, letting them think the infection had him worse than it did. "That why you only brought two guys? You knew I looked like this?"

Rosenberg squirmed, glancing away for a second.

That was what he was waiting for. He lunged. His knees protested. Pisspants shouted. He hit Rosenberg in the belly and carried him back into the hall to slam against the far wall. Rosenberg's lungs flattened with a sigh and he hammered his fists against Novak's back, but there was no air to give them power.

Novak pushed off the wall and threw a haymaker into Micah Rosenberg's exposed chin, right for one of the bruises he put there with his foot. It didn't land flush, but Rosenberg's legs gave out for just a moment. Out of the corner of his eye he saw Pisspants reach for the pistol in his belt. Had he been at a hundred percent, he might have been able to get to the little puke. As it was, he felt like he was fighting in waist deep mud. He tried to close the distance, but the gun was out of Pisspants's belt and coming up.

There was a quicksilver flicker, and the gun fell away, along with the forearm.

Pisspants screamed, but Pulaski cut that off too. Pisspants fell to the ground in several pieces.

Wheezing, Rosenberg pulled his machete, still trying to suck in air.

He hit Rosenberg with the hammer and the side of his face caved in with a wet crunch. He fell, making gurgling, mewling noises. His fingers bit into the dirty carpet as he tried to order his ruined brain to rise.

Novak turned to the last man up, Hervey: he was already running down the hall.

Rosenberg's hand gripped Novak's pantleg. Novak turned back to Micah Rosenberg and ended him with the hammer.

Stew came into the hall. "Jesus, Glen."

Harmon, with his wife protectively behind him, poked his head into the hall and both immediately gagged. "Stay in there, honey," he said to Michelle. Dr. Bloch came to the door. She looked stricken by the violence, but blood didn't bother a woman like her.

Novak said: "It's not safe here. I need to go talk to Reverend Rippey..."

"Talk?" Dr. Bloch said.

"You want me to get literal?"

"This is explanation enough."

"I need you to get Skyler and the Harmons to the rest of our people. Hole up there and if you see any of Rippey's men, act foreign."

"As in we don't speak English."

Novak nodded.

She said: "And the bodies?"

"You worry about the people who have a future."

She looked like she wanted to say something else. Maybe it occurred to her—as it had to him—that assuming anyone in the Athena had a future was highly optimistic. Instead, she turned around and spoke quietly to the room. When she reappeared, the boy's head was shielded into her pregnant belly, his arms around her.

"Harmon, you..."

"I know," he said to Novak. Harmon gathered wife and daughter and followed Dr. Bloch.

"What about the rest of us?" Stew said.

"That's up to you," Novak said. "Rippey likes to play the lamb, but we all know that's bullshit. We're talking tooth and nail against whoever's left in his gang." He tried to do the math of how many were left, but the numbers got jumbled around in his head. One face stood out amongst all of them: Jacen Ford. He was in bad shape and no match for Ford.

If he was destined to be killed, he knew Ford would make it quick.

"Boss?" Pulaski said. "You trailed off."

"Put the bodies on the balcony. Don't throw them down."

Stew and Pulaski jumped to it, dragging the corpses into the Harmons' room. Robellada hugged one of the doorframes. Novak thought in that moment, Robellada was the only man on the planet paler than him.

"Speak your mind, kid."

Robellada still couldn't look at him. "Speak my mind? You're dead."

"Yeah. I think I have a couple hours, if I'm lucky."

"You really think it was Inez Calomiris?"

"Either her or Rippey, yeah."

"So, what... you gonna kill them?"

"Yes."

"Mr. Novak... I..."

He could see it in Robellada's face. Guilt. Fear. His eyes were glued on the lumpy streaks of crimson that disappeared into the room the Harmons had vacated. The kid could take out geeks by the Mexican carload, but he drew the line at human beings. He had somehow avoided the gangs in the early days, the human predators that were worse than the geeks. Stew used to be the same way, but Novak burned that out of him. They had to in order to survive this long. But Robellada hadn't acquired that hard shell yet, and Novak didn't want to have to do that to him. Death had made him soft. Something had to. "It's okay. No one is asking you to ride shotgun. Our people need someone to look after them anyway, just in case."

He nodded. "Look after them, yeah."

"Go catch up with Dr. Bloch."

Robellada nodded but still couldn't look at him; instead, he jogged down the hall after Bloch and the Harmons.

Stew and Pulaski came out of the room a moment later. Stew said: "Where's Ricky?"

"With Judy Bloch and the others."

Stew nodded. "He doesn't have the stomach for this."

He looked at Stew with surprise. "You're not saying we should talk things over before we get wet?"

Stew shrugged. "Normally, yes. But in this case, I don't think anyone's listening."

They went down the hall.

Rippey's room was on three, a makeshift suite along the inner wall of the Athena. Hervey would have given him the heads up. Rippey would have his last remaining hard cases close by, and he'd be hiding behind the skirts of the Rippettes. Novak knew he and his guys were walking into a set position. They were outnumbered. Neither one of his guys seemed to give much of a fuck.

He was proud of them.

They made it to the stairwell that led to three. The air was as thick as the mud he imagined he was slogging through. Pulaski took a light, skipping step ahead, and his sword trailed red spots behind him. He readied a kick to the stairwell door.

Stew grabbed Pulaski, arresting his movement. Stew locked eyes and shook his head. He moved Pulaski back, pulled a pistol and got his riot shield ready.

Novak drew his gun, loaded the spare clip, and kept his hammer in his off-hand. Seven bullets left. *Make them count.*

He nodded to Stew.

Stew put his back on the smooth wall to the door's right, moved his leg out and stomped the door open.

Immediately, two gunshots exploded, the echoes driving tent-spikes into Novak's brain.

Stew dropped low, shield out, gun to the side, and fired twice.

Novak lurched forward to join him, but was too slow.

It didn't matter; Pulaski wasn't waiting. Novak hadn't expected him to. Pulaski jumped over Stew, who let out a loud curse.

Then—whistling and wet sounds.

Another gunshot.

Screaming.

And then nothing.

Novak entered the corridor with Stew.

Pulaski stood over the corpses, inspecting his arm, where a bullet had traced a black-bordered slash across his bicep. He'd have a nice coal-miner's tattoo after that.

On the floor: what used to be Hervey and another of Rippey's men, sliced apart by Pulaski's blade.

Stew said to Pulaski: "When I say hold back, hold back."

"You didn't say shit. We played some charades, then this happened."

Stew shook his head. "It's all funny till they kill you."

"Still funny then. Just not to me."

Novak turned left out of the stairwell and lurched past them. "Come on, ladies. Time's a factor."

They fell into step behind him.

Rippey's suite was ahead. He knew the Reverend would have heard the gunshots. He was giving Novak control of the situation. Rippey hadn't realized that. Losing control meant death.

Rippey's door exploded outward.

Novak was already flinging himself into a doorway. Jacob Rosenberg and one other peeked their heads out and fired down the hall.

Novak shoulder-barged the door and burst into the room. He ducked and rolled into cover behind a desk. Only then could he look out and risk finding out what happened to his guys.

Stew was hit in the calf: impossible to see how bad. He dragged a stain along the hall into an alcove.

Pulaski was out of sight, but that was a good thing.

The gunshots stopped.

He glanced back into his hiding place. Nobody was in the room. He was glad for that. He didn't need to go scaring anyone else.

Jacob Rosenberg's voice: "Glen! We only want you. If you come out and meet us, your men can go back downstairs and this never happened!"

"Bullshit!" he hollered back.

"Nobody else has to die!"

"Other than me!"

Rosenberg didn't have a response to that.

Novak stepped out into the hall, firing where he remembered Rosenberg's head had appeared. One bullet sprayed plaster into Rosenberg's face. Another pushed him back. A third dissuaded them from chancing a shot. Four bullets left. Novak dropped the gun to the floor and skinned his hatchet. He spun around the corner.

Jacob Rosenberg's eyes were wide, mouth wider. Novak split Rosenberg's face with the hatchet. His mouth had become a cross, teeth falling amongst the thick blood. Using it like a handle, Novak moved the twitching body aside to smash the other man in the face with the hammer. Hot blood spurted and he went down.

Pulaski finished Rosenberg as Novak put a foot on Rosenberg's corpse and pulled the bloody hatchet free.

Stew limped over. He kept his eyes away from the bodies. So, there was a little softness left in him as well.

They turned to the door. Closed.

Novak motioned Stew and Pulaski out of the way, then leaned in cop style, body away from the doorway.

"You in there, Rippey?"

He expected another gunshot. Maybe a shotgun blast that would shred the door like cheese. Instead, Rippey's voice, reedier than usual, barked, "Novak! You should have acquiesced to the demands of the body politic."

"Your demands." He picked up his gun. Four rounds left, he reminded himself.

Novak put the hatchet away and opened the door.

Rippey had three guys in with him, machetes out, surrounding him. Ford was in front. Rippey peeked out from behind the larger man like a little brother. The Rippettes formed a blonde cluster in one corner, weeping and cowering. Gloria Wu and Jack Finger were in opposite corners, like fighters. Finger had nail marks raked down one cheek.

"Evening, Reverend," Novak said. He tried to fake health. He knew it was less than convincing.

Gloria spoke up. "Glen, I'm sorry. I didn't know they were looking for you. I just told them you'd saved my life."

He nodded. "It's okay. You and me, we're square. Finger's yours if you want him."

Finger let out a squeal and shrieked, "Reverend! Jacen! Do something! Kill him!"

Rippey, getting bolder: "No hope for you in here, Novak. Everyone in here knows what you did."

"True. They don't know everything you did, though."

Rippey's face contorted. "You can twist the truth if you like. We recognize it unblemished."

"You made your little deal with the devil, and now you're trying to fuck the devil over. I'm here to say that's not possible. If I'm going back to Hell, I'm taking you with me."

Only Ford didn't take a step back.

"Blasphemies aside, you killed Walter."

"After you hired me, yeah, I did."

"You're lying!"

"Wasn't the only thing you did, either. You had that deal with the nomads to kill Calomiris. When they didn't, that's when you hired me. You sent them in here to die!"

"The righteous must make sacrifices!"

Novak looked up at Ford. The pain was written large across his face. "Ford, you know what happened. You know the rights and the wrongs of it. I'm going to settle up with Rippey. If you think I'm not justified, you feel free to stop me. I'm pretty sure you can."

Ford looked him up and down. He took a lurching step forward. Ford wrung the neck of his machete. Novak took another step. Ford looked for a way out. Novak took another step. Ford looked at floor and ceiling and found nothing. Novak took another step. They were breathing the other's breath.

Ford stepped aside.

Rippey, terrified, said, "Jacen, what are you doing?"

"He's telling the truth."

Novak took another step.

Rippey quailed. "He's going to kill me!"

"I know. I'm sorry, Reverend."

"God will—"

"I'll make my peace with the Lord on my own. You should do the same."

Ford left the room, followed by the other two. Finger split, too, leaving Gloria. As they left, they stayed out of arm's reach of Novak, advancing past like a whirlpool, as if skimming the edge of a maelstrom. The Rippettes watched, transfixed. One had the tiniest grin. The little one looked terrified.

"Glen... please."

"Run, Reverend."

He blinked, uncomprehending.

Novak pulled his gun and cocked it.

Rippey turned to run.

Novak shot him between the shoulder-blades. The Reverend tried to crawl away, making little prey sounds in his throat.

Novak holstered the gun. Rippey wasn't worth two bullets.

He drew his hammer and bashed Rippey's head apart.

Gloria made a gagging sound and left the room.

He pounded until Rippey's head was nothing but a frothy pink paste, hammering until his arm wasn't capable of rising any more. Then Novak collapsed on his ass and looked at a hairline crack in the wall where the Athena bled her life into the room.

- 22 -

THE RAIN HAMMERED IN TIME with the sobbing women. Novak could barely summon the strength to care. He felt hands on him, helping him up. It was the thousandth time that day, after a life of never needing hands like that. Black crept in at the corner of his vision, cutting off peripherals. His knees seemed to lock in place whenever he straightened them fully, needing concentration to move them again.

He looked back and forth to the faces of his men. Stew appeared stricken.

Pulaski's eyes roamed over Rippey's corpse, strangely introspective. "Come on, Glen. We need to leave them."

The Rippettes descended on the body as soon as Novak reached the threshold. Their grief had turned them into vultures, fearful of the lion that made the kill but ready to gorge as soon as he turned his back.

Stew and Pulaski escorted him past the other bodies. He started to think of how many people had died since the bite. He tried to count them. He couldn't.

Each step sent blades through his feet. He remembered the story of the Little Mermaid. She was given legs to live on land, but every step was like walking on razors. He knew exactly how she felt. It was a reminder that she didn't belong and never would.

It was mortality.

Stew and Pulaski helped him down the stairs. He hated the

weakness he showed, but he had to conserve what little strength was left. He felt himself slipping away into the bite, the growing chasm that pulsed venom green.

They almost descended another flight, but he stopped them. "No. Don't want to go all the way down. Find me a room."

The men didn't respond, but they opened the door onto two for him. Some of the doors were open, some closed. They chose one on the northern end of the Athena.

Stew limped from his gunshot wound. Pulaski was strong, but there was a fatigued hitch in his step. Pulaski forced it and settled Novak in the bed.

"What now, boss?" Pulaski said.

"Just want to catch my breath." He sank onto the unkempt stained bed. "Then I can go after Inez."

Stew said: "How are you feeling?"

"Like a fuckin' peach. How do you think?"

Stew's voice was admirably steady. "No. How close are you? If you turn, someone should be here with you."

"Right." Novak tried not to fall into himself. "Stew, get the Doc up here."

"Answer my question first."

"I don't have much time. Probably less than I need."

"Then I'm staying. Dave, could you get Dr. Bloch? Ricky too."

"Fuck that," Pulaski said. "I promised the boss I'd kill him."

"No. That's my responsibility."

"With that grip? It would take you two swipes at least. I can do it clean."

"Jesus, Dave. You just promised Glen that I was in charge."

Novak nearly exploded. "Fuck, if I'd known both of you assholes were this keen to off me, we'd have had it out years ago. Pulaski, Stew told you to get Bloch and Robellada. Go fucking get them, *please*."

"Sure thing, boss."

When Pulaski left, Stew sat down on the bed, shaking his head. "How the hell do you control him?"

"You don't. You just point him."

"Guess that's got to be enough." Stew ducked his head and Novak saw the tears rolling down his cheeks.

"You're not going fag on me, are you?"

Stew chuckled. "My friend's dying. I'm sorry I couldn't be more stoic."

"Nah. It's nice to know someone'll cry for me. Shit, when I met you, I never thought you'd give a fuck about me."

"Same here. You weren't very nice back in the world."

"I'm still not."

"True." Stew thought about what he was going to say, then spit it out. "I always liked Susan, though. I used to wonder what she was doing with you."

"You and me both."

"Glen?"

"Yeah?"

"I'm sorry my sweetgum trees fucked up your lawn."

"I'm sorry I used to call you a fag."

"Used to?"

"I stopped about twenty seconds ago. You weren't there for that?"

Stew laughed. "I'm going to miss you."

"Yeah."

Stew was silent then. They had said everything they wanted to say to one another. Anything else would have ruined the moment. Stew couldn't leave, even though both men wanted him to. He had to stay against the inevitable death and stillborn rise.

Pulaski came in with the Doc, but Robellada was nowhere to be found. Novak didn't mind. Robellada probably couldn't bear to see his old coach in the state he was in. Novak understood and gave the kid his silent blessing. There was a little bloodshed left to be done. Best the kid stayed clear.

Dr. Bloch settled next to the bed.

Novak said to his guys: "Get out. Please."

Pulaski shook his head. "Sorry, boss. We stay."

He drew his gun. He was proud of the way that no one in the room flinched. It said he had at least earned the trust of three people in the world. That alone validated some of what he'd done. He flipped the weapon around and handed it to Judy Bloch. Her brow furrowed, laugh lines deepened. The dark arch over brow— that aristocratic line that he could never ignore—cast a sad shadow over her brown eyes.

She looked at the gun. He knew her well enough to realize that she was weighing the oath she took in the old world. Finally, she nodded. "It's okay. I can do it."

Stew left without another word. Pulaski's eyes lingered on Dr. Bloch's back for a long moment, before he nodded to himself and left after Stew.

"Your chin isn't bleeding."

Novak nodded. "I think it's scabbed."

"No. There's no blood."

"Oh."

She thought about what she was going to say next. Then: "You told them to get me?"

He nodded. "I needed to talk to you. Before. You know."

"Before you do, can I ask you something?"

"Of course."

"Have you ever noticed that you call men by their last names and women by their first names? Why is that?"

"It's an old habit. I taught gym, so I called my students by their last names. That's what they wrote on their shirts, so that's what I called them. Didn't teach girls."

Bloch smiled. "But you call me by my last name."

"Don't take it as an insult. I don't think you look like a man."

"No?"

"No. I think you're beautiful."

Her voice caught. "Am I?"

"I wanted some... distance. Between you and me. Call you by your first name, maybe that kid's mine."

"And you can't have that."

"I thought so. Now, I think I was wrong. Means shit now, but I wanted to tell you."

"I'm glad you did."

She leaned down. She didn't kiss him on the mouth: that would be alive with the dead plague. She veered off and touched warm lips to an icy forehead. He wished there could be more. He wished he could have taken her in his arms. He couldn't. Too late for that.

He said: "I want this to mean something."

"You saved Skyler. He's downstairs with Jeanette Sorensen right now."

"You wanted samples. Here I am."

"Are you certain?"

"As I am of anything."

She opened up her medical bag. "I need some blood."

He rolled up his sleeve. She shook her head.

"You have no blood in your arms. It's settling. It'll be in your legs and ass. The infection is running you now."

Novak shuddered. For the first time he was certain that his body was not his own. His thoughts, his desires, his memories, none of it was him any more. It belonged to the infection. *Only my willpower borrows it for a little while longer.*

"How long?"

"It's close."

She rolled up his pantleg. He didn't feel the needle as it went in. He didn't feel the thick blood as it left his body. He could only hope that it helped her in some way.

"Thank you, Glen."

"You're welcome, Judy."

He put the stiff legs under him, fought the shards of ice that speared muscle and bone from both sides of every joint. He held out a hand. "I need my gun."

She handed it over. "Goodbye."

"Get to my body first. If you can use it, use it." He took a step toward the door. "If not, I don't know. Bury it or something."

She never said anything else to him. Novak hoped that she cried for him, but he never turned around to look.

He cried for her, but they were cold tears and he barely felt them.

- 23 -

NOVAK LEFT HIS MEN BEHIND. One way or the other, this was the final climb up the Athena. He would confront and kill his murderer, or he'd die there. As he ascended, he was either getting closer to Heaven or farther from Hell. Either one was fine by him.

He opened the door to the hall upstairs. The few candles formed brilliant lights, while the rest of it was shrouded in darkness. He was swallowed by the shadows, looking through layers of black gauze.

He turned the corner and nearly tripped over Barrett Cheeseman, stretched out along the floor of the hall like a speedbump.

"Jesus, fuck. You look like a wet fart," Cheeseman said.

"I've been bitten."

"That's some fuckin' honesty right there." Cheeseman reached into the cooler next to the wall, picked out a Coke and cracked it.

"No point in lying. Gonna die soon."

"No shit. What are you doing up here?"

"Gotta have a talk to Inez."

"Can she talk with your dick in her mouth?"

"I lost track of how many people I killed today, Cheeseman. I'll make it one more. Or half more."

Cheeseman stood up to his full three-foot height. "Fuck off, Novak. Take a fuckin' joke, why don't you?" He picked a door and opened it, walking straight for the back of the room.

Despite himself, he followed. Something in him wanted to know what the crinkled little gnome was going to do next. He opened up the sliding glass door. The wind and rain blew outward from the Athena. Novak knew that he should be shivering, but there was nothing left of anything in him that could feel the cold.

Cheeseman got up onto one of the chairs outside and used that to climb onto the stucco railing of the balcony. "Nice fuckin' day to die, you ask me."

"You asking for a push?"

Cheeseman undid his pants and started pissing on the swarm below.

Novak wished he could hear someone from the second floor swearing when he realized that the rain that hit him was yellow and body temperature, but Novak couldn't hear anything over the rain.

"Nah, just trying to make you less scared, you gimpy faggot."

"Why the fuck do you care how scared I am?"

Cheeseman shook his penis and tucked it away before jumping back down. "If you get too scared, then maybe you won't do the right thing when the time comes."

"Aren't you going to ask me why I haven't yet?"

"Don't need to ask. I always knew you were a pussy." Cheeseman took a drag off his Coke.

"Where did you hide those things, anyway?"

"If it was up your ass, you'd know."

Novak laughed. It turned into a cough. He looked into his hand. No blood, just something pink and jellylike, like layers of skin. He was about to leave, when Cheeseman said something: "This fucking apocalypse."

He couldn't help himself. He turned. "What?"

"You know what high fructose corn syrup is?"

Novak vaguely recalled hearing it somewhere, but couldn't place it. "Not really."

Cheeseman wiggled the Coke. "It's some shit they made from corn. Tastes like the inside of a camel's ass. They used to use real cane sugar in pop, but right before the dead stopped staying dead, they started to change over to high fucking fructose corn syrup."

Novak wasn't sure what to say. He didn't know where Cheeseman was going with his little rant.

Cheeseman went on: "If this fucking thing happened maybe five years before it did, I could still be drinking the good shit, instead of finding maybe one crate in a blue-goddamn-moon. This fucking apocalypse." Cheeseman sighed and flopped his tiny body into a chair.

Novak turned and left the little dwarf to his soft drinks.

At the end of the hall was Inez's room.

He forced that door.

Empty.

"Inez?"

Nothing.

A little bit higher. Somewhere that he could see the face of Heaven, maybe.

He took the stairs up and emerged out onto the roof. Overhead, the storm roiled. Wind pounded inland from an ocean he could no longer see. Calomiris's tarps cracked and rain hammered. The dinner setup was still there, soaked and wind-blown. Walter Calomiris was still slumped by the wall, bloodless, his body surrounded by rain-thinned red.

He turned back, around the small door. The roof stretched to the west, where it fell directly to the ocean.

Dimly, he saw shapes moving around in the darkness as the rain whipped his face. Distantly, their voices floated on the wind, but he couldn't identify words or people.

He staggered toward them on stiffened legs toward that group.

They stopped moving. One approached, resolved itself into

Inez. In her face, he saw concern, fear, and something else. "Glen? Glen, are you okay?" She lightly gripped his left arm, a solicitous touch.

He nodded.

The other two shapes at the end of the south wing were still. He had the impression they were watching him, but he couldn't be sure. He shook Inez off and took two more agonizing steps.

He tripped over something.

He didn't fall. Something in him, the infection maybe, stabilized him, found the crunchy gravel under his feet. He looked down.

Bodies.

Not stretched as far as the eye could see. Not like those old shots of battlefields in Vietnam where the ground was invisible under the stretched flesh. These were countable. These had not disappeared into the haze of statistics. These were real and immediate. They still had names.

He looked up at the end of the roof. Rudolfo Marcos and Tigran Gamburyan stood there, a body held between them. Novak took another step forward. He recognized the beaten and bruised face of the nomad leader. It bothered him that he couldn't think of the man's name.

Marcos and Gamburyan threw the body over the side, into the Pacific.

"Glen, wait."

He saw her, washing her hands raw in the little basin. She had done it then.

"You killed them."

Inez had the decency to look guilty. "I ordered it. You have to understand. They weren't here as settlers, though. Rippey's men found them out there. They were here to kill Walter and help Rippey take over."

"I know."

"You know? Then you understand. I had to do this."

"Why not just let them do it? Why get me to do it?"

"You think they would have stopped with Walter?"

She actually had a point. The nomads might have butchered everyone in the Athena. Still, that didn't excuse: "Skyler."

"What?"

"Skyler. Little kid. Hulk t-shirt. He was there for the slaughter. He's a little fucking kid, Inez."

"He's not here, is he?"

"There were other children. You killed them too!"

She turned into the rain. "It was that or let them grow up into someone that wanted me dead."

The sick logic burned in Novak's limbs. There was precious little strength in them. She had two men with her, both of whom he had beaten when he was healthier and who were probably itching for payback. He wondered if he could kill her before they got to him and finished him off.

He got closer. She hadn't recognized the danger yet, opening her arms for an embrace. "Wherever you did that. I'm guessing some of the rooms up here are wallpapered in blood. You brought the bodies up here for disposal. Am I right?"

"Glen, you need to sit down. You look terrible."

"You know why, don't you?"

"What?"

"You sent Booker to kill me, didn't you?"

She shook her head. "No!" A pause. Then, realizing she had nothing to lose: "I sent him to kill your man. Pulaski."

"Why him?"

"You're only seeing the edge of this thing. We were going to remove Rippey. Your man, Tom Martinez, was supposed to kill him last night, but Pulaski killed him first."

"Because he was bitten."

"I thought maybe Rippey had figured it out. He'd used Pulaski to head off his own assassination. I was wrong."

It clicked into place. That was why Martinez had talked about changing things. The balance of power would have been altered if not for that one geek.

Inez went on: "I never wanted you dead. You were going to run this town."

But there was something else. Though it pained him, he said, "You planted the head. The head that bit me."

Her eyes got big. The shock in them seemed genuine, but Novak couldn't read anyone any more. He wanted to believe she was the one who killed him. She was there. She was within arm's reach. If he could still feel body heat, he might have dimly felt hers. She said: "You're... you're bitten?"

"Like you didn't know."

"Novak. Get the hell away from my cousin," Marcos said. His voice was pinched from the broken nose Novak gave him.

He turned. Marcos and Gamburyan had abandoned their grim work and now stood about five feet distant, each holding their weapons. Both men carried the marks from fighting him earlier in the day, cut lips, bruised faces, black eyes, and bandaged noses. It was somewhere in their eyes, wondering if somehow Novak had beaten the infection into them.

He swayed on his feet and focused on his enemies. Gamburyan still carried his baseball bat, but Marcos held that huge metal mace he'd last seen in the hands of the nomad leader. Abruptly, he remembered Marcos in the lobby, right before the manhunt. He recalled that Marcos had a metal handle over his shoulder. At the time, it had bothered Novak, but he hadn't realized the awful implication until Skyler.

"Hey, Marcos. Did you help with this shit too?"

"This was Athena business. Doesn't concern you."

"Maybe not before. It does now."

"You're in no shape to take me on."

"Was it you? Did you plant the head?"

"The fuck are you talking about?"

Inez grabbed at Novak's arm. "No one planted anything, Glen! Whatever happened, that doesn't matter. We heard that Reverend Rippey is dead. With him and Walter gone, we can start our Republic. We can bring it back. We can take it back. We can have the world again."

Novak shoved her away.

Marcos—or the shape that Novak had to focus on to make sure it was Marcos—swung that huge mace.

Novak backpedaled. His ligaments had been replaced with broken glass. Somehow, his legs didn't give out underneath him.

He pulled his hatchet and hammer.

Inez backed away, head down. Disappointed. She didn't stop her men.

They fanned out like hyenas. Gamburyan was unsure. He was Stew's friend, playing in that obsessive D&D game every week with those others. He had beaten Gamburyan earlier, but the web of relationships was complex. He could use that.

He feinted toward Marcos and lunged at Gamburyan. Earlier in the day, when he still had his knees, before the infection tore them away, he could have gotten to the other man. Gamburyan swung the bat around like a staff, hitting Novak in the mouth with the butt end. He felt the crunch and give of some of his teeth, but there was no copper taste of blood.

He had none of that left.

He swung the hatchet low. It bit deep into Gamburyan's knee. He heard the crunch, heard the cry. He turned, barely in time to see Marcos barreling toward him. When the sun was still up, he might have had the speed to get out of the way.

Instead, he took the hit, dropping the hatchet as Marcos carried him from Gamburyan to slam into the sharp gravel.

Novak felt as though every point of every piece of gravel had torn him open. The frozen water was his blood. The rain would dissolve him entirely into something thin and red.

Marcos rose up and punched him in the face.

It was a bad place. Beyond the infection, it was the loss of control. He had no leverage, no speed with which to spin out and gain a dominant position. He saw the move in his head: slip his right leg under Marcos, spin, get to his knees, rise and lunge. In the old days, it would have been fluid, and even as the gravel tore his knees to ribbons, he would have reversed it on Marcos and pounded the other man into unconsciousness.

Marcos rose up again and landed another haymaker.

Novak coughed on something hard. It was a tooth.

"Tiger! Get the fuck over here!"

Marcos punched him in the face again. The blackness moved in closer.

Marcos was a pinpoint at the end of a long tunnel, flying farther into the light.

Novak knew that if he let go at this moment, if he gave in, the infection would take him and Marcos would be a dead man.

Give up control and his last enemies would die.

No.

Marcos hit him again, and then hauled him to his feet.

His joints rebelled as they remained locked in place from where they were. The hammer dropped from his ruined left hand.

Then both men were on him, holding him under numb armpits, dragging him toward the edge of the roof. Over the few corpses of the nomads still left on the roof. Suddenly, the stormy Pacific bloomed in his vision at the end of that tunnel.

Still holding him, they moved back, getting ready to thrust him out into space.

He planted his feet firmly on the surface, crying out when he could no longer ignore the agony of his ravaged knees. He straightened his left arm and threw outward, using the right to hang on to Marcos. Tigran Gamburyan pitched forward, but it was not a strong enough push to send him over the side.

Novak whirled, too slow in his mind, and punched Marcos in the face.

Marcos staggered backward.

Using his weak momentum, Novak turned, planted a foot on Gamburyan's ass and shoved. He smiled as the scream faded into the storm's howl.

Marcos pulled his mace.

Novak pulled his gun. Two shots went into Marcos's chest. He fell. Dead.

He turned. His vision exploded white. He felt the crunch of his nose, but tasted no blood.

Dazed, he fell on his ass, and a new agony shredded into him.

Inez stood over him with a baseball bat. Pieces of his skin were stuck to the side. Her black hair hung around her face, showing only glittering eyes.

"Glen! Please!"

Novak tried to make a sound. His jaw felt loose somehow, but there was no pain.

"You killed me," he said, but it came out mushier than he intended.

"Glen. Just let me finish you. It won't hurt. I promise."

Two bullets into Marcos. One for Inez. That left one for... he knew.

He raised his right hand, but the gun was no longer in it.

He heard the crack and saw white again. He was on the ground, his face full of white gravel and rainwater. Inez had just finished her second swing. She readied another.

He saw his gun, rain beading along the surface. Just out of reach.

She swung. He tipped over, reaching hard.

The bat hit his ribs. He heard and felt the crack, but no pain that went with it.

His hand touched the gun.

Another crack. His ribs moved freely.

The gun found its home.

He sat up.

She froze.

"Glen. No."

One shot. She fell.

He crawled to one of the air conditioning boxes. He was nearly blind. He couldn't feel the metal behind his back. He tasted the metal of the gun. It was over. He could finish it.

He thumbed back the hammer.

In that silent moment, he realized that he couldn't hear his own blood. He couldn't hear a heartbeat. The only sounds came from without. Nothing from within. He had to give it up.

He shut his eyes.

Then, a voice: "Mr. Novak?"

- 24 -

ROBELLADA STUMBLED INTO VIEW, HAND vainly trying to fend off the storm. He appeared to Novak at the end of his tunnel, but the light was fading. The kid reached the dead nomads and stumbled once. Novak couldn't make out Robellada's face from that range, but he imagined the horror that washed over it. The kid would never have the stomach for killing.

He removed the gun from his mouth. His right arm weighed a thousand pounds. His left seemed to be missing. He felt nothing. The pain from the bite was gone. The pain from his wounds was gone. There was only one thing left to do.

"Get back downstairs, kid." That was what he tried to say, but his ruined mouth spat the words out in a thin slurry.

Robellada paused, too far away to see his face, but Novak heard the disgust, the horror, and the fear in his voice. "Mr. Novak?"

"Go 'way, kid. I gotta finish this. I don't want you seein'."

Robellada took a step forward.

He didn't have the strength to shove him away. He wasn't sure he had the strength to stand at all. All power was gone in him, and he wanted to cry like a child. But he couldn't.

"Mr. Novak. Why aren't you dead?"

"Gimme a minute. Just... just go downstairs."

He saw Robellada reflexively turn, obeying out of habit, obeying because that's what he did. Then he paused. Turned around. Hunkered down. "No. I have to stay. I have to tell you something."

The helplessness burned through what was left of Glen Novak. He couldn't do this, not with an audience. "Godammit, kid. You don't want to see this."

"No."

Novak wanted to cry in frustration, but he didn't think his body would even do that. Let the rain do it for him.

"Why won't you let me alone?"

Robellada was moving, but Novak could hardly see him any more. The kid was nothing but a grainy silhouette.

"Mr. Novak. I didn't mean it."

"Didn't mean it...?" Ice speared Novak to the roof. The wind seemed to fall away for a moment. There was no mistaking the tone in the kid's voice, even if he couldn't see the look in his eyes. "You?" Novak groped for it. He saw:

The rage in Robellada's eyes at the Barricade.

The fear in Robellada's eyes that horrible Thursday.

The visit, right after he was bitten.

Then, he saw nothing at all. His vision was nearly gone.

Through the gray rain, Robellada's eyes were shadowed pits, deep and uncaring as the sea. "I tried. I tried to stop you. I tried to warn you. I thought maybe I could take it back. Get the head out of the locker. You would never have even known it was there."

"You?"

"I didn't mean it." Novak heard the pain there. It broke through the top layer of ice, gasping for big lungfuls of air.

"You killed me."

"I'm sorry."

"All because I left you that day?"

"Yes. And no."

Novak felt the infection sinking its claws into him again, dragging him away. "Then why?"

"When I got here, the group was… it was like a family. We were a group. But you weren't… there. You didn't want anyone close. It was lonely. Then I started seeing Janelle Ford and she took me to church. The Reverend… he was there. Whenever I needed him, he was there. He listened. And he talked."

"About me."

"He didn't say anything that wasn't true. He said that you were a thug and a tyrant. He said you were a rapist and a murderer. He was right about all of it. How are we supposed to make a new world with people like you? People who just take whatever they want. People who just make up the laws as they go!"

Robellada gathered himself, and when he continued, he fought to keep his voice even. "I took the head weeks ago. I smuggled it back into Devon in my pack. I kept the thing in a cooler. I thought maybe I'd never use it, but I had it. I knew, I knew that no matter what you thought, that I could kill you. And that made me feel better."

Robellada shut his eyes, and for a moment, Novak saw the tears rushing out of them. "But then you let Tom die. You said those things at the funeral, and you let Tom die and you didn't care."

"I cared."

"You didn't show it! You didn't cry! You didn't say nothing about him! It was like you were flushing a goldfish! So, I got the head and I put it in your locker and I waited. But then I thought about what I did and I thought I could take it back, but it was already too late." He swallowed. "You always said that if you get the bite, you do the right thing. I thought you'd do the right thing, but you didn't."

The pain was there, branching and molding into something else: indecision. Regret. More than that, terror. It was the terror Novak had seen earlier in the day when the Barricade had come down. To Robellada there were constants. The geeks had torn one down and that had been bad, but he had destroyed the other constant, Novak, and that was nearly more than he could bear.

"Why are you telling me this, kid?"

"Jacen Ford found me. He told me what happened. He told me..." and here Robellada's voice broke. "He told me that the Reverend hired you to kill Walter Calomiris. I knew the Reverend had lied. He was just as bad as you were. Killing you wouldn't accomplish anything if everyone else is just as bad. The Reverend used me to kill you. Used me like a puppet, and I let him."

Robellada was silent. Novak listened to the pounding rain, getting distant in his ears.

"Please, Mr. Novak. Say something."

"You killed me."

"I'm sorry. Please, you have to forgive me. I didn't mean to."

"No?" Novak expected the cold rage to take him again, as it had when he killed the others he blamed for his murder. But, for the cold and shivering boy in front of him, there was only pity.

"That day... after you left us, they attacked the school. Only a couple of us made it out. We lasted a little while, but one by one they died too. Then only I was left."

Novak saw the kid that had been in the gym that Thursday. He saw the wide eyes. He saw the patchy facial hair that couldn't even grow into a proper five o'clock shadow. He saw the tears wobbling over the boy's irises. The choice that doomed Robellada had doomed Novak at the same time, and all for nothing.

"We can't take things back, kid. No matter how much we want to."

He felt himself falling. The rage was no longer buoying his body. The infection was going to win, and it would be soon. He had time for one more thing before he ended it.

"Please. I'm sorry. I take it back. I take all of it back."

"Come here," he said.

Robellada hesitated.

"Come here," Novak said again.

Robellada moved forward. Novak held his arms out. "I forgive you, kid."

Robellada fell into Novak's arms. Through the layer of rain and ice, Novak dimly felt the boy's shoulders shaking. He tried to comfort the kid. Robellada was helpless in his grief and guilt. He shushed the kid and brushed his hair.

Then he put the pistol under Robellada's chin and pulled the trigger.

His last bullet blew the top of the boy's head off, showering Novak's face with hot blood that made his stomach come back to life, if only for a moment.

He dropped the pistol.

Robellada's body slumped across Novak's legs.

With his last reserves, he shoved the body away and used the air conditioner to give him purchase to get to his feet.

The storm howled. The rain spat in his face.

He could no longer take his own life. That power was gone, along with all the rest. It had been gone as soon as the infection had taken root. Before that, even. Gone as soon as he abandoned his kids to save Susan, an errand that was already a failure before it began.

He had no power left. He pulled himself along, staggering to the westernmost point of the Athena. Below, there were the balconies, but he could not see them. There was the thin shelf of land, but he could not see that either. Then there was the dead drop to the rocks and the Pacific below.

There was a single thing yet to do, and he could not do it himself. If he was lucky, he would be smashed to pieces against the rocks below. If he turned, it would be for a split second and the infection would die with his body.

He would have to trust.
He took a step into oblivion.
And knew nothing else.

ACKNOWLEDGMENTS

Like anyone else who creates a piece of zombie fiction, I'm playing in the house George Romero built back in 1968. Romero shares the blame for this book with noir writers like Chandler, Hammett, and Ellroy. If I end up even half as good as any one of them, I will be exceeding my wildest dreams.

ABOUT THE AUTHOR

Much like film noir, Justin Robinson was born and raised in Los Angeles. He splits his time between editing comic books, writing prose, and wondering what that disgusting smell is. Degrees in Anthropology and History prepared him for unemployment, but an obsession with horror fiction and a laundry list of phobias provided a more attractive option. He is the author of more than 10 novels in a variety of genres including detective, humor, urban fantasy, and horror. Most of them are pretty good.

He and his family reside in Los Angeles with too many cats, and extensive book, comic, and DVD collections.

BOOKS BY JUSTIN ROBINSON

The Dollmaker
Everyman
Nerve Zero
Undead on Arrival

City of Devils Series
City of Devils
Fifty Feet of Trouble

Fill in the _____ Series
Mr Blank
Get Blank

League of Magi Series
Coldheart
The Daughter Gambit

The Ahriman Cycle
The Last Son of Ahriman
The Dark Price of Ahriman
The New Dawn of Ahriman

Daughters of Arkham Series
(with David A. Rodriguez)
Daughters of Arkham
Mother of Crows